Jorn Lier Horst is one of Scandinavia's most successful crime writers. For many years he was one of Norway's most experienced police officers, with the result that his engaging and intelligent novels offer a realistic insight into how serious crimes are investigated, and how they are handled by the media. The critically acclaimed William Wisting Series has sold more than one million copies in Norway, and is translated into thirty languages. Jorn's literary awards include the Norwegian Booksellers' Prize, the Riverton Prize (Golden Revolver), the Scandinavian Glass Key and the prestigious Martin Beck Award; *The Caveman* won the United Kingdom's Petrona Award in 2016.

Anne Bruce lives on the Isle of Arran in Scotland and studied Norwegian and English at Glasgow University. She is the translator of Jorn Lier Horst's *Dregs, Closed for Winter, The Hunting Dogs, The Caveman* and *Ordeal,* and also Anne Holt's *Blessed are Those who Thirst* (2012), *Death of the Demon* (2013), *The Lion's Mouth* (2014), *Dead Joker* (2015), *No Echo* (2016), *Beyond the Truth* (2016) and *What Dark Clouds Hide* (2017), in addition to Merethe Lindstrøm's Nordic Prize winning *Days in the History of Silence* (2013).

The William Wisting Series
Published in English by Sandstone Press

CLOSED FOR WINTER

Jorn Lier Horst

Translated by

Anne Bruce

SANDSTONEPRESS
HIGHLAND | SCOTLAND

First published in Great Britain in 2013
This edition 2019
Sandstone Press Ltd
Dochcarty Road
Dingwall
Ross-shire
IV15 9UG
Scotland

www.sandstonepress.com

This translation has been published with the financial support of
NORLA.

The publisher acknowledges subsidy from Creative Scotland towards
publication of this volume.

ISBN: 978-1-908737-49-6
ISBNe: 978-1-908737-50-2

Cover by Freight Design, Glasgow
Typeset by Iolaire Typography Ltd, Newtonmore

WILLIAM WISTING

William Wisting is a career policeman who has risen through the ranks to become Chief Inspector in the Criminal Investigation Department of Larvik Police, just like his creator, author Jorn Lier Horst. *Closed for Winter* is the seventh title in the series, the second to be published in English, and finds him around fifty years old, the widowed father of grown up twins, Thomas and Line. Wisting's wife, Ingrid, went to Africa to work on a NORAD project but was killed there at the end of *The Only One*, the fifth title in the series.

Thomas serves in the military, in Afghanistan at the time of *Closed for Winter*. Daughter Line is an investigative journalist based in Oslo, whose career frequently intersects with that of her father. Wisting, at first apprehensive, has come to value how she is able to operate in ways that he cannot, often turning up unexpected clues and insights.

After Ingrid's death Wisting became involved with another woman, Suzanne Bjerke, a child welfare worker but, for Wisting, Ingrid remains the absence around which all else revolves. Subsequent books, including this one, cover the development of this new relationship.

Crucial to the series are Wisting's colleagues in the police. Audun Vetti, the arrogant Assistant Chief of Police who is also the police prosecutor, came to the fore in *Dregs*, when the question of how much information to divulge to the press was bitterly contested between the two. Wisting has more positive relationships with certain trusted colleagues: old school Nils Hammer, whose background in the Drugs Squad has made him cynical, the younger Torunn Borg whom Wisting has come to rely on thanks to her wholly professional approach and outlook, and Mortensen, the crime scene examiner who is usually first on the scene.

The setting is Vestfold county on the south-west coast of Norway, an area popular with holidaymakers, where rolling landscapes and attractive beaches make an unlikely setting for crime. The principal town of Larvik, where Wisting is based, is located 105 km (65 miles) southwest of Oslo. The wider Larvik district has 41,000 inhabitants, 23,000 of whom live in the town itself, and covers 530 square km. Larvik is noted for its natural springs, but its modern economy relies heavily on agriculture, commerce and services, light industry and transportation, as well as tourism. There is a ferry service from Larvik to Hirsthals in Denmark.

At the beginning of *Closed for Winter*, Wisting, worn down by over thirty years of police work, has returned to work following a breakdown. The many changes in society, and the increase in organised crime that has come with globalisation and improved communications, have prompted him to reflect on crime and police work. These thoughts, the intuition he has developed over many years in the force, as well as his acute awareness of human nature and social shifts, all underpinned by Jorn Lier Horst's deep experience of police procedures and processes, bring a strong sense of these novels being grounded in reality.

Closed for Winter won the Norwegian Booksellers' Prize in 2012.

Further information on Jorn Lier Horst and the earlier books is available in English at http://eng.gyldendal.no/ Gyldendal/Authors/Horst-Joern-Lier

1

Swirling sheets of fog drifted inland, settling on the wet asphalt and forming blurred haloes around the streetlamps. Ove Bakkerud drove with one hand on the steering wheel as the surrounding darkness drew in. He particularly enjoyed this time of year, just before autumn leaf-fall.

This would be his final trip to the summer cottage at Stavern, to nail closed the window shutters, drag the boat ashore and shut the place for winter. He had looked forward to it all summer long; this was his holiday. The actual work took no more than a couple of hours on Sunday afternoon, and the remaining time was at his disposal.

He swung off the main road and rolled onto the crunching gravel, the car headlights sliding over the briar hedge bordering the road all the way to the parking place. The dashboard clock showed 21.37. He switched off the ignition and emerged from the vehicle to inhale the fresh tang of salt sea air, listening to the waves boom like distant thunder on the shore.

The rain had eased and harsh blasts of wind were gusting to disperse the fog. The Tvistein light swept the landscape, glimmering across the rocks.

As he wrapped himself more snugly in his jacket, he stepped behind the car to haul the shopping bags from the boot, savouring the prospect of rare steak for dinner and fried bacon and eggs for breakfast. Man's food. Thrusting his free hand into his pocket to check for the keys he ascended the path to his cottage on the rocky outcrop. A slight incline,

1

and then the entire ocean stretched before him. His sense of the enormous panorama filled him, as always, with a special feeling of peace.

The cottage had been a simple, red-painted wooden cabin, without insulation and damaged by dry rot, when his family bought it almost twenty years earlier. As soon as he had sufficient funds he demolished the entire structure and rebuilt, and gradually he and his wife created their own little paradise. From the years when he had spent all his free time on construction work, this location had become his place to relax, breathe out, and take things easy. A place where time meant nothing and where the hours could pass according to the dictates of wind and weather.

Placing the shopping bags on the flagstones fronting the cottage, he took the keys from his pocket. The lighthouse beam struck the exterior wall and Ove Bakkerud froze and caught his breath. His grip tightened on the keys, his mouth felt dry and goose pimples spread from the nape of his neck to his forearms.

The bright lance from the lighthouse again cut through the darkness, confirming that the door was ajar, its frame shattered, the lock tumbled to the ground.

Glancing around, he perceived only darkness, though a noise, a twig snapping, rose from the undergrowth. Further off a dog barked; then nothing but the wind rustling through autumn leaves and waves breaking on the shore.

Ove Bakkerud stepped forward a few paces, holding the top edge of the door to push it open. Fumbling his way towards the light switch, he turned on the exterior lamp and the ceiling light in the hallway.

He and his wife had discussed the possibility of something like this, having read accounts in the newspapers about gangs of youths breaking into cottages to rampage through the furnishings, as well as more professional outfits ransacking

2

entire communities of summer cottages in their search for valuables. Nevertheless, he could not believe his eyes.

The living room had taken the worst: drawers and cupboards lay open, contents strewn over the floor, smashed glasses and dishes, and settee cushions scattered across the room. Everything saleable was gone: the new flat screen television, stereo system and portable radio. The cabinet where they stored wine and spirits was completely bare, a half-empty bottle of cognac the only item left behind. It felt as though their special place had been violated.

He stooped to lift the ship in a bottle, usually displayed on the mantelpiece but now lying on the floor, a large crack disfiguring the glass. Two of the masts had fractured. He recalled the many hours he had watched his grandfather's calloused fingers transform the tiny fragments into a fully-rigged ship. The moment the craft was installed inside the bottle, his grandfather had pulled the threads to hoist its sails.

His voice trembling, he phoned the police and introduced himself.

'When were you last at the cottage?' the operator enquired.

'Two weeks ago.'

'So the burglary took place after the 19th September?' Ove Bakkerud suddenly felt totally drained. 'Do you know if they've broken into other cottages?' the police officer asked.

'No,' Ove Bakkerud replied, gazing through the window and spotting a light at Thomas Rønningen's cottage in the distance. 'I've just arrived.'

'We can send out a patrol to have a look in the morning,' the police operator continued. 'Meanwhile it would be best if you disturb things as little as possible.'

'Tomorrow? But ...'

'Will you be at this number? Then we can phone when we have a car available.'

His mouth opened in protest, to demand that the police come immediately with dogs and crime scene technicians, but he held his tongue. Swallowing, he muttered a thank you and drew the conversation to a close.

Where should he start? He headed for the kitchen to fetch a dustpan and brush before remembering the policeman's admonition to leave the crime scene undisturbed. Instead he peered down at the living room window of his neighbour's cottage.

He was wondering about that light being on, since Thomas Rønningen rarely visited during autumn, having enough on his plate with his successful Friday-evening chat show. All the same, he had taken time off to celebrate the opening night of the season in August, sitting beside Ove Bakkerud at the barbecue pit drinking cognac, telling stories about the events behind the scenes before, during and after each broadcast.

A shadow flitted across the window.

Perhaps the burglars had broken in there as well. For all he knew, they might still be there. Stepping swiftly towards the doorway, he picked up the torch from its usual shelf. The police might well adjust their priorities if Thomas Rønningen was involved.

The footpath's descent to the sea curled between dense undergrowth and the impenetrable branches of crooked pine trees. Shining the torch beam on glossy tree roots and pebbles did not prevent him from scraping against pine needles and twigs.

On this side, the brightly lit cottage windows were too high for him to look in. Zigzagging the torchlight over the terrain, he approached the steps leading to the front entrance, where a blast of wind caught the door, slamming it against the verandah railings. The intense silence sent shivers down his neck and spine when he realised that he was completely defenceless.

The torch beam shed light on the doorframe, revealing similar evidence of a burglary. However, this time there was something more. The edge of the door was spattered with blood.

2

It had been a long day. William Wisting leaned forward on the settee, eyes fixed on the key lying on the table before him. Coated in verdigris, it had obviously not been used in ages.

Standing up, he crossed to the window to look through myriad droplets of rain onto the town of Stavern below. An emergency vehicle drove through the streets, its blue light slicing through the darkness, though it was impossible to tell whether it was a police patrol car or an ambulance. When it disappeared from Helgeroaveien he took a bottle from the corner cupboard; Spanish, with the date 2004 emblazoned on the label in gold lettering. He thought he remembered receiving it the previous autumn after delivering a lecture to the Trades Association. It looked expensive, and letting it sit there had probably done no harm. Though he was fond of wine, he never had enough time or interest to bone up on grape varieties, producers, wine growing areas, what suited food or which type of wine could be drunk on its own. It was enough to recognise a good vintage when he tasted one.

'Baron de Oña?' He glanced in the direction of the sofa.

Suzanne smiled, nodding towards him, and he returned her smile. She had entered his life a couple of years earlier, filling an immense void. The previous week, a water leak had sprung at her house, so she had arrived to stay with him and, though he had not told her so, he enjoyed having her here.

Picking up two wine glasses, he squinted through the window again but now caught sight only of his own reflection, a broad coarse face with dark eyes. Turning his back, he returned to the settee and settled beside her.

On the television screen, Thomas Rønningen's studio couch was occupied by enthralling guests expressing a variety of viewpoints on a common topic. Wisting enjoyed this type of programme, in which serious subjects were mixed with light entertainment, and he particularly liked this presenter. With boyish charm, Thomas Rønningen created an intimate, personal and unassailable ambience in front of the studio lights. He had transformed himself into an investigator who always posed well-constructed, intelligent questions to his guests, and instead of boxing interviewees into a corner with critical probing, coaxed disclosures from them simply by allowing the conversation to flow.

Relieving him of the glasses, Suzanne placed them on the table as he went off to fetch a corkscrew. Before returning to his seat, he peered through the window once more. Yet another emergency vehicle was heading in the same direction. He glanced automatically at his watch, noting the time: 22.02.

'Congratulations, then,' Suzanne remarked, holding out her glass as he poured.

'What do you mean?'

'About the cottage,' she smiled, nodding towards the key on the table.

Wisting plumped himself on the settee again. The day had started at a lawyer's office in Oslo in the company of his uncle, Georg Wisting. Seventy-eight years of age, Uncle Georg had spent most of his adult life building an engineering firm that specialised in energy conservation. Wisting had never quite understood what this involved, but knew his uncle had developed and patented equipment for sterilising and purifying water and air.

Uncle Georg had also made it his life's work to challenge

7

the establishment, and his inbuilt aversion to rates and taxes had led to several rounds in the law courts, resulting in penalty taxes and suspended prison sentences.

The meeting in the lawyer's office concerned Georg Wisting's last will and testament, his final attempt at ensuring the state would not benefit in any shape or form after his death. The lawyer, a specialist in inheritance matters, had drafted a fairly complex scheme to organise Uncle Georg's estate prior to his death.

Wisting's involvement meant he became owner of a holiday cottage at Værvågen outside Helgeroa, valued at the most artificially low price permitted by the legal system and so reducing inheritance tax to a minimum. This had brought Wisting a degree of affluence, though in general money posed no problem. His earnings were satisfactory and the job did not allow time for much in the way of consumption. Moreover, there was the other money, the money from Ingrid. He and the children had received a million kroner in compensation when she died while working in Africa on an assignment for *Norad*, the Norwegian aid organisation, four years previously. Although that money was sitting in a special account, increasing each month, he could not bring himself to touch it.

When they were newly married, and Ingrid was expecting their twins, bills had piled up, and sometimes they had to collect bottles to redeem the deposits when wages did not stretch to the end of the month. Now he had stopped looking at prices when shopping for groceries.

Uncle Georg's lawyer had offered to sift through his private finances to devise a plan to minimise his tax liabilities, but he had declined.

The celebrities on the television screen were laughing. 'I envy people like that,' Suzanne said, nodding in the direction of the television set. Wisting agreed, though he was not sure what kind of people she was talking about. He was content merely to sit with her on the settee. 'People who do just whatever they want,' she continued. 'People who dare to take risks, breaking free from everything permanent and secure to do something new and exciting instead. Like that woman Sigrid Heddal.'

Wisting glanced at the screen, where a woman of around fifty was declaiming enthusiastically about something called *Safe Horizon*.

'Just think, she's more than fifty, yet she leaves a secure job as a project manager in industry to travel to Addis Ababa and undertake voluntary work with orphaned children. That takes courage.' Wisting nodded, warming to this facet of Suzanne. 'Tommy's like that too.'

She was referring to Wisting's daughter Line's Danish boyfriend, Tommy Kvanter, who had resigned the year before from his steward's job on a factory trawler, selling his flat and moving in with her. In partnership with a few friends, he had invested the money from the sale in a restaurant in Oslo. Wisting agreed that Tommy was a dreamer, not adding that this was not necessarily a quality he appreciated.

Following the meeting with the lawyer, he and Suzanne had dined with Line at Tommy's restaurant, Wisting's first time. Now he understood that it was more than an eating place: a restaurant building on three storeys called *Shazam Station* with a nightclub in the basement, a coffee bar at street level and the restaurant on the top floor.

Tommy, who had responsibility for the kitchen and restaurant, had been unable to eat with them, but ensured they were served a substantial four-course meal. The food was delicious, that was not the problem, but where were all the customers on this busy Friday afternoon? Only a handful of tables were occupied. If this was the case every day, it did not augur well.

He had never really understood what his daughter saw in Tommy. It was true he could be thoughtful and talkative, and even Wisting could see how charming he was. He did not trust him though, and not simply because he had a drugs conviction. Not even because he was obstinate and egotistical. Wisting simply felt that he was not the kind of character on whom his daughter should hazard her future.

Sometimes he wondered whether his scepticism stemmed solely from Line being his daughter. He did not really think so but, on the last few occasions he had seen them together, it did seem that Line had begun to notice some of Tommy's shortcomings. He seemed to irritate her, and Wisting had to admit ruefully to himself that he was delighted.

'If you don't take the chance to try something new, you can't expect to achieve anything,' Suzanne went on. 'What have you got to lose? No matter how many times you go wrong, you always learn something new each time. All experience is valuable, both good and bad.'

One of the guests on the TV show had been asked a question he could not answer immediately, and in the ensuing silence Wisting could hear the sound of a distant police siren.

He clutched his glass in his hand. 'Would you think of starting up a restaurant?' he asked.

'Oh yes,' she replied, surprised but smiling back at him. 'Not exactly a restaurant, but perhaps a little café with an art gallery. Life is too short to continue the way things are. Turning up at the office every morning. Meetings, budgets, cutbacks, projects.'

Suzanne was a child welfare officer who had worked for years with young, single asylum seekers. Recently her job had become increasingly administrative, and now she spent the majority of her time sitting in an office.

'What would you call it?' he asked, replacing his glass without drinking a drop.

'What do you mean?'

'If you've dreamt about opening a café, you must have thought of a name for it.'

She shook her head.

'Maybe something different from *Shazam Station*?'

She smiled.

'In fact, that's an amusing name.'

'Do you think so?'

'*Shazam*'s a magic word. It's Persian. "Sesame" in English. Open sesame.'

'Sesame Station?'

She laughed and a gossamer web of fine wrinkles radiated from her eyes and the corners of her mouth across her temples and cheeks. Her walnut brown eyes took an entirely individual, luminous glow from the candles on the table.

The telephone rang. *OPERA*, the internal abbreviation for the police centre of operations, appeared on the display. Wisting answered briefly, and the operator introduced himself in similar style. 'Several holiday cottages out at Gusland have been broken into,' he said. Wisting understood there was more to come. 'A dead body has been discovered in one of them.'

3

Slamming the car door behind him, William Wisting tugged his jacket lapels together against the cold sea breeze. His breath formed a delicate, pearly haze around his face. Already two police patrol cars and an ambulance were installed on the narrow parking spot, as well as two civilian vehicles.

At the far end of the parking area a path led into the undergrowth, and fifty metres later the coastal vista opened up, its rocky edge merging into the murky ocean. The light-house beam glittered on the restless surface of the water.

Immediately beside the sea he could make out the outline of a cottage, a faint light visible at a few windows, flashlights flickering in the darkness. An electric generator rumbled into life and the front section of the house was suddenly bathed in light. Red and white crime scene warning tape fluttered in the wind, reflective tape twinkled on police uniforms. The muffled sound of radio transmitters, telephones and subdued conversations mingled in the cold, starless, autumn night.

Wisting dipped into the bitter wind. He had been summoned to similar assignments countless times before but the first encounter with any crime scene was never routine, and he never became immune to the sight of lacerated skin, dead human beings, and the bottomless despair of relatives. All too often he had seen the consequences of senseless violence that seemed more brutal and ruthless each time. The recurring thoughts made him irritable and withdrawn.

He encountered two paramedics on the descent to the crime scene. Empty-handed, they approached him with sombre expressions, greeting him with nothing more than a brusque nod as they passed. The policeman in charge of crime scene operations raised the warning tape to let him pass.

The front door of the holiday cottage was wide open, exposing the splintered frame damaged in the burglary. Inside he could see the corpse's legs, with lumps of clay clinging to the soles of its boots. He was given a concise update which added nothing to the resumé he had heard over the phone twenty-five minutes earlier.

Espen Mortensen, the young crime scene technician, was already donning a white overall. 'Are you coming in?' he asked.

Wisting nodded, but contented himself with pulling on rubber overshoes before following his colleague upstairs.

Conspicuous damage had been inflicted on the area surrounding the lock, with wood shavings strewn in all directions and the striking plate torn loose . Blood was splattered over the stone steps, and above the door skewed smudges were visible, as though someone had supported himself there with a gory hand.

Espen Mortensen took a couple of establishing pictures before progressing further, with Wisting following him along the narrow hallway, while the policeman who had greeted him remained outside.

The male victim was sprawled on his stomach in an oddly contorted position, one arm beneath his body, the other pointing directly to the side, the hand in a thick, black, heavily blood-stained glove. Wearing dirty boots reaching almost to his knees, his upper body was clad in a black jumper, and a black balaclava covered his head.

Wisting took a few steps around the body.

A pool of blood spread underneath the corpse, flowing over the timber floor, forcing him to take long avoiding strides.

13

The victim's head was turned to one side, the balaclava showing a perpendicular tear at its front edge, about the middle of the forehead, where pale folds of skin hung down at each side and splinters of skull protruded from the open wound.

Outside, one of the police dogs was barking keenly, eager to start the search. Wisting hunkered down, resting his hands on his knees.

The eyes looking out from the mask were open wide, eyeballs bulging, the lips retracted as though gasping for air.

Wisting contemplated the death for almost a minute before standing to survey the scene. Blood had sprayed along the panelled walls. The remains of a bloody handprint were visible in a number of places, as on the door. It appeared the victim had tried to support himself before keeling over.

A pair of sticky footprints led from the pool on the floor to the doorway. Whoever had been here had trampled through the blood before fleeing.

'Who found him?' Wisting shouted the question to the policeman standing at the foot of the stairs.

'The neighbour.' The policeman pointed towards a cottage further up the hill. 'There had been a break-in there too.'

'Did he come inside?'

The uniformed policeman shook his head. 'He didn't go any further than the top of the stairs.'

Wisting remained standing, silently trying to form an overall impression, at the same time attempting to fix details in his mind that could prove crucial for their subsequent investigation. This was normally something he excelled at. First impressions of a crime scene could, aided by his years of experience as a detective, often lead to the construction of a slender framework which would eventually underpin a theory. A crime scene resembled a work of art where every

14

tiny detail in the picture, from a single brushstroke to the finished painting, reveals something about the artist.

The summer cottage was stylishly furnished with a combination of contemporary and antique furniture, the colours sharp, bright and tastefully coordinated. Evidence of burglary was obvious. Drawers and cupboards lay open, loose wires hung from a low corner table where the television set had been located, and pale patches showed along the walls where paintings had hung.

Sighing and shaking his head, Wisting returned to the corpse. He could not make sense of all this, but neither could he pinpoint what did not tally. 'Has the weapon been found?' he asked.

Espen Mortensen shook his head, relaying the question to the policeman outside. 'The dog patrol is searching now,' he clarified.

'What about the housebreaking tool?' Wisting asked, indicating the damaged doorframe.

Mortensen shook his head. 'That might be the murder weapon. The forensic specialists will probably have more to say, but it looks like a heavy blow from a sharp instrument, a crowbar, for example.'

'Don't you think he's the burglar?' Wisting asked, nodding at the body.

'Perhaps he was surprised and the crowbar was taken from him?'

Wisting shook his head doubtfully. There was nothing to suggest there had been any kind of struggle, apart from the fatal blow. Two small paintings were hanging neatly on the wall, a pair of training shoes was positioned methodically at the door, two windcheater jackets were hanging tidily from a row of coat-pegs, and further inside the house no damage was evident other than what Wisting had witnessed previously at countless burglary scenes.

'Where are the stolen goods?' he asked, taking a few steps further inside.

'Maybe he returned for more?' the policeman standing outside suggested. 'Came back to pick up some more stuff?'

'Maybe,' Wisting muttered, deep in thought. 'Who actually owns the cottage?'

'Has nobody told you? It's Thomas Rønningen.'

'The TV celebrity?'

His colleague nodded.

4

Entrusting the crime scene to Mortensen, Wisting stepped into the open space in front of the cottage. It was raining again, and water was dripping from the brim of the uniform cap worn by the officer in charge. 'Which other cottages have been burgled?' he asked.

The officer turned northwards, pointing to a summer cottage further inland, its contours outlined against the sky, windows brightly lit, with an elevated flagpole flying a pennant that flapped in the wind.

'The owner's name is Ove Bakkerud. He arrived from Oslo an hour ago and discovered he had been burgled. When he went to check the neighbouring cottages, he found the body and raised the alarm.'

Wisting rubbed his hand across his rain-soaked face. 'What others?'

The policeman, turning his back on the weather, produced a notebook. 'Jostein Hammersnes.' He gestured over Wisting's right shoulder. 'He has a cottage over on the point and phoned the police station to report a break-in about the same time we heard about the body. There may be more, but those are the two we know about. We're doing a door-to-door search now.'

'What have you done with the cottages?'

'Cordoned them off.'

Wisting nodded. They had at least three connected crime scenes, giving them more than three times the opportunity to detect traces of the culprit, a rare benefit as a starting

17

point. 'We've called in crime scene technicians from the entire region.'

'What about the owners?'

'We're in the process of installing them at a hotel in Stavern. You can question them there tomorrow morning.'

'Did any of them see anything?'

The officer shook his head, on the verge of saying something when they were interrupted by dogs barking and simultaneous crackling from his earplugs. He nudged them further in to improve sound reception. 'The dog patrol has found an exit on the eastern side. They've discovered a mobile phone on the track,' he relayed, 'and are wondering what they should do with it.'

'Mark the spot and bring the phone here,' Wisting ordered.

The officer in charge passed on the message and, shortly afterwards, a young policeman arrived at top speed, carrying the phone in a sealed transparent plastic evidence bag.

'There isn't much battery power left,' he explained, handing it to Wisting. 'You should read it before it goes dead. We might need the pin-code to turn it on again.'

Wisting accepted the bag and, through the plastic, located the button to illuminate the display. Familiar with the menu options on the Sony Ericsson, he rapidly reached the call list. It was empty: no incoming or outgoing calls. Returning to the menu, he found his way to the text messages. There was only one, received at 16.53. All it indicated was a number: *2030*.

The message had been sent from a nine-digit number abroad.

In the sent folder there were two messages to the same number: the first transmitted at 16.54 – *OK* – and the next message dispatched at 20.43 – *I am here*.

Wisting searched through other folders, but the three text messages were the only information stored. He interpreted

2030 as a message about a particular time of day, with the response being *OK*, and thereafter the owner of the mobile phone had sent a message suggesting he was at the agreed meeting place. *I am here.*

'I'll take it with me and put it on charge,' Wisting said, tucking the phone into his jacket pocket. 'Perhaps more messages will come in overnight.'

A snell gust caused Wisting to shiver as he surveyed the area in the night darkness: black rocky slopes, a grove of windswept pine trees, and clumps of juniper bushes tossing in the breeze. No more than three hours had passed since the fateful encounter resulting in a man's death. The perpetrator might still be around.

'We're getting helicopter support,' clarified the policeman in charge, whose thoughts must have coincided with his.

'Good,' Wisting nodded, not intending to wait. He would return home for a change into dry clothes before driving to the station.

Retracing his steps along the path, he discovered a group of journalists huddled beside the parking place. One of the photographers pointed his camera at Wisting's lined, determined face. As he opened the car door, his ears were bombarded by the racket of an approaching helicopter, flying low from the east, its searchlight skimming the landscape, and deflecting the interest of the reporters.

He turned his wet jacket inside out, dumping it on the passenger seat before settling behind the wheel. As his car headlights pierced the darkness, they illuminated the dense woodland beside the narrow gravel track.

A sudden thump battered the windscreen. Wisting slammed on the brakes, and the car skidded across the gravel. Blood and black feathers smeared the glass: he must have collided with a bird. Spraying the windscreen wash, he watched as the wipers removed the mess.

19

He restarted the engine, but had not travelled any distance when another bird struck the car, a black ball hurtling through the air before bouncing off the bonnet and disappearing above the windscreen. A few hundred metres later the track terminated at the main road between Helgeroa and Stavern, where Wisting turned right.

A veil of mist hovered above the dark asphalt, and rain-sodden autumn leaves were buffeted by the wind, plastering themselves on the windscreen and becoming trapped in the wipers.

One hundred metres further along, he reduced his speed as he spotted a movement at the road verge, and a man appeared, walking unsteadily towards him on the opposite side, using his hand to shield his face from Wisting's headlights. Automatically, he dimmed his lights, and at the same moment the man clutched his free hand to his chest and keeled over. Wisting halted the car, glanced in the rear view mirror and stepped out. This stretch of road, flanked by black ploughed earth and fields, was deserted. Wisting crouched down beside the man.

'Are you all right?' he asked. No reply.

He grabbed hold of him to pull him around. The man turned abruptly to face him, his eyes defiant although anxious and fearful. A fist shot out, smacking Wisting on the nose. Another two furious punches followed before the man got to his feet.

Wisting tried to hold on but the man wriggled free and swung out again, ineffectually this time. Wisting retaliated. His fist struck the man's abdomen and he doubled over, gasping for breath. Wisting hurled himself forward in an attempt to knock him off balance but was himself pounded by a series of blows, one of which caught him on the chin, knocking his teeth through his lips. He slumped to his knees as his mouth filled with blood.

20

Sprinting to the car, the man flung himself behind the steering wheel, hit the gas pedal and accelerated violently, aiming directly at Wisting. The headlights blinded him, but he rolled off the road and lay still as the car roared past. After a few seconds his eyes adjusted to the darkness. The surrounding area stretched out in variegated grey tints, but he saw the glowing rear lights of his own car as they disappeared into the distance.

He stumbled to his feet, spitting blood and cursing loudly as it dawned on him that he had left his mobile phone inside the vehicle. He could hear the helicopter searching the coastline. Spitting blood again he glanced backwards, trying to remember the location of the nearest house, before deciding to head in the same direction as the car. Ten minutes later farmhouse lights appeared and he increased his speed, jogging the final few metres.

The farmhouse, a two-storeyed white building with broad staircase, red-painted barn and a couple of outhouses, had an ancient oak with a colossal crown of leaves in the middle of its yard. Inside the barn, horses whinnied as they stirred restlessly, aware of his presence.

A grey and white cat stared at him from the top step before lifting a black bird from the doormat and slipping away.

On one side of the blue-painted door a large ceramic sign gave the residents' names. Pressing the doorbell, Wisting felt at his bruised face while he waited. A man with a luxuriant red beard opened the door, planting himself in the wide doorway to scrutinise his visitor.

'I'm from the police,' Wisting explained, fumbling in his trouser pocket before realising his identification card had vanished with his car.

Nodding, the man stepped back to allow him through. Wisting had been responsible for so many cases highlighted in the media that most people in the area knew him by sight.

'What's happened?' the man asked, closing the door.

Wisting took no time to explain. 'I need to use a phone,' was all he said.

The man produced a mobile phone from his pocket. 'You don't look too good,' he commented. 'Do you want to use the bathroom?'

Shaking his head, Wisting took the mobile and tapped in the number for the police central switchboard. His description of what had taken place was short and succinct. The bearded man stood, eyes popping as he listened and, when Wisting ended the call, asked whether he could offer any assistance.

'Do you have a car?'

The man nodded, reaching for his jacket. 'It's in the barn.'

Wisting requested the man drive him home, but he had no keys for the house either, as they were on the same key ring as his car key, and this also applied to his admittance card for the police station – tucked into his wallet with his ID. He was forced to ring his own doorbell. Suzanne cautiously opened the door. 'My God,' she fussed, taking him by the arm. 'What on earth do you look like?'

'It's madness,' Wisting replied, smiling for the first time. Heading for the bathroom, he wrenched off his wet blood-stained clothes while explaining quickly. 'Can you get me some fresh clothes?' he asked, stepping into the shower.

She agreed but first began to gather up his dirty, discarded clothing. 'Don't wash them,' he said, turning on the water. 'Hang them up to dry. Some of the blood might be his.'

The water heated rapidly, and he closed his eyes, leaning back into the spray.

'You should see a doctor,' Suzanne advised.

Wiping a streak of moisture from the glass door, he peered out at her. 'I'll see. Can you phone for a taxi?'

'At least let me have a look at it before you go.'

22

He made no protest and finished showering. She handed him a towel from the cupboard before leaving to fetch the first aid kit. On her return, he stood naked before her as she examined his face.

'Do you think it was him?'

'Who do you mean?'

'The killer!' She pressed antiseptic-soaked cotton wool on his wound. 'Do you think he was the man you were fighting?'

It was the same question he had already asked himself. 'I don't know.'

'That cut doesn't look too good,' she said, taking out a small sticking plaster. 'But I think it'll be all right.'

He kissed her to express his thanks, and she stroked his chest with her hand, moving it down over his stomach, as though to remind him what he was missing. Smiling, he kissed her again and began to dress. 'Have you phoned for a taxi?'

'I can drive,' she replied. 'I didn't have any more to drink after you left.'

5

Nils Hammer helped Wisting into the building. A bulky man with rugged features, Hammer was about five centimetres taller than his boss. Though he had the reputation of being a loner, he was a capable investigator who took his job very seriously, never giving up, always throwing himself intensely into his work. Like Wisting himself, Hammer could become obsessed with solving a case, and they had spent countless night hours together at the police station, battling their way through huge wall charts, complex theories and cups of bitter coffee. Nils Hammer was always one of the first personnel Wisting requested when an enquiry group was assembled.

'Torunn's on her way,' he said through a faint whiff of beer. He did not appear intoxicated; quite a number of police officers had been forced to change their plans that Friday evening.

'Okay,' Wisting nodded. It was reassuring to hear Torunn Borg, would participate in the introductory phase of the enquiry. Efficient and thorough, she was always extremely professional. 'We'll hold a meeting when she arrives.'

'I've initiated a search for your mobile phone,' Hammer went on, as they climbed the stairs to the criminal investigation department.

Wisting's mobile phone was continually transmitting a radio signal and the telephone company could locate it through their base stations. The very thought made him both enthusiastic and optimistic.

'It's somewhere here in town,' Hammer continued.

'*Telenor* is currently disconnecting individual antenna towers to home in more precisely.'

'When can we expect a result?'

Hammer shrugged his shoulders. 'Fifteen to twenty minutes, I suppose. We just have to hope the car isn't on the move.'

Thanking him, Wisting entered his own office, where he switched on the computer. While he waited for it to set up there were a couple of phone calls he had to make. The first number he dialled was for Christine Thiis, the lawyer newly appointed as successor to Audun Vetti, who had moved up the ranks and left the police station behind.

A distinguished defence lawyer from Oslo, she had switched career and relocated from the big city. Clearly the best-qualified applicant for the post, she had accepted the far less lucrative position as Assistant Chief of Police. Now she was in charge of all cases, and automatically assumed responsibility for the investigation.

Christine Thiis answered after a single ring. 'I've been trying to get hold of you,' she said, her tone tense and slightly irritated. 'I need to know what's going on.'

Clearing his throat, Wisting spent three minutes explaining the case. He could envisage her as he spoke, cheeks tinged pink with annoyance, brown eyes alert.

'Are you okay?' she asked.

'Oh yes, fine thanks,' Wisting reassured her.

He could hear her leafing through papers; she had probably been taking notes while he spoke. 'What do we have to go on?' she asked.

'We don't have anything specific yet, but it's still early days.'

'Okay, then I won't come in. The children are sleeping, and I can't leave them on their own.'

'We're going to need a lawyer here,' Wisting commented.

'Do you want me to check if someone else can take responsibility for this case?'

'No.' The reply was blunt. 'I've phoned my mother. She's coming from Lillestrøm and will be here in a few hours. For the moment I'd like you to keep me posted by phone.'

Assuring her he would be in touch if anything dramatic happened, Wisting wound up the conversation. The next person he needed to contact was Thomas Rønningen. Assuming the famous television talk show host's phone number was unlisted, he called the television company, *NRK*. Introducing himself, he explained it was of critical importance that he be put in touch with Thomas Rønningen.

The woman on night duty at the switchboard sounded experienced. Apologising, she responded by saying she did not possess his contact details, but asked him to wait. He could hear her tapping at a keyboard.

'I have a mobile number and email address for his agent, Einar Heier,' she clarified. 'Would you like those?'

'I'll take the phone number.' She read it out to him. 'Thanks. Tonight's broadcast, do you know when it was recorded?'

'It's a direct broadcast.'

'What does that mean?'

'We used to record the programme one day in advance, but that meant we lost some of the topicality. Now the programme is recorded four hours before the start of the broadcast, and goes out unedited.'

Wisting did a mental calculation. 'So that means the recording was finished around six o'clock this evening?'

'That's right.' She hesitated. 'Is this something you should be discussing with security?'

'Oh no. If I do, I'll phone back later.' Terminating the conversation, he keyed in the number for the agent, who replied with feigned affability. Wisting introduced himself once again, requesting contact information for Thomas Rønningen.

'I can give you a mobile number, but it's not certain you'll get an answer.'

'No?'

'I always phone him after the broadcast to tell him what I think about the programme, but tonight he didn't answer.'

Wisting glanced through the window as he spoke, spotting a helicopter flying low above the fjord. 'When did you last speak to him?'

'Yesterday. May I ask what this is about?'

'His holiday cottage in Helgeroa has been broken into.'

'Oh well. Then I'm sure he'll be grateful for your call.' The agent read the number aloud. 'If he doesn't answer, send a text message instead to let him know.'

'Thank you.'

'Is there anything I can do; something practical in connection with the burglary?'

'Not at the moment. I have your number now.'

Outside, the helicopter was hanging aloft, a cone of light directed inshore, where it hovered expectantly. Wisting keyed in Thomas Rønningen's number before standing up and crossing to the window. Immediately, an automatic answering machine clicked on and Wisting stored the number after disconnecting the call.

Nils Hammer's voice on the intercom system broke the silence in the room: 'They've located your phone. It seems to be out at Revet.' The helicopter outside tilted as it turned in an easterly direction. Revet was originally a sandbank situated between Lågen and the Larvik fjord, but nowadays it was a significant industrial and harbour area. It offered many possible hiding places for a vehicle, but only one exit route. 'We're setting up a cordon around the canal quay,' Hammer explained.

Wisting took his eyes off the helicopter, staring instead at his own reflection in the window. Raindrops distorted his facial contours, making him a stranger to himself. His heavy eyelids closed, and he kept them shut as he gathered his thoughts.

This would be his first large-scale investigation since returning from a lengthy period of sick leave. He had always considered his work challenging and stimulating, but last summer, confronted with a steadily increasing burden of work divided among ever fewer resources, he had become unwell. The constant overload had resulted in physical and mental exhaustion.

He had been off work for three months and when he returned, realising he was far from indispensable, he had managed to transfer more responsibility and share out an increased number of tasks to his colleagues.

Now he stood, aware of his body, wondering if he was ready for this, before reaching a decision. Lifting the jacket hanging on the back of his chair, he strode determinedly towards the door.

6

A barrage of rain battered the windscreen as Wisting drove out of the police garage. As he switched on the wipers, the raindrops were swept aside, returned, vanished again. Water tumbled over the kerbs, forming deep puddles where the drains could not cope. A drizzly haze enveloped the deserted streets.

The journey out to Revet took no longer than three minutes. He was stopped at a roadblock, where two patrol cars were positioned bonnet to bonnet, with another police vehicle in front of them. A helicopter was searching in wide circles overhead.

A rain-coated police officer approached, his arms resting on a sub-machine gun suspended on his chest. When Wisting wound down his side window, his colleague saluted with two fingers raised to his cap.

'Any news?'

The policeman shook his head. In his mirror, Wisting spotted the lights of another car. The police officer straightened up, peering in the same direction. A red Golf drew to a halt and Garm Søbakken from the local newspaper jumped out. 'What's going on?' he asked, turning his back to the rain. The uniformed officer did not reply so the journalist directed himself to Wisting.

'We're searching for a stolen car,' he explained.

'With a helicopter and guns?'

The armed policeman tramped back to his post at the barrier. Wisting nodded. He should have prepared a press release before leaving, but assumed that someone at headquarters was already on the job. Pressure from the media would be intense as soon as the few details in their possession became known. News editors could not wish for more. A criminal case and celebrity story combined.

'A statement will be made to the press very shortly,' he said, winding up the window.

He was not usually so dismissive, but was embarrassed that the presumed killer had escaped by stealing the car belonging to the policeman leading the investigation. The journalist from *Østlands-Posten* pointed his camera at the barrier with the helicopter in the background.

Suddenly the enormous machine swooped like a falcon, plunging towards its prey, before climbing once more, hovering in the air, its spotlight pointing down vertically. The helicopter pilot summoned the police officers on the ground: '*Fox 05, this is Heli.*'

'*Fox 05,*' crackled through the police radio.

'*We have sighted a suspicious vehicle under the light. Thermal imaging indicates that the engine is warm. No sign of life.*'

'*Received, we see where you are.*'

One of the cars at the barrier started its engine. Wisting rushed over and clambered into the back seat.

The man behind the wheel turned and nodded before moving off, heading for the helicopter's cone of light. They drove past the Color Line terminal building and out towards the container harbour, passing warehouses, workshops and crawler cranes. In the rain, the high lamps lining the road were encircled by golden light.

Wisting's stolen car was parked in the open, beside a trolley stacked with stone blocks awaiting shipment. Gusts of wind were driving the water in horizontal cascades across the asphalt. It seemed totally abandoned.

A police car arrived from the other side, stopping twenty metres from Wisting's car. Three men stepped out and brief messages passed across the two-way radio. They approached the vehicle with weapons drawn, while the two police officers from the car that had brought Wisting to the scene formed a kind of perimeter defence.

Rapidly ascertaining that there was no one inside, one of the men positioned himself with the barrel of his gun pointing towards the boot lid, while another opened it from inside. Followed immediately by the crackling message: *'All clear.'*

One of the officers in the other patrol car led out a dog as Wisting stepped forward to take a look. His sodden jacket was lying on the passenger seat and he opened the door to remove it. Underneath was the evidence bag with the mobile phone. There was still a trace of battery power remaining, but no new messages or calls.

One of the policemen shone a Maglite into the driver's compartment. 'What should we do with the car?' he asked.

Wisting surveyed the interior. The keys were still in the ignition and the pale fabric on the driver's seat was smeared with mud and clay. 'We must get it towed in for forensic examination. Will you see to that?'

His colleague nodded as he probed the interior of the vehicle with the beam of light. 'Did you injure him?' he asked, pointing with the light towards a number of dark stains on the seat.

Wisting skirted around the car. 'Not significantly.'

'That looks like blood.'

Wisting inwardly reconstructed the events: the play-acting when the man fell to the ground, dark clothing and gloves, nothing to indicate that he was injured. In the brief fight he had glimpsed his face, but it was only the expression he remembered. The man had looked terrified; panicked.

31

'Wonder why he drove out here,' the policeman said, interrupting Wisting's train of thought. 'He must have been picked up by accomplices.'

The helicopter above them soared off to continue its search. Wisting turned up his jacket collar and returned to the patrol car. This trail was about to go cold.

7

On the return journey Wisting located the number he had saved for Thomas Rønningen and tried one more time. The voice on the answering machine sounded just as bright and cheerful as it did on television. He left a brief message giving his mobile number.

Torunn Borg was sitting in her office with only the desk lamp for illumination, a yellow ring of light spilling onto her papers. One hand was placed in the middle of the spotlight, the other supported her head. A long, soft lock of hair hung over her right shoulder. She sat up straight when Wisting entered.

'Good to see you,' he said.

She swiftly tucked her hair behind her ear. 'I've asked Benjamin Fjeld to come too.'

Wisting nodded. That was a good idea. Benjamin Fjeld came from the law enforcement section, but had been a probationer in Criminal Investigation for almost six months and had made a good impression. Motivated and knowledgeable, he possessed an enormous capacity for work, as well as a good eye for detail and a rare ability to pinpoint connections and relationships. He was inquisitive and had a particular talent for thinking out of the box. Against all that he lacked experience of a major case, a case such as this. Also, Wisting had a weakness for the purposeful and idealistic twenty-six year old. There was something about him that reminded him of himself at the same age.

He sat in the visitor's chair.

'What do we know so far?' Torunn Borg asked.

'Not much.' Wisting replied. Nils Hammer joined them and stood leaning against a filing cabinet, sipping at a cup of coffee. 'It looks as though this started with three burglaries in summer cottages.'

'Six,' Hammer interjected. 'The dog patrol has followed the trail and discovered three more cottages with the doors broken open.'

'More work for the technicians,' said Wisting.

'There's a whole team out there now,' Hammer elaborated. 'They're going from cottage to cottage.'

'I've checked the background of the guy who found the body,' said Torunn Borg. 'Ove Bakkerud runs an accountancy firm in Oslo. He's had the cottage for more than twenty years. Married, with two grown-up children. No criminal record.'

Wisting nodded. Often, the person who raised the alarm with the police about a serious crime turned out to be more deeply involved than he suggested. So far they had been unable to pin down any inconsistencies in Ove Bakkerud's story. 'What about the other neighbour at the cottages?'

Torunn leafed through her papers. 'Jostein Hammersnes: recently separated, has two small daughters, the cottage is in joint ownership, works in an IT company in Bærum. He has a few traffic offences, that's all.'

'The most interesting thing is probably the identity of the murder victim,' Hammer suggested. 'It could have been a private quarrel. Two burglars fall out about something and one of them kills the other.'

Wisting agreed. It need not be any more complicated than that.

Hammer went on, 'The murderer leaves, attacks a random motorist and hijacks a car.'

'But why didn't he use his own car?' Wisting asked. 'They must have had a van or truck loaded with stolen goods.'

34

'It might still be there,' Torunn Borg suggested. 'Perhaps the keys are in the murder victim's pocket.'

'In that case we'll need to wait until after the post mortem to check it out,' said Hammer. 'Mortensen wouldn't even try to lift the balaclava for a glimpse of his face.'

'I don't think that would help us anyway,' Wisting said. 'His face is probably completely destroyed.'

Standing up, he produced from his pocket the evidence bag including the mobile phone found near the cottages.

'Can you look into that?' he asked, handing it to Hammer. 'Where it has been located during the last twenty-four hours – the way you tracked my phone?' Putting down his coffee cup, Nils Hammer took hold of the phone. 'But remember to charge it before the battery runs out,' Wisting added.

'Give me a couple of hours,' Hammer said, disappearing out the door.

Torunn Borg turned towards the computer screen.

'What are you working on?' Wisting asked, leaning against the doorframe.

'I've brought up a list of all the housebreakings at cottages in the Østland area in the past three weeks. There could be a connection. They come in a series. Six or seven burglaries in one place one day, and a similar number somewhere else the next.'

'East Europeans?'

'Probably.'

Wisting remained standing in the doorway. Aggravated theft committed by people from the poor part of Europe was a growing problem for the police. New gangs and fresh trends cropped up continually. Some gangs specialised in stealing cosmetics and razor blades from shops, others filched boat engines from marinas. Some specialised in electronics stores, while others concentrated on private homes or remote groups of holiday cottages. The gangs were increasingly professional, and the police constantly lagged behind. 'Are there any clues or information in the other cases?'

'Not so far. I'm in the sifting process.'

Expressing his appreciation of her initiative, Wisting headed for his own office but his mobile rang before he reached his destination.

'Press release?'

Wisting recognised the voice of the person in charge at operational HQ in Tønsberg, where most of the media enquiries were directed. The issue of a press release would reduce pressure on the central switchboard. 'Any suggestions?'

'The usual.' The operational leader rustled a sheet of paper, reading aloud: *'An investigation has been initiated by Vestfold police district after a person was found dead in a cottage near Helgeroa in Larvik. The police received a report of the death on Friday 1st October directly after 22.00 hours. At this point no further information can be issued concerning the case. A press conference will be held at Larvik police station at ...?'*

Wisting sat behind his desk, glancing at the clock on the wall.

'Ten o'clock,' he decided. 'We can probably give them a little more information. Confirm that we have started a murder enquiry and that searches are being conducted with helicopter and police dogs for one or several perpetrators.'

'Fine. Is there anything we're seeking information about? Movements, vehicles or such like?'

Wisting decided it was too early to ask for specific observations. They had provided the public with the time and location of the murder. Experience suggested that anyone who had noticed anything out of the ordinary would make contact. 'No. Not just now. Will you send me a copy when it's issued?'

'Yes. It's going in a few minutes.' The operational leader hung up without rounding off the conversation.

Wisting switched on his computer and leaned back in his chair while waiting for the display to appear.

When he had started in the criminal investigation department in the mid eighties, all the report writing had been done on typewriters. Not until ten years ago had every single detective been allocated a personal computer. Notebooks from the major cases he had worked on, containing complete logs of the investigation of cases in real time, were stacked on the shelves of the cupboard behind him. Names were noted and crossed through, some circled, or connected to others using lines and arrows. Thoughts and reflections were jotted down, tasks distributed. Many cases had approached a resolution through complicated mind maps on paper.

Now this aspect of police work was digitalised. Dedicated computer tools had been developed and an electronic project room created, sharing the information among all the participants in an investigation. Information gathered was intended to provide a foundation for a particular analysis of the case. All the documents concerning the case were recorded and all the individuals involved in the investigation or mentioned in some way were entered in a special register. Data programs ensured the execution of a comprehensive and effective investigation from the initial phase until the conclusion of the enquiry, the aim being to provide a full overview, verifiability, objectivity and professional quality.

He logged into the data system and waited while the machine worked its way through its start procedure. Rotating his chair, he opened the cupboard behind and hauled out an unused hardback notebook. He extracted a grey pencil from the desktop holder and opened at the first blank page, writing a caption: *Who?*

For the present he was not so preoccupied by motive or

37

method, as the main challenge was to discover the victim's identity. The answer could lead them directly to the killer.

Fishing out the spectacles he was now dependent on, he continued to make notes. For almost an hour he wrote down key words about urgent tasks. Important elements more imperative than others he underlined or allocated additional comments in the margin, individual clues were elaborated with explanations and amplifications. He sketched arrows and symbols, and numbered the priorities and the less essential aspects.

High on the list was the collection of electronic evidence, valuable information that had to be recorded as soon as possible. CCTV tapes from petrol stations were wiped after one week. Recordings of vehicles in transit through various tollbooths were stored for slightly longer. The same applied to traffic data on the mobile phone network. Often they were unsure what they were looking for at this early stage of information gathering, but if they failed to secure all electronic material, it would soon be irretrievable.

The forensic examination of the body would be crucial. Above all to establish the identity of the victim, but it might also be possible to find strands of hair, fibres or other traces that could link him directly to the perpetrator. Wounds, accumulations of blood and postmortem bruising were also crucial pieces of information that could shed a great deal of light on the sequence of events.

Often the forensic examinations provided answers about what had taken place, but investigators never knew in advance what types of evidence would emerge, and they could never depend on the possible acquisition of forensic evidence. Focus had to be placed on the tactical investigation.

A strategy had to be devised with respect to the media as well. As yet, that consisted of two bywords: openness and honesty.

This was going to be the first press conference Christine Thiis had led. From that point until the conclusion of the case, she was the one who carried formal responsibility for the investigation. It was going to be a steep learning curve, and he hoped she would be equal to the task. This crime, involving a dead man discovered in the summer cottage belonging to one of the country's most well-known TV personalities, was going to create an explosion of media interest.

Once more he attempted to phone Thomas Rønningen, but was again connected to an answering machine. Intending to leave a new message, he nevertheless decided to hang up and send a short text message instead.

Rising from his chair, he stretched himself before stepping into the corridor and across to the conference room where he found a half-full pot of coffee sitting on the hotplate. He fetched himself a cup from the shelf and filled it, glancing towards the door when he heard footsteps.

Espen Mortensen appeared. Handing him the cup, Wisting filled another for himself. 'Finished at the crime scene already?'

The crime scene technician shook his head. 'We've removed the body. I'll prepare some photographs and write a summary report to accompany it to Forensics. I've made an appointment with the ID group at *Kripos*. They'll attend the post mortem.'

Kripos was the national criminal investigation department, where certain aspects of crime investigation were centralised. They sat down at the conference table. 'Have you discovered anything more?' Wisting enquired.

Mortensen nodded. 'It isn't as we thought initially.' Wisting looked at him. 'He's been shot. When we turned him over, we found a large entry wound in the stomach region.'

Wisting pictured the bloody entrance to the cottage where the man was found: blood dripping onto the steps and smeared on the upper part of the door, gory gloves and the pool of blood underneath the corpse. 'He must have been shot before he entered the cottage. We have an undetermined crime scene.'

Mortensen confirmed: 'The shots were fired in another location. He managed to drag himself to the cottage where the struggle continued. The way the blood was splashed over the walls suggests he was struck at least three times.'

'Have we found the weapon?'

Espen Mortensen got to his feet. 'No, neither the gun nor the weapon that caused the blows.' He crossed to the door with the cup in his hand. 'And it's difficult to say what the actual cause of death was. He's been shot, and then battered unconscious. He might have bled to death from the bullet wounds, but the blows could have been fatal in themselves. And it isn't certain that the man who shot him was also the man who delivered the blows.'

8

Line was reluctant to go to bed, but so bleary-eyed that she had to stretch out on the settee and pull a blanket over herself. She was wakened by her mobile phone when the clock display showed 04.23. Her neck was aching and throat dry.

Initially, she thought it was Tommy sending his usual message, apologising for being late and telling her he would be home soon, but she was wrong. Instead it was a red alert from *NTB*, a service she subscribed to, notifying her of breaking news. They called it red alert because, when it rolled over the news feed on the enormous screens in the editorial offices, the letters were in bold red font. There was always great excitement when a news story the journalists had worked on hit the public domain and the newspaper was given the credit in a rushed message from the news bureau.

She squinted at the display: *NTB: The police in Vestfold confirm murder enquiry after body found in holiday cottage. Armed police searching for perpetrator with dogs and helicopter.*

She opened her laptop to read what her newspaper had to say about the case. They had already published a dramatic photograph of an armed, uniformed police officer standing in front of flapping police crime scene tape with a helicopter suspended in the air behind him. A freelancer had taken the photo. The headline warned the public about a fleeing killer. She checked the bye-line and saw that one of their more experienced journalists, on duty in the online newspaper's editorial office, had got the scoop. Since the police had been armed, it

41

was natural to query whether the situation was dangerous for the public and, as long as the police could not guarantee safety, this strikingly effective headline was legitimate.

She skimmed the brief article, noting that it did not add much more factual information than the hurried message from *NTB*. The police were unforthcoming, and the *VG Nett* online newspaper would provide further details later.

She checked the other newspapers. *Dagbladet* had illustrated their report with a map, while *Aftenposten* was text only. As far as content was concerned, neither of them had any details to add.

Line had been employed at *Verdens Gang* for just over two years, but during this short tenure she had won several journalistic awards. She could not conceive of doing any other kind of work. It had become more than a source of income for her. Being a journalist was her way of life. Envisioning the busy editorial office, she felt pleased she had just taken some time off. She enjoyed working on such cases, but at present had too much on her mind.

A car door slammed in the street and she crossed to the window to look. The streetlamps swayed in the wind, and the asphalt three floors below was running with water though the rain had at last subsided.

Tommy had parked in an empty space directly opposite their block of flats. Standing beside the car, he fumbled in his jacket pocket for a pack of cigarettes before selecting one. His clean-cut features glowed as he lit up. His mobile phone rang in his trouser pocket and he hurried to answer, gesturing with his hand as he spoke. When he glanced up she withdrew slightly from the window.

Line collected her cup and plate from the coffee table and carried them to the kitchen as Tommy let himself in. He smiled when he caught sight of her. 'Haven't you gone to bed?' he asked.

She shook her head, avoiding his speckled brown eyes. Something still stirred inside her when he entered, but she had made her decision and would let common sense triumph.

He attempted to give her a quick kiss, but she turned away to avoid the tobacco smell. Laughing at her, he threw his leather jacket on a chair. Underneath he was wearing only a tight white T-shirt that was stretched around his upper arms.

Opening the fridge, he helped himself to a beer before producing an opener from the drawer and leaving it lying on the worktop together with the bottle top. The taut sinews in his neck stood out as he drank. 'How did dinner with your father go?' he asked, leaning against the kitchen worktop. 'Did it taste good?'

Taking a deep breath, Line carefully enunciated the sentence that had been waiting, ready, inside her head, for some time. 'This isn't working anymore.'

He stared at her in surprise. 'What do you mean?'

'You're hardly ever home, and I don't know where you are or what you're doing.'

'I'm running a restaurant.'

'You're hardly ever there either. I don't know what you're doing. I don't know your friends or the people you spend time with.'

'You haven't been particularly interested in getting to know them either.' His Danish accent was more noticeable when he was riled.

Line flung out her arms expressively. 'The ones I have met I haven't been especially interested in getting to know better,' she admitted. 'But that's not the point.'

'What is the point?'

'The two of us. Don't you see that we're drifting apart?'

'That's not only my fault. I don't always know when you're home either. You're sometimes away for days on an assignment.'

43

'That's my job.'

'And *Shazam Station* is my job. I'm doing it for us, you know, even though I'm not paid for every hour I'm there.'

'For us? What do we have to show for it? There aren't any profits. You're living in my flat and driving around in my car.' She grabbed the bottle top from the counter and hurled it into the rubbish bin. 'You don't contribute much at all.'

He set down the bottle and stepped towards her. 'It will get better,' he said, making a move to embrace her.

She wriggled free. She had heard him say that too many times before.

The first six months with Tommy had been ecstatic. She hardly ate, hardly slept, and every hour away from him had felt like a meaningless waste of time. She was head over heels in love, and the protestations of her girlfriends were simply irritating. Kaja, one of Line's best friends from the newspaper, had appeared at the flat one evening, clutching a bottle of wine, full of good intentions. After a couple of glasses, Kaja delivered pragmatic advice together with remarks about Tommy's background, his lack of education, his family relationships. She thought it obvious that he was not a suitable life partner for Line. The evening had ended with Line showing her the door, offended by her lack of faith in her, and more certain than before of her love for Tommy.

Now the intensity of their love had diminished she reluctantly had to admit that Kaja had a point. Lack of education and a few mistakes in his past were not in themselves problematic, but it felt as though large parts of Tommy's life were hidden from her, and in recent months anxiety had overwhelmed her happiness. A week earlier she had done something she could have sworn she would never do and checked Tommy's text messages when he was in the shower.

Trembling, she had scrolled through his inbox, searching for answers to the questions that troubled her night and day, but had emerged none the wiser. She had found no sign of infidelity, only business appointments and innocuous messages from people involved in *Shazam Station*. Afterwards, she had felt ashamed, and the only way she was able to forget her disgrace and disquiet was to lose herself in Tommy's arms.

She completely recognised how clichéd her situation was, but that did not improve matters. Accustomed to being in control of her life, even after her mother's death she had understood who she was and what was right for her. However, she was now on the verge of disintegrating and needed to be alone for a while, to renew contact with old girlfriends, go for walks, take exercise, and discover what kind of life she really wanted. In Tommy's company she lived from day to day; she had adopted his habits, and it was becoming clear that this was not the route to a harmonious life. She was robust, but needed some measure of predictability at home. As her job was full of surprising twists and turns and grotesque assignments, she needed to feel secure with her nearest and dearest, but she did not feel even safe with Tommy. He held his cards too close to his chest, communicated physically rather than verbally, seemed troubled and restless but refused to concede that something was worrying him.

'This isn't working anymore,' she repeated.

'What do you mean?'

'The two of us,' she said, pointing from him to herself. 'I no longer know if this is what I want.'

He did not speak, but simply continued to stand, clasping the beer bottle he had picked up again, clutching it to his chest as he looked at her.

'I need some time to myself,' she declared.

This was a tentative method of articulating her intentions. Nevertheless she noticed a glimmer of anxiety in his eyes.

She gave all her thoughts expression through words and once they were set free, they continued to spill out. She had to make a determined effort to remain calm.

'I don't understand,' he said, shaking his head.

'Maybe that's the problem,' she suggested.

He was about to say something, but was interrupted by a signal from his mobile phone. He read the message and glanced up at her. 'Can we talk about this tomorrow?' he asked, putting down the beer bottle.

'Are you going out again?'

'There are some problems down at *Shazam*,' he said, lifting his jacket. 'They need me.'

She wanted to say that she needed him too, but that was no longer true. 'I won't be here when you come back,' she said instead.

He sighed, continuing to stand with his jacket in his hand. 'Can't we discuss this?'

'I've said all I've got to say. I'm going home for a while.'

'What is it you want, then?'

'I want you to come back and pack your belongings, and find yourself somewhere else to stay.' She stood with her arms folded as Tommy continued to stare at her. Then he lowered his head, turned on his heel and left.

9

Just before six o'clock Wisting leaned back in his office chair and closed his eyes. He had gathered his strength like this many times before, and knew that a doze of only half an hour would put him in better shape for the rest of the day. He drifted into sleep but was wakened twenty minutes later by a knock at the door. Straightening up, he cleared his throat and greeted Christine Thiis.

The newly appointed Assistant Chief of Police sat at the opposite side of his desk, looking intently at him. Her state of mind was always revealed by her eyes. Open and straightforward, her eyes were like those of an intelligent child, eager to learn.

'How are the children?' Wisting asked before she had broken the silence.

For a moment it appeared that she had not understood his question, and then she smiled, 'They're fine. Fast asleep. My mother's arrived and will stay for the weekend. Next week too, if necessary.'

'That's good.'

In the four months she had been with them Christine Thiis had never mentioned the children's father. All they knew was that he was a corporate lawyer in Oslo, but there was never any suggestion of the children staying with him. Wisting had the impression that her former marriage was something she did not want to discuss, as though it comprised only unhappy memories she would prefer to forget.

'How are things going here?' she asked.

47

Wisting stroked his chin. 'Situation normal: complex and confusing.'

Apprehension appeared in her eyes, and it dawned on him that she had never previously participated in such an investigation. 'It's always like this in the beginning,' he said. 'Gradually we get a grip on things.'

He clarified the overnight developments in the case, letting his eyes slide over her instead of meeting her penetrating gaze. Her hair was short and chestnut-coloured with unruly curls. She had soft and generous lips and her nose was sprinkled with freckles. He suddenly felt that he had lost concentration, struck by an abrupt, involuntary thought about what type of man could let her go, before continuing his report and concluding with the discovery of the bullet wounds in the murder victim.

'Have we any theories?' she asked.

'Not really,' Wisting answered. 'This early in the case all we have are speculations.'

'But you must have some thoughts about what might have happened?'

Wisting considered the implications of her question. Building a case on mere speculation was like pouring sand into your petrol tank, the road to ruin. 'What is obvious, of course, is that there's some connection between the burglaries at the cottages and the murder. It will all become much simpler once we establish the identity of the victim.'

'And when do we get to know that?'

'That can take time. The post mortem will begin in a couple of hours. We'll have people from the ID group at *Kripos* joining us there. They'll start by undressing him. As soon as we have a picture of the face behind the balaclava, we'll know a great deal more, but it's far from certain that it'll tell us anything valuable. He won't necessarily be someone already known to us. He may not even be Norwegian. If we're lucky he'll have an ID card of some description, or something else in his pockets that takes us further. If we're really lucky, his details will be in the fingerprint register. Then we'll have our answers before this day is done.'

Christine Thiis stood up. 'Okay,' she said. 'When are you meeting with the investigators?'

Wisting glanced at the clock. 'In half an hour. In the conference room.'

'Then I'll see you there.' The Assistant Chief of Police stepped towards the door.

'There's one thing more,' Wisting called after her.

'Yes?'

'The prosecutor's responsibilities also include liaison with the media.' Christine Thiis nodded with what Wisting thought was a trace of uncertainty. 'A press conference has been arranged for ten o'clock.'

'You'll accompany me, I hope?'

'Yes.' Wisting smiled. 'I'll come with you.'

A few minutes before seven, the investigators gathered in the conference room. Wisting paid a visit to the toilet, where he splashed his face with cold water and looked at his reflection in the mirror for several seconds. His pale face was swollen, his hair untidy and his eyes fixed. Tearing a paper towel from the holder, he dried himself before tossing the paper in the bin and leaving to join his colleagues.

Someone had switched on the television and Wisting stood in the doorway following the news report about the case in progress. On the screen, four policemen carried a covered stretcher, placing it in the rear of a hearse as a reporter gave an account of what the News Channel knew about the case. In the lower corner of the picture, his commentary was summed up in bold text: *MURDER ALARM IN LARVIK*.

The report continued with alternating photographs of the police helicopter, dog handlers, and police officers wearing bulletproof vests and carrying weapons while they played the recording of a telephone interview in which Christine Thiis made a few concise comments. Wisting recognised his own words from his briefing of her. The reportage was rounded off with photographs of the hearse leaving the scene accompanied by Christine Thiis commenting that the victim had not yet been identified and that the investigation would make considerable progress as soon as the post mortem had been carried out, establishing the identity of the murder victim.

She managed well, Wisting reflected, her voice betraying no trace of the uncertainty he had read in her eyes.

The newsreader promised viewers that they would continue to pursue the story in the course of the day and return with a live broadcast from the press conference at ten o'clock.

The TV set was switched off as Wisting stepped into the room where a rapid head count showed twenty-two people in total. The dog handlers were sitting on chairs lining the wall, together with others from the operational force who had worked through the night. The investigators who would progress the case were seated around the conference table. At the top, the Chief Superintendent had already taken his place, with Christine Thiis in the chair Wisting normally occupied at such meetings.

He sat in the vacant chair at her side. Outside, the autumn darkness would persist for another hour yet. 'Welcome,' he said, going on to thank the officers who were on overtime duties.

Nils Hammer started the ceiling projector, and an overview map showing the area between Hummerbakk fjord and Nevlunghavn illuminated the screen. At a point on the inside of the cove described as Ødegårdsbukta, a cottage by the edge of the sea was highlighted.

Wisting cleared his throat before delivering as succinct a

50

summary as possible, appreciating from the expressions surrounding him that everyone in the room was already familiar with the case. Locating the leader of the operational force in his seat beside the row of windows, he nodded in his direction.

'What's the latest from the crime scene?'

Placing his coffee cup between his legs, the burly officer produced his notebook. 'We called off the search for the presumed perpetrator half an hour ago,' he explained as he flicked through the pages. 'As you know, it was fruitless and we have neither an arrest nor the murder weapon. In the meantime, a couple of interesting things have cropped up. The crime scene technicians will probably say more about those, but I will say this much. There have been a lot of people out there. The dog handlers have tracked in every direction, from cottage to cottage. I think we're talking about four or five sets of unidentified footprints at least.'

Wisting made a few notes. Although information would appear in a report later in the day, it was nevertheless useful to record it now.

'The prints frequently end up at one side road or other, so they had a vehicle.'

'Have you found any cars?'

'We've checked several. There will always be a few cars parked at a group of cottages like that, but they are all accounted for. You'll receive a detailed list, but we're talking about cottage owners, fishermen, birdwatchers and farmers, all of whom have seen or heard zilch.'

The operations leader grabbed hold of his cup and leafed through his notes.

'The most interesting discovery is one we made just before we finished,' he said. 'Out at Smørvika we found three empty cartridges.'

Wisting turned to the map hanging on the wall behind

51

him. Nils Hammer placed the cursor on a little inlet east of Ødegårdsbukta. The surrounding area was shaded green, indicating a nature reserve. The cottage where the body had been found was the nearest habitation, at a distance of five to six hundred metres.

'They're lying in the middle of the path and can't have been there long. At one side of the path there's a patch of woodland, and two of the cartridges are lying on top of newly fallen leaves. We've cordoned off the area and have covered them with a tarpaulin, so the technicians can have a look at them when they have time.'

'That's good,' Wisting remarked. 'Excellent.'

He had not previously heard about the discovery of the cartridges, and his spirits were lifted by the operational leader's account. Magazine clips, firing pins, strikers and fingers all left traces on gun cartridges. This discovery represented the securing of vital evidence.

He assigned a further fifteen minutes of the meeting to the officers who had worked through the night to relate their thoughts and impressions, before thanking them for their attendance, thus reducing the number of assembled participants. In this type of case, there was always some information he was reluctant to share with more colleagues than absolutely necessary. What he had christened the *Telephone Trace* on his notepad fell into this category.

He gave a brief account of the mobile phone found by the search dogs.

Nils Hammer placed the mobile, still inside a transparent plastic bag, before them on the table. 'I've managed to charge it now,' he said, looking at Wisting. 'There's a message in the inbox,' he continued, directing himself now to those who were not familiar with the details. 'It was received at 16.53 yesterday. *20.30.*'

'A time of day?' Christine Thiis suggested.

52

'Probably. The message was answered by *OK*. Later, at 20.43, the owner has sent *I am here*.'

Christine Thiis gave voice to her thoughts. 'First a message about a meeting time, and later a confirmation that the person in question had arrived.'

Leaning forward across the table, she lifted the mobile phone, as though it could provide further answers in itself.

'I interpret it that way as well,' Hammer affirmed.

'Is it at the correct time?' Torunn Borg asked.

'Approximately. It's thirty-seven seconds slow.'

'Who's the subscriber?' Christine Thiis asked.

Hammer removed the phone from her hands, as though afraid she might damage it. 'That's interesting,' he replied. 'It makes this case bigger than it's been up till now.' Leaning forward, Wisting eagerly waited for him to continue. 'There's a Spanish pay-as-you-go card inside it,' Hammer explained.

'Spanish?'

'Yes, the numbers are Spanish, both the sender and the receiver, and registered to the same person. Carlos Mendoza in Malaga.'

Wisting jotted down *SPAIN* in large capitals on his notepad. They had a name, but he was not sure he liked the sound of it. International ramifications posed great challenges.

'I'll follow it up today,' said Nils Hammer, 'but I think I've found something else of significance.'

Wisting nodded as a sign that he should continue.

Nils Hammer held up the phone as he spoke. 'When the first message was received, the phone was located in Oslo. The text message was registered by a telephone base station in Havnelageret. Three hours and fifty minutes later, when the owner texts *I am here*, it's in Nevlunghavn.'

'An Oslo connection,' the Chief Superintendent concluded. He had been sitting in silence, listening intently, until this point. 'Where's the other phone located?'

'In Nevlunghavn also, but we can get more out of this.'

Crossing to the flipchart, Nils Hammer picked up a pen and wrote *20.43* at the foot of the sheet of paper before drawing a line to the top of the page and writing *16.53*.

'If the person concerned sends *I am here* when he arrives in Nevlunghavn ...'

'Then he's almost a quarter of an hour late,' Christine Thiis interrupted him. 'And he has taken nearly double the length of time it usually takes to travel from Oslo.'

Nodding, Nils Hammer continued. Wisting, understanding where he was going with this, leaned forward on the table.

'Here and here,' Hammer said, drawing two crosses on the line between Oslo and Nevlunghavn, 'there are tollbooths. The normal travelling time from the tollbooth on the E18 at Langåker is twenty-five minutes, and from the toll station at Sande one hour and ten minutes. All vehicles in transit are registered with a photograph of the number plate or a subscription chip.'

The Chief Superintendent concurred. 'All vehicles that pass through the toll station at Langåker about twenty-five minutes before the text message was sent, could be connected to the case.'

'As Christine pointed out,' Hammer went on, 'he arrives nearly fifteen minutes late, and it's hardly believable that he has taken a break on the last part of the journey, or waited to send the message about having arrived. Nevertheless, if we give him a few minutes slack, he ought to be among the cars passing through the tollbooth between 20.00 and 20.20.'

'That's quite a number all the same,' Torunn Borg piped up. 'On a Friday evening there must be several thousand vehicles an hour passing through?'

'Yes, that's true, but our man is coming from Oslo, and

we're only looking for the cars that have also passed through the toll station at Sande. In addition, it's reasonable to assume that he drives back the same way, that same evening.'

Christine Thiis recapped, as though to demonstrate that she had understood: 'So you'll begin with the vehicles that pass through the toll station at Sande around 19.30 and at Langåker around 20.15, and additionally registered on the return journey that same evening.'

'Agreed,' Wisting said. 'Prioritise that task.'

Every single electronic trace contained potential evidence in such a case. Wisting considered all the kinds of stored data that were the silent witnesses of the modern age, all to be selected and analysed.

Espen Mortensen entered the room, crossing to the coffee machine to help himself before sitting in a vacant seat.

'Any news?' Wisting asked.

'Not really. The body's en route to Forensics. You've heard about the gun cartridges?' The others nodded.

'Thirty-eight calibre. Our man has lost a lot of blood, so we're searching the area for blood, but it's difficult because of the rain. There are several footprints on the ground close to where the cartridges were discovered, but they've been ruined by the rain as well.'

'Do you think he was shot out there and then managed to make his way to the cottage?' Christine Thiis enquired.

'Yes. His bullet wounds are in the stomach region, but the blows to his head are probably what killed him. I estimate three blows. From the blood spatter on the walls in the hallway, it looks as though he was first struck twice while he was standing upright, and then a last, more violent blow after he had fallen to his knees.'

The crime scene technician was drinking his coffee. 'Have you managed to get hold of Thomas Rønningen?' he asked.

William Wisting shook his head. 'I tried him again just

55

before this meeting, but I'll get a patrol car to drive out to his home.'

'I think he's staying at his cottage, writing a book.'

'A book?'

'Yes, there are papers all over the living room floor. They look like the manuscript for a book.'

'What's it about?' Christine Thiis asked.

Espen Mortensen shrugged his shoulders. 'You can read it once we've gathered up the pages,' he suggested. 'There aren't very many, but it looks like some kind of documentary novel. There were quite a few famous names mentioned.'

Wisting moved the meeting on, ending after barely an hour. The detectives rushed out, eager to work on their allocated tasks. He detained Espen Mortensen.

'This manuscript,' he said, recollecting that he too had seen some typewritten pages in Thomas Rønningen's cottage. 'What names does it mention?'

Espen Mortensen resumed his seat. 'Celebrities,' he replied. 'It looked as though it had to do with people who have been guests on his show: actors, musicians and politicians. Why?'

Instead of responding, Wisting let his gaze drift thoughtfully towards the window. Outside, the darkness was lifting.

10

Wisting instructed his police colleagues in Bærum to drive out to Thomas Rønningen's house in an attempt to make contact with him.

There was something unsettling about this case. He was not certain what it was, but it was something more than the usual gnawing perplexity typical of the initial stage of an investigation. There was something cool and calculated about the entire business, but simultaneously something that indicated a kind of desperation, or failure of organisation.

Wisting forced himself to be optimistic. Despite everything, the case had picked up momentum. There were a number of loose ends that needed to be tied up, but they were making their way towards something specific. Investigating a murder case with an unknown perpetrator was like picking the label off a beer bottle. It was never possible to remove it in one piece. Instead it had to be torn off one ragged little section at a time. Nevertheless, a case like the one facing them now was among the simplest to solve. The distinguishing factor was that nothing was planned. One act had led to another, and everything that happened subsequently was part of a sort of domino effect. The investigation followed the same pattern. If they could discover the original act the rest would fall into place. He had no idea what it was, and this was what he was searching for as he read through the bundle of reports.

An hour later he walked into the conference room, where he filled a cup with coffee and crossed to the window. The press had already arrived and stood in groups on the hard area fronting the police station, waiting to be allowed inside.

Wisting glanced at the clock. He and the Chief Superintendent had been asked to a meeting in Christine Thiis' office half an hour in advance for a final review. Having five minutes left, he sauntered back to his office to gather his notes. The telephone on the desk was ringing when he entered. Wisting remained on his feet to take the call.

'This is Anders Hoff-Hansen at Forensics,' a shrill voice barked into his ear. 'We're waiting for the body.'

'What do you mean?'

'I'm working overtime here. Asbjørn Olsen from the *Kripos* ID group is too. I received a fax requesting a post mortem, but I don't have a body.'

'Are you sure?' Wisting enquired, picturing the television images of the hearse leaving the crime scene. 'It should have been with you several hours ago.'

'I'm quite sure.'

Wisting performed a quick mental calculation. The body had been collected just before five o'clock that morning. Mortensen had been in the police station preparing folders of illustrations and writing a preliminary report to accompany its transfer to Forensics. The plan had been to begin the post mortem at nine o'clock. 'Let me check this out,' he said, sitting down at his desk.

'Okay. We'll have a cup of coffee while we're waiting.'

Wisting put his own cup aside as he replaced the receiver, and then dialled Espen Mortensen's number. He replied abruptly at the other end, as though concentrating deeply on something or other. 'Forensics is waiting for the body,' Wisting explained.

He heard Espen Mortensen changing the phone receiver from one hand to the other. 'What did you say?'

'The body hasn't arrived.'

58

'Have you spoken to the undertakers? They came to collect the documents about six o'clock.'

'Which undertaking company?'

'Memento. The driver was a new man. They should have got there by eight. There's hardly any traffic on a Saturday morning, of course. Do you want me to phone them?'

'I can do that.' Wisting was familiar with the company, as he had used them for Ingrid's funeral. 'Is there any news from the crime scene examination?'

'Not really. There were good footprints in the blood in the hallway, when I managed to illuminate the floorboards properly. I've checked them against those of the neighbour and they aren't his shoes. He hadn't gone very far inside, so they must be from the killer. The pattern on the sole is so clear that the type of shoe can probably be traced. It will all eventually come to you in a folder with photographs and a written report.'

Wisting was listening with only half an ear while he tracked down the telephone number of the undertaking company. Having drawn his conversation with Mortenson to a close, he dialled the emergency number listed in Yellow Pages. The funeral director introduced himself by announcing the company name.

Wisting recognised the calm, earnest voice of Ingvar Arnesen, the third generation proprietor of the business. 'Your car hasn't arrived,' he explained. He had to repeat the message so that Arnesen understood what he meant.

'I don't understand that.' Some of the composure in Ingvar Arnesen's voice had vanished. 'Ottar left just before six o'clock. He should have arrived long ago. Have you checked whether there have been any road accidents or anything of that nature?'

'No, I haven't,' Wisting admitted. 'But maybe you could phone him?'

'Yes, wait. I can do that from the other telephone.' Wisting heard him keying in the number at the other end, followed by the voice on an automatic answer phone. 'No,' Arnesen stated. 'Might there have been a road accident?'

'I'll find out. What's his name, other than Ottar?'

'Ottar Mold. He hasn't worked for me for very long. To be quite honest, I'm not sure if I'll keep him on after his probationary period.'

'Why not?'

'There have been a number of things. He's newly separated, and has been off work a lot in connection with that. That's okay in itself, but he doesn't always give notice, and we can't do with that in this line of business. People rely on us.'

'Could he have done that now, do you think? Gone home to his ex-wife instead of driving to Oslo?'

'I don't really think so, but I can ring her and find out if she's heard from him.'

'Great. Do you have the vehicle registration number?' Wisting waited while Ingvar Arnesen leafed through papers before reading out the registration number.

'It's a black Voyager,' he added.

'With a cross on the roof?' Wisting asked.

'A cross on the roof and the company logo on the side. It shouldn't be too difficult to spot.'

Wisting called for Torunn Borg over the loudspeaker. He brought her up to date on the situation and asked her to investigate whether the hearse had been involved in an accident. He then glanced at the clock. There were twenty minutes to go before the press conference. He looked out of the window and saw that the fog had dispersed. The leaden sky was overlaid with scudding clouds that were perpetually, but almost imperceptibly, changing shape, dissolving and then merging once more.

The phone rang again. It was Arnesen. All the restraint had disappeared from the funeral director's voice. 'I've spoken to his wife. She hasn't heard anything. I've tried to phone him several times but I don't think his phone is switched on.'

'Okay,' Wisting replied. He could not think of anything more sensible to say, concluding the conversation just as Torunn Borg appeared at his office door.

'He drove through three police districts on his way to Forensics,' she explained. 'Søndre Buskerud, Asker and Bærum, and then Oslo. None of them have any reports about a road traffic accident involving personal injury, or any other kind of accident.'

Wisting ran his hand over his hair. A feeling of disquiet gnawed deep inside him.

'What should we do?' Torunn Borg asked. 'Search for the vehicle?'

There were only fifteen minutes until the press conference, when they would have all the attention of the media directed at them. However, he had no desire to sit facing the camera lenses, forced to announce that the body had vanished. 'Send a car on the same route,' he requested, rising from his chair. 'Full emergency status. Perhaps the hearse is stopped by the roadside somewhere with a flat tyre, and that idiot behind the wheel has let his phone battery run down.'

Torunn Borg nodded her head and disappeared. Lifting his suit jacket from the chair back, Wisting headed for the preliminary meeting with Christine Thiis. Several members of the press corps were already in the building and being directed to the conference room on the second floor. A couple of them threw a few questions at him, but Wisting hurried past.

Christine Thiis' desktop was bare, apart from a printout of the progress report Wisting had emailed her, and a ballpoint pen she had used to make corrections and additions.

61

The report summarised the parts of the case he felt they should inform the public about, expressed in general terms, but nevertheless containing sufficient detail to satisfy the press. He sat in the vacant visitor's chair beside the Chief Superintendent. 'We may have a problem,' he said, and told them that the hearse had gone missing.

'What shall we do?' Christine Thiis asked.

'I suggest we leave this until after the press conference,' the Chief Superintendent said. 'Shall we go through the statement?'

Accepting this, Wisting let Christine Thiis read it out. They discussed individual points before coming to an agreement.

'Have we made contact with Thomas Rønningen?' she wanted to know.

'No. He lives in Bærum. I've instructed the police there to drive to his house but haven't heard back from them yet.'

'Do you think the press know about his involvement yet?' Christine enquired. 'That his cottage is the crime scene?'

'I don't know,' Wisting answered. 'But if they do, none of them will ask you about it. That's a headline each one will want to keep from the others. It's probably only a question of time before it's out in the open, but we can't give out any information yet.'

They divided out roles and tasks. It was the young police lawyer's duty to lead the press conference, and Wisting could see that she was unused to the situation. 'It will go all right,' he said as they stood up. 'If there's anything you can't answer, you can pass the question to me.'

She gave him a swift, friendly look before crossing to the mirror beside the door. Tidying a few wisps of hair, she assumed a serious expression before nodding to her two colleagues to indicate her readiness. Wisting glanced fleetingly at his own reflection. His face was swollen on one side and the skin surrounding the sticking plaster on his chin had developed a bluish tinge. His encounter with the previous night's assailant had produced visible results, and the bruise had started to throb.

His phone rang as they left the office, with his daughter's name illuminated on the display, but he declined the call, wondering at the same time whether he would see her at this press conference. She had covered some of his cases, and he always felt uncomfortable about it.

Nonetheless he had to admit that she was a competent crime journalist. She understood the different phases of police work and had a particular talent for interpreting the developments in a case. Her articles had sometimes led to progress in an enquiry. He had to concede that he was proud of her.

Wisting remembered the crowded press conferences during the summer of the previous year, when four severed left feet had washed up along the coastline in his police district. That was then. Now, the room was no more than half full, and he could not spot Line among those present. There were only two camera teams and one journalist from newspapers in the capital. The other nationwide media outlets would be taking reports from the news bureaux.

The journalists turned to face them and some of the photographers captured their arrival on their cameras. His phone rang. If it was Line calling it might be something important, but it was a different number. He answered, intending to ask the caller to phone back later.

'It's Hoff-Hansen at Forensics,' explained the man at the other end of the line. Wisting gesticulated to Christine Thiis to let her know he had to take the call. 'He has been here,' the pathologist continued, 'but he drove off again without delivering the body.'

'What on earth do you mean?'

'One of the women in the lab saw the hearse from Larvik

and presumed it was to do with the case they've been talking about on the news.'

'So?'

'It drove away from the car park when she arrived, at top speed.'

'She's sure it was from Larvik?'

'It said so on the side. Anyway, we're not expecting any other deliveries today. It was here, but turned around and disappeared.'

'And you don't have the body? Perhaps delivered and put in the wrong place or something like that?'

'I guarantee that's not happened.'

Wisting was unsure what this might mean, other than providing confirmation that the most essential evidence in the case, the body, had gone missing.

'What do we do now?' the pathologist asked.

'I don't know,' Wisting replied. 'I'll phone you back.'

He disconnected the call and turned his phone to silent before entering the room for a second time. He took his place beside Christine Thiis, stroking his chin thoughtfully. The pain was increasing.

The Chief Superintendent welcomed the press group and introduced the platform party before handing the microphone to Christine Thiis. Point by point she reiterated the statement they had prepared, and only occasionally did she steal a glance at her notes, looking comfortable in her role.

As soon as she had finished, the journalists were ready with their questions. A female reporter from the local paper was sitting in the front row. 'What clues do you have?' she asked.

Christine Thiis hesitated momentarily. 'We have secured a number of interesting pieces of evidence,' she responded. 'However, the crime scene work is still in progress.'

'What was interesting about it?' the reporter followed up.

Wisting cleared his throat. The police prosecutor had opened a door. They had decided in advance not to provide information about what evidence had been found. The public had no need to know, and it could damage the investigation if they disclosed too much. All the same, he appreciated the police lawyer's need to show the press and the public that their work was already producing results and that they were making progress towards a resolution.

'For one thing, footprints,' he heard Christine Thiis announce.

Wisting regretted neglecting to brief her better. Inexperienced, she had not realised how words can catch you out.

'Do you have the murderer's footprints?'

Now she understood clearly the consequence of what she had revealed, as the perpetrator might be following the press coverage. 'Wisting?' she said, passing the question over to him.

'Obviously it's too early to say.' He paused dramatically and cleared his throat to indicate that he had something else. 'However, a special situation has arisen,' he continued, fully aware that his words would shift the press focus. 'The hearse has not arrived at the Forensics Institute. It was expected to arrive at the National Hospital around eight o'clock, and we have a witness who saw it leaving the hospital at top speed, though the driver had not made contact with any of the staff at the forensic pathology department. We have not succeeded in contacting the driver, and we now need to search for the vehicle.'

Wisting read out the registration number and gave a description of the car. Cameras flashed and hands shot into the air. Wisting closed his eyes. They were not going to have a single moment's peace from now on.

11

After the press conference Wisting rushed from the conference room. He knew the assembled journalists did not share his misgivings but, as far as he was concerned, the press conference most resembled an amateur dramatics production. The reporters flocked around the police lawyer, anxious to obtain individual interviews, but she knew no more about the vanished hearse than his brief description had indicated, and could therefore not say anything stupid.

Shutting the office door behind him, he stood at his desk while dialling the number for Arnesen at the undertakers. He explained about the initiated search and warned him to prepare to be inundated by phone calls from journalists. He then called together the remaining investigators for a meeting.

Wisting installed himself at one end of the long conference table, extending his arms to grip both sides of the tabletop. 'The case has taken an unexpected turn,' he said. 'At the press conference, we have just announced a search for the hearse that was supposed to convey the body to the Forensics lab.'

The eyes around the table, bewildered and astonished, fixed on him. Wisting continued, fleshing out the few details they possessed, and concluded by putting words to something lingering at the back of his mind. 'We may be facing a hijacking, which would mean the perpetrator has set the investigation back considerably.'

No one around the table uttered a word. He could see from their expressions that the development had produced a similar feeling of unease in them. In most cases, the perpetrator normally kept his head down, remaining hidden in the hope that everything would pass. Now they were confronted by an adversary actively working to conceal his tracks and hamper their task.

'One more thing,' Wisting continued. 'The hearse also contained the photographic documentation from the crime scene, together with a written report by Mortensen for the Forensics team, summarising our knowledge of the case. I don't need to explain to you how damaging it will be if these have fallen into the wrong hands.'

'What'll we do?'

Standing up, Wisting crossed to the kitchen counter, where he filled a glass of water. 'What we always do,' he answered. 'Investigate. It's a setback, but we have a fresh crime scene. We need to find the car, and the body.'

He pointed at Torunn Borg and Benjamin Fjeld who were sitting side by side at the table. 'Get hold of a vehicle and drive out there. The Oslo police are sending a crime scene examiner to Forensics and they've said they'll interview the woman who saw the hearse, but I want more than that. Interview everybody and check the CCTV footage – the whole kit and caboodle. I don't want as much as a cigarette end left lying on the ground outside the National Hospital.'

The two detectives nodded as they took notes.

'And one more thing,' he declared, making eye contact with Nils Hammer. He knew that the experienced investigator was already overloaded, but he was the best digger he had. 'I want to know everything there is to know about the driver of the hearse.'

Hammer met his gaze with a steady, earnest expression. 'Right, I'll get on with that.'

There were no questions, only a scraping of chairs, and the meeting was over.

12

At half past eleven on the morning of Saturday 2nd October, Wisting returned to the crime scene, twelve hours after he had left. Everything looked different in daylight. More exposed than he had imagined, the landscape was thick with juniper bushes, mostly gnarled and mauled by the wind, and barely a metre high. The spot where he parked afforded him a panoramic view over the sea. A bitterly cold, damp wind whistled ashore.

Wisting broke through the red and white crime scene tape. On the main road behind him, another tape kept the press contingent at a distance. The terrain down to the cottages was rough and steep, and he had to tread warily as the path was covered in slippery roots. On his way he passed two techni-cians, crouched down studying something that appeared to be a scrap of paper at the edge of the path. Trampled into the heather, it was nothing anyone else would have noticed but, for crime technicians inspecting the tortuous path metre by metre, every fragment was potential evidence, and some-thing that seemed unimportant now could turn out to be vital later. What seemed obscure and unconnected at present could prove to be the decisive detail.

Directly beneath them lay a dead bird, its head snapped backwards, wings spread to one side. 'Have you seen this?' Wisting enquired.

The elder of the two technicians nodded as he stood up. 'There's another one lying further down,' he said. 'Do you think it has anything to do with the case?'

68

'Do you?'

The man shook his head. 'No,' he replied decisively, nudging the bird off the path with his foot.

Wisting halted at the clearing in front of the cottage to gain a better impression. In daylight it seemed peaceful and well maintained. Crime scene examiners were busy here too. One of them, on his hunkers at the front door of the cottage, picking at something, stood up when he caught sight of Wisting. The black, coagulated blood and chalk outline of a human body on the uneven timber floor bore witness to the crime.

The investigations Mortensen had conducted suggested that the scenario was entirely different from what they had envisioned the previous night. The man had been bludgeoned to death in the confined space of the hallway, but had already been mortally wounded before he stepped inside the door.

Having brought a map indicating the discovery sites for the mobile phone and empty cartridges, Wisting followed the path until he arrived at the locations.

He positioned himself on the spot where the gunman had stood and surveyed his surroundings. Several broken branches were visible in the nearest grove of trees, but it was questionable whether the damage had been caused by police dogs or by someone fleeing in panic at night.

Raising his arms, he took aim over the desolate landscape, as though clutching a pistol in his hands. Tensing his body, he pulled the trigger of the imaginary weapon, but this simple reconstruction gave him no greater understanding. He folded the map and tucked it into his inside pocket before returning to his car.

A sparrow approached, wings flapping, and settled in front of him on the car bonnet, looking exactly as though it was staring at him. Before it took off again Wisting thought he detected a trace of fear in the tiny bird's black eyes.

On the return journey, he decelerated as he passed the site of his attack and car hijack. At the farm where he had received assistance, the owner was standing on the road, sweeping something onto a spade and dropping it into a wheelbarrow. Wisting wondered whether he ought to stop to thank him for his help, but decided against this. At the same moment, his phone rang, and noticing that the call was from Line, he answered using his hands-free kit.

'Hi, Dad,' she said, 'it is me.' He could hear from those five words that something was wrong. 'How's it going?'

'Hectic,' he replied. 'How are you?'

'I was thinking of coming down for a visit.'

'Are you going to write about the case?'

'No, I'm on holiday. I was just thinking of coming home for a while. Is that okay?'

Wisting grasped the nettle. 'Is there something wrong?'

'I just need to get away for a while. Chill out.'

'Are things okay between you and Tommy?'

'No.'

Wisting remained silent, noticing how he used the hiatus in the same way as he did in his professional life, when he wanted people to elaborate a point.

'It's over,' Line said. 'It's really only been a question of time. I thought I should come home so Tommy could have a few days to pack and find himself somewhere else to stay. Is that all right?'

'Of course,' Wisting answered. 'Suzanne's living with me just now, of course. Her house is full of tradesmen, but it'll be fine. Your room is available.'

It went quiet at the other end of the line. 'Maybe I could stay at the cottage?' Line suggested.

'The cottage?'

'Yes, the one you took over from Uncle Georg.'

'I don't know, Line. It's been years since anybody was there.'

'Then it's about time,' she said. 'I can clean and tidy. That'll give me something else to think about.'

'But I don't know if I have time to come out there with you ...'

'You don't need to. I know where it is, and there's electricity and running water.'

Wisting could hear how the idea of staying at Uncle Georg's cottage had lifted her spirits. Her voice was livelier. 'The key's at home,' he said. 'You can help yourself to whatever cleaning materials you need.'

'I'll buy some *en route*, and food as well.'

Wishing her luck, he wound up the conversation. In his thoughts he envisaged the map hanging on the wall in the conference room, with the cottage where the victim had been found marked with a red circle. The distance from there to Uncle Georg's cottage in Værvågen could not be greater than four kilometres, and they still knew nothing about the killer roaming through the bleak autumn landscape.

13

Wisting found a box of *Paracet* with one remaining tablet in his desk drawer. He pressed it from the blister pack, washing it down with cold coffee from the cup on his desktop.

Nils Hammer entered the office with a pale, shy man in an anonymous charcoal suit following behind. Wisting recognised him as Ingvar Arnesen from Memento undertakers. Hammer slapped a printout of an enlarged passport photograph on the desk. 'Ottar Mold,' he announced.

Wisting picked up the photograph of the vanished hearse driver: a broad face with dark close-set eyes, high forehead, wide jaw, and strong, bearded chin. 'What do we know about him?'

The funeral director remained standing while Hammer sat in the visitor's chair. 'A lot,' he replied, leafing through his notebook. 'Forty-six years old, two grown-up sons, recently separated and now living in a studio flat in Torstrand.' Wisting waved him on. These details he already knew. 'The most interesting fact is that he's been inside.'

'In prison?'

'Twice: three months in 2002 and six months in 2004.'

'What for?'

'Receiving stolen goods.'

Ingvar Arnesen took a step forward. 'I didn't know anything about it,' he said.

Hammer produced a number of stapled sheets of paper. 'I have details of the last court case. He had bought stolen computers, televisions and DVD players and sold them on.'

Wisting fastened his eyes on Ingvar Arnesen, wanting to ask how he could have employed such a man. If there was one time when people really needed to rely on others, it was in connection with a funeral.

Ingvar Arnesen cleared his throat. 'He approached me,' he explained, without waiting to be asked. 'He'd been unemployed for three months and was tired of having nothing to do. I had registered a vacancy for additional staff at the unemployment office, but it's a special kind of work, and no candidates had declared an interest. I valued his initiative and wanted to give him a chance.'

'Did he have references?'

'I spoke to a courier company he had worked for. They gave him a good recommendation. He worked hard and always turned up and that's what I needed: an assistant to collect from the hospital or nursing home, and accompany me during the night. He was taciturn and polite, but had little contact with our clientele. I take care of that myself. Besides, I know his family. I buried his grandparents and know his mother well. She's an active church member.'

Wisting gazed steadily at the man, who evaded his eye, causing Wisting to suspect there was more. He waited for him to continue.

'There are certain circumstances I should tell you about,' Ingvar Arnesen said, after Wisting had made the silence oppressive. 'Ottar Mold seems to have considerable financial problems. I've been given instructions by the tax authorities and enforcement officers to make deductions from his wages.'

Wisting wondered whether he should invite Arnesen to bring a chair across from the door and sit down, but decided to keep him on his feet.

'And there's one more thing,' the funeral director continued. 'Things have gone missing from the deceased.'

'What do you mean?'

'Last weekend, Ottar collected a man who had died relatively suddenly from the nursing home in Stavern. Afterwards, his son reported several thousand kroner missing, money he thought his father had kept in a wallet in the bedside cabinet drawer. It could have been one of the care workers or one of the surviving family members who had taken it, but I'm not so sure.'

'You think Mold took it?'

'I've no reason to claim that, but other things have gone missing as well. I get to know quite a lot in my conversations with the relatives. There's been talk about jewellery they can't find or banknotes that have disappeared. I never suspected him, but now this has happened, I'm beginning to wonder. As I told you on the phone, there's been too much trouble with Ottar, too many absences without notice. I won't be keeping him on after his probationary period.'

'Does Ottar Mold know that?'

Ingvar Arnesen nodded. 'I've told him that I don't need enough help to justify a permanent post.'

'When did he find out about that?'

'Yesterday.'

Wisting leaned back in his chair. A picture was building of a person backed into a corner who might behave irrationally from sheer desperation, but he simply could not see what Ottar Mold had to gain by stealing the body in a murder enquiry.

Twenty minutes later, William Wisting and Nils Hammer let themselves into Ottar Mold's basement flat with the landlord's keys.

A glass door led from the porch into a combined kitchen and living room. With all the curtains drawn, the air was heavy and muggy. The kitchen section contained a refrigerator, washing machine, and utilitarian hotplate beside the sink. From the living room a tiny corridor led to the open door of the bedroom, where a quilt with no cover was folded on top of the bed. It seemed as though Ottar Mold spent his nights under a blanket on the settee.

The place showed signs of only a couple of months' habitation, with bare walls and belongings still packed in cardboard boxes.

On the coffee table, Wisting noticed an empty glass and a half-eaten slice of bread on a plate. The meat spread was desiccated, the bread curled at the edges. Beside these lay a bundle of envelopes of varying shapes and sizes, payment reminders and collection notices, together with a number of unopened letters.

The sparsely furnished flat told them little, testifying only to a lonely man's uneventful existence. Nothing shed any light on what might have happened. Nevertheless, there was something unsettling about the cramped flat. Wisting could not quite put his finger on it, but it reminded him of a sailing vessel hurriedly and for no discernible reason abandoned by its crew, left like a ghost ship drifting on the sea.

14

When Wisting returned to his office, he regretted not stopping at a pharmacy to buy a new pack of *Paracet*. The single tablet he had found in his desk had eased the pain, but not eliminated it entirely. He rubbed at his tender chin as he logged into the electronic project room where an endless stream of information poured in from all the caseworkers. Sometimes the sheer amount was so overwhelming that it blinded him to the intended focus of his attention, but there was no method of sifting the facts. He was forced to absorb it all and attempt to sort out the most pressing elements, knowing well that the answers often lay in the details.

Before beginning to read, he phoned Suzanne.

'How are you getting on?' she asked.

'It's sore, but I'm okay.'

'You should have let a doctor look at it.'

He navigated around the computer screen while talking. 'If it gets worse, I will,' he said. 'I've taken a *Paracet*.'

'Are you coming home tonight?'

'Yes, but I'll be late.' He cleared his throat before continuing. 'Line phoned. She'll be popping in.' The silence at the other end told him Suzanne was waiting for an explanation. 'She's finished with Tommy. She's coming down to take things easy for a while.'

'Oh, that's a shame. Is she upset?'

'More relieved. She's the one who ended it. She's given him a few days to pack and find somewhere else. In the meantime, she'll stay at the cottage.'

'At the cottage? But it's not been fixed up.'

'This is what she wants to do. She'll pop in to pick up the key.'

'Okay. Do you think I should go with her to give her a hand?'

'I think she wants to be on her own.'

'Then I'll stay here and prepare something for us to eat, in the hope that you can find the time.'

Wisting promised to come home if he could and replaced the phone on his desk. His landline and his mobile were constant sources of interruption, and the conversations were too often unnecessarily prolonged. He keyed in his out-of-office message on the office phone's voicemail, and pushed his mobile aside, not risking a complete disconnect from the outside world.

Over an hour passed before the decisive call came in.

15

Unable to catch the name of the man who phoned, Wisting understood he worked at the central HQ of Oslo police district. 'The good news first,' the voice said. 'I think we've found the hearse you're looking for.'

Wisting leaned his head back, fixing his eye on a spot on the ceiling. 'And the bad news?'

'It's on fire.'

Wisting closed his eyes; the thought had occurred to him. 'What else can you tell me?'

'We received a report from some hikers at two minutes past twelve about a vehicle on fire on the eastern side of Vettakollen.'

Frowning, Wisting glanced at the clock. Forty-eight minutes earlier. Vettakollen was only a few kilometres from the National Hospital, at most a drive of ten minutes. Nevertheless, several hours had elapsed from the time the vehicle had vanished until it had been set alight.

The man at the other end continued. 'Police and fire service are on the scene, and it's swarming with press.'

Wisting clicked onto the Internet to check whether the news had reached the online outlets. Fires were sources of excellent photographs, even when they were extinguished. 'Are you sure it is our vehicle?' he asked.

'Yes. The folk who phoned in the report read out the registration number.'

Verdens Gang newspaper had written about the case under the caption *HEARSE SET ABLAZE*. A reader's mobile phone photograph accompanied the report. Wisting squinted at the screen. The firefighters had completed their work, and the police had cordoned off the area surrounding the burnt out vehicle.

Wisting clicked further into the story to a series of photographs. Steam was rising from the mangled wreckage of blackened metal, but the damage did not appear to be as comprehensive as he had feared. 'Are there any witnesses?' he enquired.

'Nobody who's seen anything other than the actual fire.'

'How does the car interior look?'

'The compartment is empty, but your body seems to be still lying in the rear. If he'd been conveyed in a coffin, perhaps more would have been saved. The plastic of the body bag melted and fed the flames.'

Wisting closed his eyes once more. He had seen enough charred bodies to fear fire more than anything else. If he had to choose between a body from the sea and a fire victim, he would prefer the drowned body's swollen, formless mass to the fire victim's carbonised, flaking remains.

'We're sending technicians to the scene,' the man from headquarters continued. 'As soon as is practical though, we'll tow the vehicle here and examine it. The Forensics team might get the body early tomorrow.'

Wisting thanked him and asked to be kept informed.

The online report had been updated with the newspaper's own photographs. The photographer had used a wide-angle lens. In addition to the wrecked car covered in foam, he had captured the firefighting crew packing away their equipment, spectators covering their mouths and noses from the stinking smoke, and the surrounding area. The discovery site was a clearing beside a gravel track. In the background, the yellow foliage of autumnal trees stretched up to a leaden sky.

He skimmed the text, establishing that this was indeed

the missing hearse. The newspaper reporter had spoken to a hiker who had passed through the site half an hour before the fire was discovered, when the area had been deserted. The big question was: where had the car been during the hours between disappearance and being set on fire?

The newspaper neglected to pose the other unanswered question. Where was the driver?

16

The rain had begun after Line collected the cottage key. Now, as she drove towards the coast, fog swirled in from sea and she activated the wipers. Overhanging clouds reduced visibility, obscuring the roadsides so much that she took a wrong turning three times before finding the right gravel track, full of bumps and murky puddles. Another vehicle had left behind deep, muddy tyre tracks which made it difficult to manoeuvre.

The track twisted and turned for three quarters of a kilometre through dense woodland before climbing to an elevation which gave her a view of rocky slopes as they rolled down to sea. Fog erased the silvery contours of the landscape.

The track terminated at an open area about thirty metres from the cottage and a footpath continued from there, the final stretch covered in crushed seashells. A large silver van, its sides splattered with mud, was parked in the middle of the clearing. Stopping in front of a thick dog rose bush on the opposite side, Line stepped from her car and took deep appreciative gulps of the salt sea air.

The location of the cottage was exactly as she remembered, slightly secluded, the building painted red with a tiled roof and green window shutters. At the bathing jetty down by the sea, a seagull stood on a mooring post, its beak jutting towards the horizon. Several rungs on the ladder leading to the diving platform had by now rotted away, but the sight nevertheless evoked happy childhood memories of summer visits here at Uncle Georg's cottage.

A man wearing a black, ankle-length raincoat was standing on Steinholmen a few hundred metres off, holding a pair of binoculars to his eyes and looking in a northeasterly direction. Obviously he had not seen Line approach. She looked in the same direction, but could see nothing beyond the monotonous grey mist. The seagull on the jetty took flight, rising in a circling, gliding motion, hovering on the air. She carried the bags of cleaning materials and food to the wide wooden staircase which led to the timber verandah on the cottage's south face.

A dead bird lay on the top step. She prodded it warily with her foot, causing its wings to spread out. Slime oozed from the yellow, sharp beak, forming a small stain on the timber. She unbolted the door, inserting the key in the lock with some difficulty. It had been so long since anyone had been here that it had become somewhat recalcitrant. Inside she found herself in semi-darkness. The cold and stuffy air had a nauseating smell of mould.

Leaving the door open she located the light switch. The shade was full of dead flies and moths, subduing the light. She would need to remove the window shutters before she could fully inspect the place and to do that she would have to go outside.

The furniture in the living room was covered in white sheets. An ancient, sun-bleached maritime map of the Oslo fjord hung on one wall beside three framed black and white photographs. On the opposite side of the room, an overfull bookcase covered the entire wall from floor to ceiling with books stacked untidily and with no discernible system. Hand-woven rugs were thrown across the wooden floor. A large open fireplace divided the living room from the adjacent kitchen. Apart from cold, grey ashes and the remains of a few burnt logs, everything was spick and span.

The cottage contained four other rooms: a bathroom,

storeroom and two bedrooms, one almost as large as the living room. As well as a wide bed, it was furnished with a writing desk and high-backed winged armchair. Two large windows overlooked the sea. She noticed that the fog was now even more impenetrable; rendering the man on Steinholmen invisible.

Returning to the kitchen, she turned on the tap, sending cold water into the sink. She located the hot water tank underneath the worktop and switched it on, but it would take several hours before she had hot water for washing, unless she boiled some in the kettle.

The refrigerator had been pulled back from the wall and its door left ajar. She plugged it in before pushing it back into place and filling it with her purchases. In the living room she removed the dust sheets from the furniture and somehow sparked some life into an old portable radio.

Standing at the windows staring into the fog, she thought about Tommy, his dark, warm eyes, sinewy forearms, and the intensity of his embrace.

She had never felt so close to anyone before, and had become dependent on this closeness. Possibly she had become more dependent on their physical intimacy as the mental distance between them increased. The impossibility of remaining in the relationship had struck her with full force only a few weeks earlier, and although it had been painful she had also felt a sense of relief. She needed to reclaim her life; she needed to stand on her own two feet. Deep inside, she had known for some time that life with Tommy would end in sadness, possibly worse; it had been clear for all to see. His dark sides, so attractive initially, were now the very aspects that drove her away.

She shivered as though freezing, and it struck her that this was how it often went. The qualities that the first intensity of passion masked with an indulgent veil became impossible when that initial intensity subsided. Tommy's hidden life, his nightly jaunts and whispered telephone conversations in the bathroom simply created mounting unease and frustration.

Outside, the mist began to clear. The trees were being buffeted by the wind, which also blew away the fog.

Sitting down, she reached for a book that was sticking out from a bookshelf, one of Agatha Christie's crime novels. A chocolate wrapper near the back had been used as a book-mark. She read a few lines before closing it again.

Her head was filled with chaotic thoughts: doubt, amaze-ment, and a mixture of memories good and bad. To spend a few days at the cottage was at least to try to escape these thoughts, but she would need more than an old crime novel to help her. The silent solitary feeling now enveloping her did not exactly help, but perhaps this was something she could not escape. Perhaps it was something she had to face. She fetched her laptop, intent on expressing these discon-nected thoughts and feelings in words.

She liked herself better now than she had before she met Tommy. Previously, she had been immature and uncertain. Now she was still uncertain, but in a different way. She knew more about what she wanted and who she was, and had more awareness of what life could offer. She had learned what passion could do to people; how invigorating and destructive it could be at one and the same time. She was more mature, and knew it was time for her to move on.

She was twenty-seven years of age. Once she had believed a person of twenty-seven must be an adult and ready to settle down. How wrong could one be? It was time to grab life by the throat, time to live. Not inside her head, in the past or the future, but in the here and now.

Therefore she could not look back, but had to turn to a new chapter. Glancing again at the Agatha Christie novel, she picked it up and flicked through its pages. Everything was so elementary, so easily understood. A community or family is shaken to its foundations by a murder. Miss Marple enters the picture, gathers information, analyses the situation, exposes the murderer, and harmony is restored in a carefully controlled universe that is unambiguous and transparent. She might wish for someone to take control of her life in the same way, arranging it so that everything could be brought to a simple, logical and happy resolution.

She lifted her eyes to the window again. The sea was about to vanish into the blue-grey twilight. Remaining seated, she let her thoughts drift before deleting everything she had written about herself and beginning again with a fresh sentence:

They retrieved the body on the eighth of July, just after three o'clock in the afternoon.

Satisfactory; an excellent opening for a crime novel.

17

Benjamin Fjeld's photographs of the burnt out hearse, with an overview of its stowage space, filled Wisting's computer screen. They gave no grounds for optimism. Nothing remained of the dead man's clothing, and the blackened skin was covered in enormous, burst blisters. Wisting opened an attachment and homed in on a close-up of the head: a few tufts of hair still clung to the cracked skull but the nose and lips had been burned away and the eye sockets had become gaping holes.

Forensics could ascertain little from the charred corpse. Dental records might assist in establishing identity, but very few other clues would be available. He now regretted their reluctance to remove the balaclava at the crime scene to allow photographs.

Nils Hammer appeared at the door, rubbing his eyes with the thumb and forefinger of his left hand. 'That's what our job has become,' he said. 'Sitting staring at a computer.'

Wisting laid aside his glasses and rubbed his painful jaw. 'What progress have we made with the toll stations?' he asked. 'Have you received the data files?'

'Yes indeed, and I'm beginning to form an overview, but it's a slow task sorting the information.' Hammer sat down. 'There's more traffic than I anticipated. If we keep within a twenty-minute time window, there are 378 cars passing both tolls on the way south. Of those there are actually as many as 216 that return the same night. The problem is that the data we receive from the toll company only includes the registration numbers. I have to look up every number manually in the vehicle registers to identify the car model and owner; that done, it starts to get interesting. I just need a break at the moment. Far too many letters and numbers at one time, my head's spinning.'

Christine Thiis entered the room. 'It's out now,' she said. 'The media have discovered that the cottage where the crime took place belongs to Thomas Rønningen. They can't get hold of him either.'

'Perhaps we should try to make contact with his dentist?' Hammer suggested, pointing to the screen in front of Wisting.

Christine Thiis grimaced as she crossed to the window. 'What should I say when they phone?'

Wisting opened the desk drawer to see if there might possibly be any loose *Paracet* tablets lying around. 'We can confirm it's his cottage,' he said. 'And that we have not succeeded in contacting him.'

His mobile phone rang. He closed the drawer without finding any more painkillers. Checking the display, he restrained a satisfied smile and held up the phone for the others to read: *Thomas Rønningen*. He answered concisely, nodding in confirmation to the others when the man at the other end introduced himself.

'I understand you've been trying to get hold of me,' the television presenter said. Wisting confirmed that point. 'I don't know how much you've found out about what has happened, but we need to talk to you.'

'I've heard the news. Is it my cottage? Is that why you phoned?'

'Yes.'

'I was afraid of that. I'm on my way over.'

'When can you be here?'

'In an hour, but I had hoped we could meet somewhere

87

other than the police station. I expect there are a lot of press people there?'

'Where did you have in mind?'

'Could we make it as discreet as possible?'

'We can find a solution, I'm sure.' Wisting said. 'We could meet at my house.'

'At your house?'

'I need to go home anyway.'

'If we can do things that way I'd appreciate it very much.'

Wisting had never taken such a course of action before, but had no objection to it. The most critical aspect was to create an atmosphere in which the witness felt relaxed. He gave Thomas Røningen his address in Herman Wildenvey-sgate, and an hour later was parking in the driveway.

Suzanne was working beneath the giant birch tree in the garden, raking wet leaves. She wore his black Wellington boots and a pair of gardening gloves from the shed. Straightening her back, she smiled when she caught sight of him. Resting the rake against the tree trunk, she removed her gloves as she approached.

'Great that you could manage,' she said, giving him a kiss.

'You're so clever,' he smiled, glancing over her shoulder.

'I like working in the garden. It lets your thoughts run free.'

'What are you thinking about?'

'I can tell you another time.' She laughed as she kissed him again, and then drew back to scrutinise his features. 'How are you?'

'It's throbbing,' he replied, walking to the front door. 'I need to find some painkillers.'

'Was that why you came home?'

'One of the reasons,' he smiled. 'We're going to have a visitor.'

'Who would that be?'

88

'Thomas Rønningen.' Suzanne repeated the name, without seeming to understand who he meant. 'He's a witness in the case,' Wisting explained. 'The body was found in his cottage.'

'Does he have anything to do with it?'

'That's what I'll be trying to find out.'

'And you're going to talk to him here?'

'It was a practical solution.'

Suzanne pulled off the overlarge boots. 'It's a bit strange,' she said.

'In what way?'

'We were sitting watching him on TV yesterday, and now he's actually coming here.'

Inside, Wisting filled a glass with water from the tap and swallowed two *Paracet* tablets while Suzanne boiled the kettle for tea. 'Line was here,' she told him. 'She took the key for the cottage.'

'You didn't manage to persuade her to stay here?' Wisting asked, taking a seat at the window.

'I asked her, but she said she wanted to have some time on her own.'

'How did she seem?'

'Fine, but I don't like her being out there at Værvågen by herself. I wonder whether I should take a trip out there.'

Wisting drank the tea, appreciative of the concern she was displaying for Line. 'That was what she wanted, of course,' he said. 'To be on her own for a while.'

'All the same,' Suzanne replied, nodding at the gloom outside. 'The forecast is for the weather to worsen.'

The doorbell rang before they had finished their tea, and Wisting opened the door.

Thomas Rønningen, shorter than he had imagined, was dressed in jeans and a black turtle-necked sweater underneath his windcheater jacket. As he extended his hand with a jovial twinkle in his blue eyes, it struck Wisting that this felt like greeting an old friend. He led the way inside, where the famous television host hung his jacket in the hallway, removed his shoes and said hello to Suzanne. In the upstairs living room he stood by the window while Wisting found something to write on. Daylight was dwindling in the ashen sky outdoors.

'Fantastic view here in good weather, I should think,' Rønningen remarked.

'Yes indeed,' Wisting agreed. 'Do sit down.'

'We could probably have done this over the phone,' Thomas Rønningen said, settling on the settee. 'I don't know anything about what has happened.'

Wisting sat directly opposite him and switched on the little tape recorder, prompting a more formal context. 'All the same, it was good of you to take the time,' he said.

The purpose of an interview was always the same: to obtain fresh information. Wisting often considered it a game played by two people who sat on opposite sides of a table, each with different information about a case. The police officer should take the lead to establish the terms of the interview but, occasionally, the interviewee was so proficient that he assumed control and the policeman ended up giving information instead of gathering it.

Thomas Rønningen was a professional adversary. In case he was more involved in this matter than he was admitting, Wisting decided to proceed with caution. He placed his notepad on his lap and leafed through to a blank page, mostly as a signal that a formal examination was in process.

'When did you last visit your cottage?'

'A fortnight ago. I was there from Friday to Monday.'

'Were you alone?'

'Yes.'

Wisting glanced at the tape recorder. He had learned from

the celebrity press that Thomas Rønningen was divorced. They referred to him as an attractive young man who, in recent years, had been associated with a number of famous female actors and musicians. 'No visitors?' he asked.

Thomas Rønningen took a second or so to reflect. 'No, actually not. I'm writing a book, and so I prefer to be on my own.'

'A book?'

'About what you don't get to see onscreen,' Rønningen said with a smile. 'What happens behind the scenes and after the camera lights are switched off. I've hosted almost two hundred programmes with nearly one thousand guests. All the elite of Norwegian society have been there. Industry leaders and cultural icons. I've been visited by heads of state and members of royalty, porno stars and celebrated criminals. It's obvious there has to be a book in it.'

Smiling back, Wisting continued. 'Does anyone other than you make use of the cottage?'

Thomas Rønningen squirmed in his seat. A hint of tension at the corner of his eye suggested that he felt uncomfortable about this question. 'I don't quite understand where you're going with all this. The point is surely that the people who were there yesterday weren't there by invitation.'

'Sorry.' Wisting placed his pen on the open notepad. He should have explained the purpose of the interview more clearly; an uncertain witness was a poor witness. 'This is about elimination,' he explained. 'The crime scene technicians have obtained fingerprints and DNA profiles, so we need to exclude people who have had authorised access to the cottage before we can be sure which traces have been left behind by the assailant. We will require fingerprints from you. If this becomes a lengthy investigation, it may also be necessary to take prints from your guests.'

Thomas Rønningen leaned back in his seat 'I don't

know …' he began, but broke off just as he did on the TV screen. 'Let me try to understand,' he said instead. 'My cottage is the scene of a murder.' Wisting nodded. 'I understood that the man who was murdered was found in the outer hallway. Was he killed there, or inside the actual cottage?'

'He was killed in the hallway,' Wisting clarified. 'On the way in. The assailant was already inside the cottage.'

Wisting said no more, wondering whether he had given away too much. He had to assume that Rønningen would be interviewed by the press and make reference to what he had learned.

'A burglar?'

'That's one theory.'

'What did they steal?'

'Several cottages were broken into. It appears that they were after easily marketable domestic electronics equipment. What did you have there?'

'I certainly had that kind of thing, and a portable computer I worked on when I was there.' Wisting saw the ransacked cottage in his mind's eye. 'It was on the coffee table,' Rønningen added.

'That's probably gone,' Wisting confirmed. 'There were some pages of manuscript left behind.'

Thomas Rønningen grimaced. 'It was an old computer, and I've backed up the files, of course, but I don't like the thought of the manuscript going astray.'

Wisting picked up his pen once more. Rønningen's focus had shifted and he had avoided the question of who used the cottage other than himself. Throughout the interview his hands had been fidgeting, which was unlike his demeanour on television. Restlessness suggested unease.

Wisting restated his question. 'Who, other than yourself, has been to the cottage?'

92

'I had a lot of visitors during the summer, including *Se og Hør* magazine. And I had visits from some colleagues at *NRK*.'

Thomas Rønningen rattled off a few names, and listed several summer guests, while Wisting took notes. Eventually the list contained an excess of blonde women considerably younger than the cottage owner. 'And what's more, I was visited by David Kinn and some of his friends.'

Wisting could not disguise how surprised he was. 'The investor?' he asked.

Thomas Rønningen nodded. David Kinn was described in the media as an acrobat of the financial world and a repeated bankrupt. He was involved in gambling and pyramid schemes, and several years earlier had been sentenced for receiving criminal proceeds after borrowing money that turned out to be stolen. The most recent headlines had him being pursued by thugs.

'He was a guest on my programme around Easter. We had some business meetings during the summer, but they didn't lead to any agreements.'

Wisting sat without uttering a word, hoping that the television presenter would find the silence uncomfortable and, from habit, take up the thread of the conversation.

'He borrowed the cottage for a few weeks in late summer,' the man finally said. 'I don't know if he had visitors or anyone else staying with him.'

'A few weeks?'

'Three. From the 4th to the 25th of August.'

Wisting noted the name *David Kinn* at the top of the sheet of paper. The list of visitors had become lengthy, and a furrow was digging into the TV personality's brow. 'Do you have any idea who the murdered man was?' he asked.

Again the conversation was being diverted. 'We don't have a firm identity,' Wisting said.

Thomas Rønningen indicated the notepad. 'Do you think it might be one of them?' he asked.

Wisting cast his eye over the list of names. 'Do you?' he threw the question back.

The television celebrity shook his head. 'I think it was completely accidental that it happened in my cottage,' he said, gesturing with his hand as Wisting had seen him do on TV when he wanted to introduce a new topic. 'You must have a difficult job. Challenging, is it not?'

'That's what makes it so interesting.'

'I'm fascinated by the way competent investigators like you manage to see connections that others are blind to.'

Wisting understood how television guests felt comfortable and opened up in Thomas Rønningen's company. It was natural for him to be the central person and focus of attention, but at the same time he managed to direct the spotlight towards his conversational partner. His charm and gift for rhetoric created a congenial atmosphere, a type of charisma that could not be learned or practised. Nevertheless what he said seemed more like a diversionary tactic than a genuine opinion.

'Where were you yesterday evening and last night?' Wisting enquired, refusing to go down the conversational route.

With a smile, Thomas Rønningen changed position once more. 'You would perhaps think I have the best alibi in the world – a million TV viewers, but the truth is that what everybody sees on the screen is a recording. The programme is recorded in the afternoon and broadcast unedited.'

'So where were you?'

'At home. Alone.'

'We've been trying to phone you, and even sent a car to your door this morning.'

Thomas Rønningen nodded. 'I disconnected everything,' he said. 'Mobile phone, doorbell, television, everything. I arrived home at about seven o'clock and sat down to write. I kept going until almost five, and then collapsed into bed. When I woke, I switched on my mobile, read my texts and phoned you.'

Wisting considered the possible methods of checking his alibi. If he had been sitting at a computer connected to a home network, data traffic would have been registered. Leaving this aside, he posed several additional routine questions. The hour-long interview gave him a slightly different picture of the man than he had gained from his television persona. There was something feigned and affected about him that did not find its way onto the TV screen.

Interview over, he accompanied his visitor outside, where the illumination from the street lamps was dulled by drizzling rain. 'Where are you heading now?' Wisting asked.

Thomas Rønningen pulled up his jacket zip and thrust his hands into his pockets. 'I was thinking of going out to have a look at the cottage. Do you think I'll be able to do that?'

'We still have technicians there. You'll probably not be allowed in.'

'I'll go out anyway, and drive home afterwards.' They shook hands in farewell. Thomas Rønningen sat in his car and reversed out of the courtyard.

We're not getting anywhere, Wisting thought, in a sudden attack of pessimism. We are at a standstill, stranded in a total vacuum, and don't even know what we're looking for.

18

At 21.57 Wisting brought their second working day to a close by gathering the detectives for a meeting. Despite his fatigue, he summarised the main features in the case – not fully thought through, but nevertheless weighty.

'The crime scene!' he offered as a key word to Espen Mortensen when he concluded his own summary. The crime scene technician switched on the projector.

'At the moment it's the footprints that are of most interest,' he said, showing them photographs of bloody footprints heading towards the exit. The grooves in the tread on the soles were clearly delineated in the angled beam of light. 'They're interesting because they're marked in blood and must be from the last person in the house.'

'Type of shoe?'

'We're working on that, but preliminary findings are that it's a casual shoe in size 44.'

The next photograph was self-explanatory. Several finger-prints had been found on the doorframes. 'The victim was wearing gloves, and we don't know whether they belong to the owner of the cottage or someone on a visit. A search through the records is being conducted.'

A picture of a crumpled cash receipt appeared on the screen. As the ink had run on the wet paper, the letters had blended together and were impossible to decipher. 'This was found at the side of the path leading to the cottage,' Mortensen explained. 'It hasn't been lying outside for very long, but enough to damage it. I've placed it in the vacuum container. Hopefully the text will become clearer once the paper is freeze-dried.'

Nils Hammer tilted his head, squinting at the large picture. 'I think it says *Hot Dogs*. Probably a receipt from a Statoil petrol station dropped by somebody in the dog patrol.'

His comments unleashed a burst of laughter.

'How's the video project progressing?' Wisting asked.

Hammer lifted his coffee cup. The gathering of CCTV videos was his responsibility. 'We're in the process of collecting them all, but it's a huge task. I've been in contact with every petrol station in town to make sure nothing is deleted. Some places have people working who can deal with the CCTV equipment, but in other places they have to wait until somebody competent comes on duty.' He swallowed a mouthful of coffee. 'And then things are going slightly more slowly with the toll station project. That's come to a complete standstill.'

'Oh?'

'The vehicle register is down for maintenance and won't be in service again until tomorrow morning.'

Wisting felt his irritation grow. He had become used to the outdated police data systems causing problems but, now they had reached such a critical point in the investigation, it was difficult to be patient. He progressed the meeting. Torunn Borg had been to Oslo with Benjamin Fjeld. Wisting chose to let the young probationer give an account of their cooperation with the Oslo police.

'Now at least the body has been safely delivered to Forensics,' said Fjeld. 'The post mortem starts early tomorrow, but I don't think we have great expectations. There was little to obtain from the examination of the vehicle either. There were traces of inflammable liquid, but it doesn't come as a surprise that the fire was deliberate.'

'Witnesses?'

'Nobody other than the hikers who reported it. We've spoken to the lab technician who saw the car outside the National Hospital. She can't tell us any more than that. She saw the car from the side and partly from the rear. She didn't see who was driving.'

'Anything new about the driver from the undertakers?'

'No, and that's actually quite remarkable. He surely can't simply vanish.'

'What are we doing about it?'

'We've contacted his employer and family, and have made a formal missing person report.'

The uncertainty surrounding the driver had created a vague internal ache of unease in Wisting. Something did not add up, but the whole day had been like that. Nothing added up, and their time had been spent searching for the unknown. The best he could hope for now was that both he and the investigators could get a good night's sleep, and that tomorrow would provide more answers.

19

Wisting drove through the darkness, his thoughts skipping across the events of the past twenty-four hours like an anchor hauled across a seabed without finding any grip. The tide of reflections withdrew as he approached his house in Stavern. Not until he swung the car to a halt though, did it dawn on him that he ought to phone his daughter. He stayed in the car to call. 'Hello! How are things going?'

'Fine, thanks,' Line answered. 'Suzanne just phoned to ask the same question. She was hoping you'd be home soon.'

'I'm on my way into the house at the moment,' he said, stepping from the car. 'Was the place really filthy?'

'Oh no! It smelled a bit stuffy, but now the fragrance of green soap has taken over.'

'Have you spoken to Tommy?'

'Yes, he phoned earlier.'

'What did he want?'

'I don't think he knows what he wants.'

'When do you go back to work?'

'Next Monday, but I've a few more days holiday owing.'

Wisting entered his house. 'Just phone if you need anything,' he said.

Suzanne met him in the hallway. 'Was that Line?'

'Yes.'

'I just spoke to her. We had a good chat, but I felt she was holding something back. I think she misses her mother.'

Wisting exhaled heavily. He missed Ingrid too, but said

nothing to Suzanne. Instead he gave her a kiss and whispered in her ear: 'I'm happy I have you.'

There was room for two women in his life, as he had discovered. They were not to be compared though, and love for one in a way overlapped his love for the other. Ingrid, as the mother of his children, would always be the more significant.

They sat in the living room, where Suzanne had been reading. A book lay on the table, page down and spine upwards, that had belonged to Ingrid, taken from the bookcase upstairs.

'How's the case progressing?' Suzanne asked.

Wisting shrugged his shoulders. 'We've still a long way to go before we have a breakthrough, but you never know. Something could happen all of a sudden.'

Suzanne tucked her feet underneath herself on the settee. 'Are you not scared?' she asked.

'Of what?'

'Of the unknown. What you don't know, lying in wait for you.'

Wisting appreciated Suzanne's interest in his work. 'It doesn't frighten me. I think it's probably the opposite. Not knowing drives me on.'

Suzanne appeared pensive and Wisting, lacking energy for a serious discussion, changed the subject. 'What were you thinking about?' he asked.

'When?'

'When you were raking the leaves. You said you enjoyed going out to have a think.'

She laughed, as though embarrassed to share her thoughts with him. 'I was thinking of a name,' she responded.

Wisting did not immediately understand what she meant, but then it dawned. Only twenty-four hours earlier, they had been sitting in this same spot and Suzanne had been talking about resigning from her administrative post and opening an art café. 'For the restaurant?'

She nodded.

'Let me hear then!'

She hesitated slightly before announcing, *'The Golden Peace.'*

Wisting turned the name over in his head. 'Excellent choice for an art café! When does it open?'

'It probably won't come to anything.'

'What's holding you back? Are you afraid of the unknown?'

'Perhaps that's what it is, the insecurity. It's not exactly a secure business, after all. It feels safer to sit in an office as an administrator, with a fixed salary.'

Wisting studied her. She had experienced war and fled as a refugee to a foreign country. She had sought out new challenges through education and employment. They had been plentiful, and seldom had she known the answers in advance. It was difficult to understand how such factors about insecurity could hold her back.

'Where would we be if we knew everything that lay ahead?' he asked. 'There would be nothing left. Hope and faith and dreams would all be worth nothing. I think you should go ahead. Think about how good it would be – I'd be able to have my own regular table.'

Laughter lines spread across her face and she chuckled as she stood up. 'Now we must get to bed,' she said.

Wisting followed her to the bathroom and ten minutes later was laying his head on the pillow. He had a strong sense of disquiet about what the next day had in store.

20

Line slammed the cottage door behind her. She did not usually rise so early, at least not when she had a day off, but had wakened an hour earlier and been unable to get back to sleep. Tying her scarf around the collar of her jacket, she turned into the wind and descended from the verandah onto the coastal path.

Sheets of rain and ragged clouds hung in the lowering, dismal sky. The wind had freshened during the night, dissipating the fog, though it left the air damp and cold.

The previous evening, she had written seven pages of her crime novel. She had thought from time to time that it would be fun to use her writing skills for something more than newspaper articles and in-depth interviews. She had technical competence as a writer, and had gained a great deal of knowledge about police work and investigation from her father. Thoughts of a crime novel naturally followed.

It had started as a game. She brought a fictional protagonist to life, endowing her with personal qualities and outward appearance, set her in a time and place, and sketched out her surroundings. After seven pages though, she had dried up, and when she read those seven pages she thought that much of it was good, but lacked form and direction.

She had considered how to build her narrative while cleaning the kitchen cupboards, but then thoughts kept buzzing around her head and she was too tired to put them in order. The flood of ideas had disturbed her sleep, and that was why she had wakened early. Also, too many unresolved emotions

102

jangled inside, preventing her from focusing properly, and her thoughts returned to Tommy.

For breakfast she ate two slices of crispbread and drank a cup of coffee, and then decided to take a long walk and let her thoughts wander.

She was alone, with the cold and uninviting coast before her, surf breaking over rocks and underwater reefs. On the steely horizon, a cargo ship was heading westwards. The cries of seagulls sounded like teasing laughter on the wind. They looked beautiful from a distance, graceful to watch, but she knew they would eat anything and that made her think of them as filthy scavengers, full of parasites.

The coastline alternated between pebble beaches, rocky slopes and wind-blasted woodland. Line rambled along the path between dog rose and blackthorn bushes until it petered out in the bare hillside.

Inside a cove, a flock of gulls thronged in the air above an abandoned rowing boat, the birds swooping around it, fighting over something lying on board, wrestling with their wings and tugging at the same scraps. The unsuccessful ones pecked at the more fortunate, forcing those that were too small or too weak to release their spoils. The strongest birds bolted down their loot to become even stronger.

The path brought her close to the boat, scaring off the gulls. It was a strange place to tie up, she thought. The little craft must have come adrift somewhere and been washed ashore. Now it was beached and scraped against the large, round pebbles.

She froze; someone was on board. A man was sitting on the bottom partly supported by the stern crossbench, with his head upturned. His eyes had been pecked out and his mouth was gaping.

103

21

The first phone call arrived while Wisting stood beside the kitchen worktop in the conference room, filling his cup with coffee. The caller's name was Leif Malm, leader of the intelligence section in Oslo police district. 'We have information,' he said.

Wisting strode towards his office, his mobile phone at his ear.

'An informant has told us about a narcotics delivery that should have arrived by sea from Denmark on Friday evening. The cargo should have been shipped in near Helgeroa but something went wrong. The main man is said to have suffered a loss of several million kroner and one of his men was killed in a shooting incident.'

This sounded like a breakthrough. Wisting sat down. 'Do we know the identity of the main guy?'

'He's Rudi Muller, one of the big fish at the centre of a major network that deals in weapons, narcotics and prostitution.'

Wisting nodded. Muller's was a familiar name from many intelligence reports. 'Was he here himself?'

'No, two men drove down to collect the cargo. We haven't identified them yet.'

'Do we know what went wrong?'

'Apparently this was a regular arrangement over the past six months; ten kilos of cocaine every third week. Someone got wind of it and there was a raid.'

Wisting scribbled keywords on his notepad. 'Can we arrange a meeting?'

'I think we should,' Leif Malm replied. 'We're meeting our source at eleven o'clock, and can come down to see you after that. Maybe we'll know more by then.'

They wrapped up their conversation. Wisting was unsure what this implied, but he was suddenly tense. They were on the track of something.

There was another half hour before the regular morning meeting. He could already hear a few of the detectives in the corridor and was looking forward to telling them about this new development when the phone rang again. This time it was Line. Before she uttered a word he could sense that something was wrong. 'I've found a dead man,' she said.

He heard what she said, but nevertheless asked her to repeat it. 'I'm out for a walk,' she explained. 'There's a dead man in a boat. I think he's drifted ashore.'

'Are you certain he's dead?'

'The seagulls have pecked out his eyes.'

Wisting controlled his voice with an effort. 'Tell me exactly where you are.'

A chart lay in front of him with Thomas Rønningen's cottage marked. Drawing it towards him, he scrutinised it closely while Line explained. The discovery site was situated directly west of the camping grounds at Oddane Sand. Only Havnebukta with the skerries of Råholmen and Bramskjæra separated this place from Friday's crime scene. 'Okay. Stay there,' he instructed. 'We're on our way.'

He felt almost ill. Line was alone there and it was not safe now, not safe at all.

22

Wisting took Torunn Borg and Benjamin Fjeld with him. Espen Mortensen followed in a crime scene vehicle.

At the coast he led them through dense alder trees for several hundred metres to where Line stood with her arms folded. A gust of wind ruffled her hair, leaving it tousled around her face. She was soaked and shivering.

Pulling her towards him, silently holding her before letting go, he rubbed his hands quickly up and down her arms to pummel some warmth into her trembling body. 'Are you all right?' he asked.

When she nodded, he understood she was telling the truth. She had been in similar situations before.

He stepped away to look at the boat. Scraping against the pebbles, it rocked with every wave that beat against the shore. The dead man leaned against the stern, the wounds inflicted on his face by the seagulls resembling large pustules. He wore an open, black jacket with a grey sweater underneath. The sweater was encrusted with blood. The boat had let in water, which now reached the dead man's hips.

Wisting wished his daughter could have been spared this. She was robust, but he knew how such sights return to haunt you, even years later. He had lost count of the number of times he had wakened bathed in sweat, bestial images fixed on his retina, pictures from real life. Line could not know how affected she would be by the unpredictability of their coming, how threatening darkness can be, and how what has been seen once can return and grow in your consciousness. Wisting knew all too well.

Clearing his throat, he assumed his professional persona. 'We'll need you to make a formal statement.' He turned to Benjamin Fjeld. 'Perhaps you could go back to the cottage with her?'

The young police officer nodded.

Wisting made eye contact with Line again. 'Okay?'

She smiled broadly. 'Fine.'

'Afterwards, what will you do?'

'What do you mean?'

'Will you go home? I have to work, but Suzanne is there.'

Line shook her head vigorously. 'I'm staying at the cottage.'

Wisting closed his eyes and shook his head. He did not like the thought of Line alone. Staying here probably did not constitute a physical risk, but unwelcome thoughts could come creeping at night. He understood she needed time to adjust to the break from Tommy, but sitting alone out here with all her thoughts and emotions was not a good idea.

'Come home for tonight at least, and you can sleep in your old room.'

'I like being here,' she said, telling him with her eyes how useless it was to try to change her mind.

Stubbornness: yet another quality she had inherited from her mother. Wisting shook his head. Looking earnestly at her, he made sure she knew she could change her mind at any time and that he could be reached by phone twenty-four hours a day. Line smiled back, hugged him briefly and pulled her jacket more snugly around herself.

Benjamin Fjeld let her walk ahead. Wisting followed them with his gaze until they disappeared beyond the headland, before turning to face the sea and a snell wind that blew with all its might, sending angry blasts across the land and rocking the boat. The dead man unbendingly rocked with it.

'What do you think?' Torunn Borg asked.

'There's a connection,' he replied. 'Must be.'

Espen Mortensen descended the path with a rucksack on his back, removed it without speaking, and looked down at the dead body. 'I think I recognise the tread on those boots,' he said. 'It's the same as in the cottage.'

Wisting approached more closely, balancing on a slippery boulder. The dead man's boots stuck vertically out of the murky water. He had not studied the crime scene photographs, but the pattern on the soles was chunky and seemed distinctive. 'The footprints in the blood?' he asked.

'No, in the living room. The footprints in the blood are from a training shoe or something like that. I may know what type by the end of the day.'

Torunn Borg stepped out onto the slippery stones beside Wisting. 'Where did all the blood come from?' she asked, indicating the saturated sweater.

Espen Mortensen waded into the water and alongside the boat. 'The injuries on his face are from the gulls,' he said. 'He has more serious injuries in the abdomen.'

Torunn Borg stepped closer to the boat, leaning on Wisting to do so. 'Is that a revolver?' she asked, pointing under the water and between the decking boards.

Supporting himself on the side of the boat, Mortensen bent forward and peered down into the dirty water. 'Yes, but the empty cartridges we found over in the area of the cottages were 38 calibre. This is a smaller weapon. Probably a 22.' Wading ashore again, he opened the rucksack and produced a camera. Wisting and Torunn Borg withdrew slightly. 'The boat's unregistered,' he said. 'No outboard motor or oars. I wonder what he was actually doing out there.'

Wisting lifted his eyes. The seagulls were circling low above their heads. The sea blended into the leaden sky, entirely erasing the horizon. 'What'll we do with the boat?' he asked.

'We'll get a recovery vessel to tow it to the nearest harbour. Then we can haul it up on a breakdown truck and bring it in.'

'With the body on board?'

'I think that's the simplest solution. I'll carry out an inspection here first. He's been out all night, so I don't think I'll do much further damage.'

Wisting tucked his collar up, turned his back to the sea and trudged towards his car.

23

Line opened the cottage door. 'I just need to change,' she said, heading for the bedroom.

Closing the front door behind them, Benjamin Fjeld looked around. 'It's cold here,' he said. 'Cosy enough, but cold.'

In the bedroom Line pulled off her wet clothes, the skin on her chest and along her bare arms bristling with little goose pimples. Hauling her bag onto the bed, she rummaged for something to wear, finally putting on a tracksuit before returning to the living room.

Benjamin Fjeld was crouched in front of the fireplace, stacking kindling in the open hearth. 'Is this all right?' he asked, taking a box of matches from the mantelpiece.

'Marvellous. I haven't tried a fire yet, so you need to check the damper and that kind of thing.'

'How long have you been here?' he asked, striking a match.

'I arrived yesterday.'

'Is this your cottage?'

'It's Dad's. He's just inherited it from his uncle.'

'Are you living here on your own?'

'I live in Oslo. I came down to chill for a few days.'

The kindling caught fire and Benjamin Fjeld added a couple of logs from the basket before sitting in a chair beside the window.

Line stepped across to the kitchen corner. 'I need a hot drink. Would you like a cup of tea?'

'Yes, please.'

Line looked at him as she filled the kettle. Around her

age, he was tall and broad-shouldered. Though his dark hair was slightly too short for her liking, it accentuated his clean-cut, chiselled features. She found herself thinking that she was not wearing any makeup, and had not showered or tidied herself before venturing out. 'Where are you from?' she asked.

'Bjørkelangen,' he said. 'A little place to the east of Akershus.'

Line knew where it was as she had been there on a missing person the previous year. It was an idyllic county where forestry was the main source of employment. 'Have you been working here long?'

'Almost two years. I started in Oslo after Police College, and then applied for this post. My family had caravan holidays here for years.'

'You like it, then?'

'I love the open landscape. Where I come from is mainly forest.'

'I miss it,' Line smilingly remarked. 'Oslo is really so huge and foreign. Don't you think so?'

He agreed, smiling broadly. 'Strictly speaking, I'm the one who should be asking the questions.'

She chuckled and sat down opposite him, where the warmth from the fireplace heated her back. 'Sorry,' she said, 'it's an old habit. It's part of my job too. I'm a journalist.'

When he nodded she suddenly realised it was common knowledge where the boss's daughter worked. Simultaneously, it struck her that she should tell the editorial staff about the discovery of the corpse. The news wasn't out yet, and they could be first to break it. She really ought to grab her camera and get back to the discovery site before it was too late.

'I'm afraid there isn't very much I can tell you,' she continued. 'I found a dead man in a boat, and that was that.'

111

Benjamin Fjeld produced a notebook and flipped through to find a blank page. 'Did you meet anybody?'

She shook her head. 'A lot of people go walking out here, but it was early and the weather wasn't too great.'

'Have you seen anyone else here since you arrived?'

Line remembered the man with binoculars and nodded eagerly.

'He was quite conspicuous,' she said after describing him. 'I don't know what he was looking for.'

Scribbling notes, Benjamin Fjeld lifted his gaze to look past her. 'Kettle's boiling,' he said.

Line rushed over and, filling the cups only half-full, returned with them to the coffee table. Benjamin Fjeld lifted his and raised it cautiously to his mouth. His sinewy neck contracted when he swallowed. He rose and walked past her to throw another log on the fire. The flames blazed, and the glimmer of light played in his eyes as he sat down again. They were brown, the pupils completely dark. Blinking, he returned to his notebook. 'What did he look like?'

'Hm?'

'The man with binoculars. What did he look like?'

'I only saw him from a distance. He wore an enormous black raincoat that reached below his knees, and Wellington boots.'

'Anything on his head?'

'An old-fashioned sou'wester.' Another thing struck her. 'He must have parked in the space out there.' She pointed in the direction of the area where she had parked her own car. 'At least there was a big, dirty van there, a VW Transporter or something like that.'

Benjamin Fjeld asked her to describe the van before laying aside his notebook. 'How long are you staying here?' he enquired.

'A week.'

He stood up. 'Well, I may come back. You must phone me or your father if you think of anything else.' He placed a card with his name and phone number on the table. 'Or if the man with the binoculars turns up again.'

Letting the card lie, Line collected their teacups and carried them to the kitchen sink. 'I'll come with you.'

'You don't need to do that,' he said, pulling on his jacket.

Line took down the camera bag hanging from a hook beside the door. 'I think my news editor will have a different opinion,' she said with a grin.

24

The morning meeting had been postponed until everyone returned, but the only person now missing was Espen Mortensen. Wisting had informed Christine Thiis about the communication from the Oslo police. Now he opened the staff meeting with the same information. 'Leif Malm from the intelligence section is meeting me here later with the person who dealt with the informant. I'd like Christine Thiis and Nils Hammer to join me.'

The atmosphere around the conference table became optimistic as the investigators contributed comments and suggestions on how an unsuccessful drugs deal could fit.

'And,' Wisting continued, leafing through his notepad. 'Another body found.'

Benjamin Fjeld started the projector and Wisting indicated the discovery site on the map that appeared on the screen. 'As the crow flies, it's less than three kilometres to the cottage where the first body was discovered on Friday. We have every reason to believe there's a connection. Also, the pattern on the soles of his shoes is strikingly similar to the prints found in the cottage.'

'Do we know who he is?' one of the detectives asked.

As Espen Mortensen had entered the conference room, Wisting passed the question to him. 'No,' he replied, taking up position at the far end of the table. 'He only had one thing on him that might help.' The crime scene technician took a step forward and placed a transparent evidence bag on the table. 'This photograph.'

Wisting reached forward and pulled the bag towards him. The photograph was somewhat larger than a normal passport photograph and stained with moisture. A woman in her mid-twenties, she had chubby cheeks, wore rather too much lipstick, and her smile showed slightly crooked teeth. Blonde hair lay in loose curls around her shoulders. 'A girlfriend?' he suggested, passing on the photograph.

'Maybe.'

Espen Mortensen took charge of the computer from Nils Hammer. 'I've just uploaded another photograph, which is extremely interesting.'

The investigators turned back to the screen. Wisting recognised the receipt found the day before on the path near the group of cottages. Yesterday the ink had been watery and illegible. Now the scrap of paper had been freeze-dried and was bathed in stark blue light. The text remained difficult to read, but it was possible to interpret.

The receipt was from the Esso station at the exit road from the E18. Someone had purchased a hotdog and a packet of *Dent* pastilles.

'None of our team dropped it,' Mortensen continued, crossing to the screen and pointing. 'It's dated Friday evening at 20.49, barely an hour before the alarm was raised.'

'Then it must have been the killer or the victim!' Hammer said. The burly detective stood up and made his way towards the door. 'I have the DVD from the CCTV camera at that petrol station in my office.'

Wisting leaned back in his chair, enjoying the satisfactory sound of pieces falling into place.

'Okay,' Mortensen went on. 'While we're waiting for the pictures: I've had it confirmed that the tread on the soles of the shoes tramped through the blood is from a Nike trainer.'

He clicked his way forward to display the photograph

115

of a white leather training shoe. The curved Nike logo was clearly marked in blue on the side.

'A Nike Main Draw men's shoe,' Mortensen said. 'The same print has been found in at least one of the other cottages as well.'

'Which one?'

'The nearest for one, but there are still piles of footprint samples to go through. Probably we'll find it in other cottages too.'

'There's a good chance the perpetrator has got rid of them by now,' Torunn Borg supposed. 'They must have been covered in blood.'

Wisting agreed, but avoided commenting that the remarks made by Christine Thiis at the press conference might also have done some damage.

Nils Hammer returned, holding the DVD aloft before inserting it into the computer. The images were unusually sharp and clear, and the text below showed time and date. Nils Hammer fast-forwarded.

'We can't be sure, of course, that the clock on the cash register and the CCTV camera are set to the identical time,' Mortensen reminded them.

'We'll need to keep a lookout for everybody eating hotdogs.'

Only the noise of the ceiling projector disturbed the silence as the counter on the CCTV film passed 20.45.

Two minutes later, a stocky bald man wearing fine-rimmed glasses entered the shop, exchanged a few words with the girl behind the cash desk, lifted a box of pastilles from a display stand and produced a wallet from his back pocket. The girl accepted a banknote and returned his change together with a receipt. The man placed both in the side pocket of his jacket as the girl crossed to the serving counter, where she inserted a hotdog sausage into a bread roll and handed it to him.

Hammer froze the video picture as the man opened his mouth, about to take his first bite.

'It's Jostein Hammersnes,' Benjamin Fjeld said.

'Who?'

'One of the other cottage owners. He also had a break-in. I interviewed him yesterday. He arrived at the cottage about nine o'clock on Friday night, using the same path, but didn't see or hear anything. It must have been all over by the time he arrived.'

'A dead end,' Hammer pronounced, stopping the video player. 'Damn.'

'How's the toll booth project going?'

'The systems will soon be up and running again.'

Hammer sat down at the conference table again and flicked through his notes. 'It's actually quicker getting responses from abroad than from our own data systems.' He produced a print-out. 'Carlos Mendoza,' he said, leafing through. 'The Spanish mobile account for the phone found beside the cottages was opened at a combined Internet café and mini-market in Malaga. The proprietor was imprisoned last month on suspicion of fraud and identity theft. The Spanish police believe that our accounts in the name of Carlos Mendoza are only two of many false identities he has sold to criminals. They aren't optimistic about finding the actual user. The telephone has been switched off, and the last registered use was here with us.'

It's another dead end, Wisting thought, staring through the window. The wind was still gusting, though the rain clouds had disappeared. The photograph of the woman with blonde curls had circulated around the table. Grabbing it, he rose from his seat.

'I want to know who this is,' he said, slapping it down in front of Torunn Borg. 'She meant something to the man who was carrying her portrait. I want to talk to her. She may have the answers we're looking for.'

117

25

The photographs of the man in the rowing boat were inserted into a dedicated folder in the electronic project room. Close-ups showed how extensive areas of his face had been ripped open by the seagulls' beaks and claws. Despite these ravages, those who knew him when alive should still be able to recognise him. Around thirty years of age, he was slightly built. His small face had a low forehead, narrow jaw and square chin lightly dusted with stubble.

Wisting wondered what the missing eyes had gazed on not so long ago, and when they had last looked on the woman in the photograph. How often had the man laughed unwittingly as the seconds of his final hours and days ticked away? What had he seen when the truth, inescapably and irrevocably, dawned on him?

Closing the folder, he lifted the telephone and keyed in his daughter's number.

'Are you going to scold me?' she asked.

'Why on earth would I?'

'Haven't you read the online newspaper?'

Wisting clicked his way into the online edition of *VG*, where a photograph of the rowing boat on the beach illustrated the main headline. A number of uniformed police officers had arrived after Wisting left the discovery site, and the salvage vessel was in the process of taking the craft in tow. Line's name was discreetly mentioned beneath the photo, though it had been tactfully omitted from the bye-line.

He often experienced the phenomenon of witnesses or

others peripherally involved in crimes being tempted by money to be made from major newspapers. Line though, was simply doing her job. Not only that, she had given him a greater understanding of the importance of the police being open, honest and responsible in their dealings with the press, and that positive communication with the media was the best route to follow in order to reduce criticism of the force.

Many businesses and organisations worked assiduously to gain visibility in the media, but for the police it was a different story. They were the main suppliers of news material, giving them an exceptional opportunity to steer the information. They had to adhere to their duty of confidentiality and the data protection laws, but increasingly had to think of the media as partners.

'How are you?' he asked.

The newspaper gave an excellent summary of the case. Another corpse discovered in Larvik on Sunday morning had been connected to the masked murder victim found in a cottage belonging to the well-known TV celebrity Thomas Rønningen last Friday. The police did not know the identity of the new murder victim and were still bewildered as far as the first victim was concerned. Identification work had been considerably hampered after the hearse transporting the body to the Forensics Institute had been stolen and set ablaze.

'I'm fine,' his daughter assured him. 'I don't want you to worry about me.'

'What was it like being interviewed?'

'It's not the first time that's happened, of course.'

'But it went well?'

'Oh yes. He was very pleasant.'

'Benjamin. Yes, he's smart.'

'I think he was a bit annoyed when I phoned the editorial team.'

119

'I can understand that.'

'Have you found out who he is? The man on board the boat?'

Wisting chortled. 'I'll send you a press release when we know anything further.' He changed the subject. 'Won't you come home this afternoon and have dinner with Suzanne and me?'

'Have you time for that?'

'I'll make the time.'

'Okay, but I'm going to go back to the cottage afterwards.'

They arranged a time and drew the conversation to a close.

Benjamin Fjeld indicated his presence in the room by knocking on the open door. Wisting waved him in. The young policeman glanced at the computer screen and Line's photograph of the discovery site. He seemed upset and Wisting wondered whether he should say something about his daughter's role as a journalist. Instead he waited to hear what Benjamin wanted.

'I think we've found the owner of the boat,' he said, nodding towards the photo on the screen.

'Tell me.'

'I've just had a phone call from Ove Bakkerud.' Wisting nodded. 'He saw the online article and thinks it's his. It was tied to a wooden jetty below the cottage. He hasn't gone to see whether it's missing, but thinks he recognises it all the same.'

Wisting placed one end of his ballpoint in his mouth and started to nibble. 'That makes sense,' he said, thinking how one of the men might have thrown himself aboard a fortuitous boat and fled into the darkness. The injuries he had already sustained later killed him.

'The wind had been blowing in an easterly direction,' Benjamin Fjeld replied, 'which fits with the discovery site.'

Removing the pen from his mouth, Wisting jotted down a

120

few keywords. 'Well done,' he said. 'Are you going to follow this up?'

'We've still got crime scene examiners out there. I'll get them to check the jetty. Then I thought I should talk to the dog handlers about whether all this fits in with their findings.' Benjamin Fjeld was already on his way out.

Wisting could now sit undisturbed with the case documents. Ten minutes later the telephone rang.

The caller introduced the conversation with a heavy sigh. 'This is Anders Hoff-Hansen.'

Wisting recognised the name and the slightly brusque, pleasant voice of the pathologist at Forensics. 'Have you completed the postmortem?' he asked.

'We have opened and closed the body,' the other man confirmed. 'But there's something that doesn't add up.'

'What do you mean?'

'I've studied the crime scene photographs and read the reports from your technician, and I can't understand it other than that we've performed a postmortem on a different body from the one described.'

Wisting felt an icy sensation creep along his spine. 'The body was totally incinerated of course, with charring on both skin and underlying tissue, but I'm not finding any outer lesions in the area of the abdomen as suggested by the crime scene photographs. On the other hand, there's considerable tissue damage on the neck and throat. That's where the cause of death is to be found. A projectile has pierced and penetrated the body.'

'Shot through the neck?'

'Precisely! I can find the entry wound, the projectile path and the exit wound, but it means this is a different corpse from the one described in your reports. The height and weight don't tally either. The burnt corpse is a smaller person.'

'How is that possible?' was all Wisting managed to say,

121

although the connection and explanation were already clear to him.

'This is something you really should have considered earlier,' the pathologist continued. 'There's obviously a possibility that this is the driver we've autopsied.'

'What do we do now?'

'That's up to you, but we have secured tissue samples for DNA and taken X-rays of the teeth. It should be possible to obtain reference samples and dental records for the driver for comparison. Of course, it should be the ID group at *Kripos* that deals with all that kind of thing.'

The conversation wound up with the pathologist promising to send the preliminary postmortem report by telefax accompanied by a summary and conclusion. Wisting rushed to speak to Christine Thiis who was rounding off a telephone conversation as Wisting took a seat opposite.

'I'm sorry about the footprints at the crime scene,' she said. 'That should never have been disclosed.' Brushing this aside, Wisting described his conversation with the pathologist. 'You're saying that someone killed the driver and swapped the bodies? That means we've got three murders.'

Wisting nodded. He had never heard of such a thing, but could not see any other explanation. Obviously they were dealing with an unusually calculating and dangerous adversary, someone much like Rudi Muller. Wisting felt icy fingers crawling down his neck once more. It was imperative to make good use of time now. They must not lose their calm nor allow fear to gain the upper hand.

26

Leif Malm and William Wisting were about the same age. Malm, wearing a dark blazer and pastel-coloured shirt with a stiff collar, had a lithe physique and strong, heavyset features. Wisting had seen him speak on behalf of Oslo Police in television interviews as well as read about him in the newspapers. His impression of Leif Malm as a leader with authority was confirmed as soon as he opened his mouth.

The officer accompanying him, Petter Eikelid, was about thirty years old and short in stature for a policeman. He chewed gum, thankfully with his mouth closed, and greeted them with only a nod, dislodging a lock of dark hair. He did not look at Wisting, but glanced around the room instead.

'For a while now we've been investigating a circle of people behind the importing into this country of relatively large quantities of cocaine,' Malm said. 'Given the size of their organisation they must have brought in almost a hundred kilos since May. The main man is called Rudi Muller.'

Petter Eikelid silently opened the folder in front of him to produce a surveillance photograph of a thickset man in his late thirties and of medium height, in a linen shirt opened sufficiently at the neck to reveal a thick gold chain. His smile only just lifted the corners of his mouth while the remainder of his face was immobile beneath thick black hair combed straight back. As he squinted in the sunlight, he brought to Wisting's mind the thought of a sleepy panther wakened from its slumbers at the wrong time.

'Sizeable business,' Nils Hammer commented.

Leif Malm nodded. 'Cocaine has a street value that varies according to its purity. Between two and four hundred kroner is the standard price of a gram.'

One hundred kilos meant a turnover of between twenty and forty million kroner.

'The money is laundered in the entertainment industry and reinvested in restaurants and bars as well as land and property,' Leif Malm said. 'Three weeks ago, we acquired a source close to Rudi Muller, and he's told us how the organisation functions and operates. Cocaine is only part of it. They bring in ten kilos every third week. The goods are delivered by contacts in southern Europe and transported here by boat over the Skagerrak from Denmark.'

'That fits with our Spanish connection,' Hammer noted, after explaining about the mobile phone found near the crime scene.

'That's our understanding of the operation too,' Leif Malm said. 'The arrangements are made in advance and, when the deliveries arrive, they give short messages via mobile phones which are impossible to trace. The cargo is shipped ashore and the cash payment transported out.'

Wisting recognised the smuggling *modus operandi*. This was how hash had come into the country when he started his police career almost thirty years before. At that time they had used fishing boats; nowadays, probably, large speedboats. 'However, on Friday something went wrong,' he remarked, bringing them back to the point.

Leif Malm nodded, tight-lipped. 'Petter Eikelid had a meeting with his source this morning.'

The young policeman stopped chewing. 'We don't really know what went wrong,' he said, his first contribution. 'Only that the money and the drugs are gone, and two men died.'

Wisting glanced at Leif Malm. 'You said that Rudi Muller lost one of his men.'

Petter Eikelid answered instead. 'One man failed to return with the boat to Denmark. My source assumes that the guy found in the rowing boat early today is the missing Dane.'

'I'm not quite following this,' Christine Thiis admitted. 'Are you saying that two men arrived in a boat from Denmark with ten kilos of cocaine, and two men came from Oslo with money to receive the drugs? Then it went wrong: shots were fired, we find two bodies, and both the money and the drugs have disappeared.'

Leif Malm smiled at her indulgently. 'Both we and Rudi Muller believe that a robbery took place when someone learned about the plan. They went off with both the money and the drugs.'

Nils Hammer rose from the table to fetch the pot of coffee. 'How much money?' he asked.

'Two million kroner, but Rudi is being held responsible for the drugs as well.'

'How come?'

'The goods have been delivered, but the European backers haven't been paid.'

'Have we any notion who was behind the robbery?'

Producing a packet of chewing gum from his pocket, Petter Eikelid pressed out a tab and placed it in his mouth. 'No,' was his succinct response.

Hammer returned to his seat. 'Rudi Muller must have some idea where the leak sprung?'

'He's leaving no stone unturned.'

Wisting looked up from his notes. 'Do you know who came here to collect the drugs?'

'We think we know who was killed.'

Petter Eikelid placed a photo of a round-eyed young man whose pale face was marred by acne. 'This is Trond Holmberg,' he said. 'He's the younger brother of Rudi's lady friend and hasn't been seen since Friday morning when he was with Rudi in the bar at *Shazam Station*.'

A knot twisted in Wisting's stomach. He took a drink from his glass of water.

'*Shazam Station*?' Christine Thiis asked.

'One of the restaurants Rudi Muller part-owns,' Petter Eikelid explained. 'If Holmberg is identified as the charred body in the hearse, we'll have made good progress.'

Wisting felt a blockage in his throat, only worsened by his attempts to clear it. 'It isn't Holmberg,' he said. Swallowing, he explained what he had learned from the postmortem. The corpse in the hearse was probably the driver.

Taking deep breaths, Wisting struggled to control his thoughts beneath the blur of his colleagues' discussion. Rudi Muller was a part-owner of *Shazam Station*, of which the man who had been living with his daughter was part-owner.

He swore inwardly. Where had his head been these past few years? He had distanced himself from his daughter's relationship with this Dane, the same age as herself, mostly because he knew about his past and his criminal convictions. He had remained silent until he saw how the relationship developed and, after it became well established, had remained silent. He had been too resistant to involvement.

He had to concentrate furiously to appear unruffled. He had lived long enough to know that his intuition was worth listening to – it had guided him through serious cases, but now it concerned his own daughter, the most important person in his life. For fear of losing her he had kept to himself what he actually thought about Tommy. He had allowed her to live her own life, and now was turned inside out with anxiety.

During the first period they had been together, he had more than once searched for Tommy's name in criminal records. Eventually he began to understand the qualities that Line

126

appreciated. Tommy could be attentive and considerate, a good conversationalist who listened and was reflective, but Wisting had been naïve and he cursed his weakness. He should be the first to understand that criminals can have attractive characteristics. Now Tommy Kvanter was bathed in an altogether new and uglier light. Youthful petty criminal behaviour was one thing; involvement with one of Europe's worst criminals was another. The thought of Line with such people made him feel ill.

He forced himself to participate in the conversation again.

'So, we have a rational explanation,' he said, putting into words the hypothesis that had taken shape in parallel with his own concerns. 'Rudi Muller knows how the police operate. He knew that if the body was identified as Trond Holmberg we would connect him to the case, but we announced that the murder victim was masked and that we had to await the post mortem report before we could say anything about his identity. The television even showed pictures of the hearse leaving the crime scene. We wrote the story for him.'

'All the same, it was an enormous risk to take,' Christine Thiis said.

'Typical of Rudi Muller,' Petter Eikelid said.

'What about the other man who was with him on the journey?' Nils Hammer enquired. 'Does the source know anything about him?'

'Not yet, but he is meeting Rudi Muller this evening. We might find out more after that.'

'Why did they bring the drugs ashore in our patch?' Hammer asked.

'It's possibly an established route that Rudi Muller took over, but we also know he has connections here.'

'What connections?'

'It's not on record, but he was collaborating with Werner Roos, now doing time, and he operates in the same network.'

Wisting nodded. Werner Roos was a property investor who had built up his business through narcotics. *Økokrim*, the financial crime department, led the investigation that put him away for eight years, but his outfit was still in operation.

Leif Malm held forth again. 'Our informant says that Rudi Muller is under pressure to pay. A deadline has been laid down and the pressure will increase now one of the suppliers is dead.'

Christine Thiis turned to a fresh page. 'How much of this can we use?'

'All of it is classified. If any of it leaks our source's life will be in danger. You'll have to take it from there.'

Trond Holmberg's arrest photograph lay in the middle of the table. Wisting pulled it towards him. 'Does he feature in the DNA register?'

'No, only photo and fingerprints.'

Christine Thiis seemed discouraged. 'So we have a crime scene possibly covered in his blood, but can't confirm.'

Wisting replaced the photo. 'If Trond Holmberg is reported missing we have a way in,' he said. 'It would be reasonable to take reference samples from the family and compare them with unidentified bodies and profiles in other ongoing cases.'

'With the exception of his sister, he's not somebody who keeps much contact with his family,' Leif Malm said. 'But we can start a missing person report. We could draft a summons and look up his parents.'

'Where is Rudi Muller now?' Hammer asked.

'We have surveillance on him. When we came into the meeting he was at his flat in Majorstua.'

'What about monitoring his telephone?'

'We expect to have all communications covered from early tomorrow,' Malm confirmed. 'The challenge is that we can't control what number he uses.'

'The most important thing now is to control the source,' Wisting said, making eye contact with Petter Eikelid.

Eikelid looked away.

'We need to know three things,' Wisting continued. 'Where is Trond Holmberg's body? Who was the other man he was with? What is Rudi Muller's next move?'

Leif Malm agreed.

Glancing through his notes, Wisting saw unanswered questions for himself as well. If it was true that Line had been living with a criminal for more than two years, with his silent approval, then he had many sleepless nights ahead. However, he would have to cope with that on his own.

'As the case now stands, we're looking for unknown robbers,' he said. 'But is there any chance that this wasn't what took place?'

'You're thinking of a plain and simple showdown between the supplier and the recipient?'

'Either that, or that this is all about something else entirely. Something we're not seeing.'

No one had an answer.

27

Suzanne prepared a simple and tasty meal, surprising them with puréed strawberries for dessert. 'I went home to get them from the freezer,' she explained, placing the bowl on the table.

'How are things at your house?' Line asked. 'Are the plumbers almost finished?'

'I don't really know. I don't think there was much difference from my last visit.'

Wisting sampled the dessert. 'You ought to serve this in your restaurant,' he said.

'Are you going to open a restaurant?'

Suzanne's cheeks turned pink. 'Not a restaurant, a café,' she said. 'Possibly.'

Wisting supplied additional details.

'It's going to become your favourite eating place,' Line said.

'That's what I think,' Wisting said. 'Did you go often to *Shazam Station*?'

Line talked while eating. 'In the beginning, yes,' she replied. 'At least a couple of times a week, less often after a while. Tommy was always there though. It took up all his time.'

'Were there many customers?'

'It was never full, but there was always a lot to do. He was partly responsible for the bar as well, so it wasn't a case of simply coming home when the kitchen closed.'

'Did you get to know any of the others?'

'Not many. There were constant changes, but that's what it's like. I didn't meet anyone I'd imagine becoming friends. I'm much happier with my colleagues.'

'What about Tommy? Did he socialise with colleagues in his free time?'

'Work and free time blended together, I think.' Line replaced the spoon in her empty dish. 'What's this about? You're more interested in Tommy now it's over than you were when we were together.'

'Sorry, but it's difficult to have friends in common when a relationship ends.'

Slightly ashamed, he glanced down at his dessert dish. What he was doing was actually detective work. His questions only appeared innocent.

Line cleared the table and put the plates in the dishwasher.

'Everything okay out at the cottage?' Suzanne asked.

'Absolutely fantastic, and I do enjoy wet and windy weather. It's lovely to sit at the panorama windows with the fire at my back, although what's happening to the birds is horrible.'

'What about the birds?' Wisting asked.

'Dead birds falling from the sky. Haven't you noticed? It's grabbed more headlines than your murder case.'

Line crossed over to the kitchen door and her bag to pull out her laptop. She placed it on the table facing her father.

DEAD BIRDS RAINING FROM THE SKY was the headline. Wisting recognised the man in the photograph as the farmer who helped him after he had been attacked. He stood with a shovel in his hand on which four dead black birds were laid out.

As many as a thousand birds may have fallen to the ground, dead, in the course of the weekend around Helgeroa in Vestfold, he read. The mysterious phenomenon started on Saturday morning and continued throughout the weekend.

131

Farmer Christian Nalum had experienced dead birds falling onto his house, the roof of his car, and in his fields, and had gathered more than a hundred on his property alone. The Wildlife Board had taken over collection and intended to have the birds examined at the Veterinary College.

'I ran over two like that on Friday night,' Wisting remarked.

'And I found one on the stairs outside the cottage,' Line told him. 'It's happened in other countries too,' she pointed to a lower paragraph.

The previous week, more than five thousand dead birds had fallen from the sky in the little town of Beebe in Arkansas, Wisting read. The birds had been examined at laboratories in Georgia, where experts had decided they had died as a result of internal hemorrhages and injuries to their vital organs. No real light had been shone on the mystery. There had been a similar event in Brazil.

'Yep, more hits than your murder case,' Line repeated, closing the laptop.

They discussed other matters until Line thanked them for dinner and left for the cottage. Wisting had half an hour before he was due back at the office.

'I think you should go ahead,' he said to Suzanne. 'Open that café. Follow your dream of the good life.'

'I'm living the good life now,' she said, snuggling up on the settee and leaning her head on his chest. 'I've always felt that. At least if I compare it with those who were born into the same war as me, the ones who didn't get away, and are living in starvation and poverty. I've bought a winning ticket, William.'

Suzanne, born in Afghanistan, was studying at the Sorbonne when the Soviets invaded in 1978. She had not returned, and a great deal of both their lives would have been different if she had made other choices at that time. He understood what she meant.

132

'What is the good life?' he asked.

'There's no single answer to that,' she said. 'Since we're all too different, and we all have different dreams and ideas. For the majority, it's about money and standard of living, but for me it's about realising a dream.'

'What's holding you back?'

'The road is long and difficult. I don't know if I dare change direction.' She turned to face him. 'What's the good life for you?'

He decided it was about happiness, but he was unsure where it was to be found. No dreamer, he preferred to enjoy life exactly as it is.

'Probably it's sitting at my regular table in *The Golden Peace*.'

28

The road was always long and difficult.

Behind his desk, Wisting mulled over what Suzanne had said about reaching one's goal. In a case it meant trawling through reports and other documents for a solution you could not be sure actually existed.

He alternated between reading information logged into the data system and what had been sent as original documents, and it struck him that he actually took satisfaction from this. Life was best when he felt he was doing something important, when he could follow the interplay of thoughts and actions and knew his efforts were going to make a difference. It fed his belief that his work could help create a better world.

As Benjamin Fjeld entered the office, Wisting looked up and removed his glasses to focus. 'You're still here?'

'I was thinking of going now,' Fjeld replied, 'if there isn't anything else.'

Wisting remembered his dread as a young detective of letting something slip, the fear of not being present when there was a sudden breakthrough. 'I'll phone you if anything happens,' he reassured him. 'Go home and get some sleep.'

Benjamin Fjeld was on his way out of the room when he stopped in the doorway, half-turning towards him. 'Have you seen that we're being blamed for the dead birds?'

'Are we?'

'Some birdwatcher is blaming the police,' he nodded in the direction of the computer screen. 'It's in the online *VG* pages.'

Wisting opened his browser, contributing another click to the editorial counting mechanism. The newspaper was speculating that the sudden deaths of birds were caused by the police helicopter flying low over the area. The director of the Norwegian Ornithological Association thought the birds had possibly died of exhaustion. If large flocks experienced severe stress, they could quite simply fly themselves to death, he pronounced.

'Everything is connected,' Wisting said. He reached for his coffee-cup, only to find it empty. 'How are you enjoying your work?' he asked, taking hold of the thermos flask.

The young policeman re-entered the room. 'Fine, thanks.'

Wisting filled his cup and found a clean plastic beaker for Benjamin Fjeld. 'That's clear from the work you hand in,' he said, nodding towards his tray of reports. 'You're thorough and efficient.'

Benjamin Fjeld accepted the coffee. 'Thanks,' he said. 'I hope an opening will turn up so I can stay here.'

Wisting nodded. The system was such that officers from the law enforcement section spent a six-month probationary period, taking the experience back with them into front line policing. Benjamin Fjeld, however, had detective qualities. Wisting regarded him as a natural investigator who absorbed everything and really cared about the cases and the people involved.

'We'll have to wait and see,' he said. 'You have a few probationary weeks left. If this case hasn't been solved by then we'll get to hold on to you anyway.' They remained seated, chatting about the case, Benjamin Fjeld brimming with observations, questions and arguments. It was after midnight when he left.

Returning to his computer screen, Wisting replaced his glasses and got to work with the investigation material.

Nils Hammer had completed his overview of the cars that

135

had passed the two toll stations between Oslo and Larvik, and had entered this information into the data system, noting that it had not been analysed yet.

Wisting scrolled through the long list of car registration numbers, models, owner information and the precise times of their passing. His eyes were heavy and he was rubbing them to focus more clearly when a familiar name popped up. *Thomas Rønningen*. He was the owner of a black Audi S5 that had passed the tollbooth at Sande at 19.32, the same vehicle that had been parked outside Wisting's house the previous evening.

He found the written record of the tape of Thomas Rønningen's statement, and located what he was looking for about halfway through.

> WW: Where were you yesterday evening and
> last night?
> TR: You would perhaps think I have the best
> alibi in the world – a million TV viewers, but the truth is that what everybody
> sees on the screen is a recording. The
> programme is recorded in the afternoon
> and broadcast unedited.
> WW: So where were you?
> TR: At home. Alone.
> WW: We've been trying to phone you, and even
> sent a car to your door this morning.
> TR: I disconnected everything. Mobile phone,
> doorbell, television, everything. I arrived
> home at about seven o'clock and sat down
> to write. I kept going until almost five,
> and then collapsed into bed. When I woke,
> I switched on my mobile, read my texts and
> phoned you.

Returning to the computer screen, Wisting scrolled to locate the record at the toll station on the local authority

136

border between Larvik and Sandefjord. The time was 20.17. Thomas Rønningen had passed both toll stations, in a direct route between Oslo and Larvik on the evening of the murder.

He sank back into his chair. The famous TV host had sat opposite him in his own home and told barefaced lies.

He read the account again. This was what an interview was all about, a detailed statement that could be used later to expose lies. It was true that one detail was missing from the statement. It was entirely possible that someone else had used Rønningen's car while he remained in his apartment writing, but Wisting reckoned that possibility was slight. He had encountered numerous accomplished liars and ham actors, and recognised them easily. Thomas Rønningen was one, but he could not make the lie fit with the information given by the informant to Oslo Police.

He pushed his fingers under the lenses of his glasses to massage his eyes. With increasing complexity solutions became more difficult to grasp. Deciding to switch off his computer and travel home to catch up on sleep, he noticed something else on the screen and the rhythm of his breathing changed.

Barely three minutes before Thomas Rønningen's Audi, a black Golf had passed the tollbooth. The registered owner was Elcon Leasing, but Wisting recognised the registration number of Line's car.

His thoughts whirled like autumn leaves, flitting and fluttering across his consciousness, and he was unable to grip them. On Friday at 19.29, he had been finishing the meal eaten in the company of Suzanne and Line at *Shazam Station*. Tommy Kvanter had been busy and unable to join them.

It dawned on him that he was sitting open-mouthed, unable to breathe. He gasped for air, but could not shift the icy, tight lump forming in his chest.

137

29

Banks of heavy dark clouds hung low over the horizon. Dense fog hovered above the sea, but gusts of wind repeatedly tore deep gashes in the gloom.

Line thought it a good idea to make the central character a female journalist, like herself, who inherits a large house on the skerries. The house has lain empty for many years, but the first time she visits there are fresh flowers in a vase and the clock on the wall is set to the correct time. One of the doors on the upper floor is locked, and none of her keys fits. When she finally succeeds in opening the door, she also opens a spellbinding murder mystery.

She had written late into the night and been wakened early by the seagulls' cries. Her breakfast was a cup of tea and a slice of crispbread with cream cheese. She read through what she had written and was less than happy with most of it. Some parts though, made her really proud.

Dressing for the squally weather, she slung her camera over her shoulder and stepped outside into wind that hurtled inland from the sea. Waves crashed onto the beach and the old wooden jetty.

She chose the opposite direction from the one she had taken the day she found the dead man. The terrain to the west was different, and the path led her into a tangle of dense woodland where the ground was soft and muddy, showing large, deep footprints. Someone had been here before her, either late the previous evening or early that morning.

She stopped and listened. Beyond the track the undergrowth

was so dense it was impossible to see the forest floor, and rampant clusters of honeysuckle snaked around the tree-trunks. A branch snapped in the distance, and then all was silent. A bird took flight, vanishing into the air.

Line walked until coastal rocks replaced the marshy forest and she found herself on a rocky outcrop, breathing the tang of salt and seaweed.

It was an excellent view for a wide-angle photograph, although the light was rather too dull and contrasts were minimal. She looked for some softer images to capture, but the golden autumn leaves further inland also lacked the necessary light.

Searching through the camera lens, she took a couple of preliminary shots but they were underexposed and grainy. She adjusted the shutter speed and positioned herself with legs wide, steadying the camera, and made a fresh attempt. This improved results, and she continued to look for new compositions.

When the viewfinder found two blasted, crooked pine trees on a crag, she took a photograph. Lowering the camera she spotted something jutting from a ledge beneath the pines. Something made by human hands. She zoomed in. Several wooden slats had been placed between two boulders with a green tarpaulin drawn over them. Branches had been placed in front, and a camouflage net covered the entire structure. She took a couple of photographs before packing her camera.

To investigate the slightly remote spot she had to climb around a cleft in the rock. The rudimentary shelter had stone walls at the back. It resembled a den made by children, except for its unlikely location. It was quite a distance to the nearest houses and no path led naturally to the little rocky overhang.

Two openings were carved out of the wooden boards at the front, reminiscent of firing hatches. Pushing her hands inside the net, she used them to lift the branch and inside

139

found a ground sheet and sleeping bag; at the rock face a propane lamp and a camping stove, with a water bottle and several empty cans lying beside them.

Crouching down, she crept inside. Birds' feathers had been pushed into fissures in the rock. She picked one out and rolled it between two fingers, but suddenly had the unpleasant sensation that she was being watched. Dropping the feather, she turned to face the little opening. No one was there. She hurried out, returning the branch to its former position.

As she turned her back on the little hiding place, she heard a strange rustling as the sky grew darker. An enormous flock of birds rose from the scrubby woodland behind her, manoeuvring as one single, connected organism. The roar of flapping wings grew louder as the flock veered above her and disappeared towards the west.

Line shivered. Turning up the collar of her jacket, she returned to the path and strode back hurriedly.

30

A man stood on the wide verandah with his hands cupped on the living room window, peering inside. Only when she approached more closely did she see it was her father.

'What are you doing here?' she asked.

'I wanted to see how you were getting on.'

'At nine o'clock on a Monday morning?'

'I was in the vicinity.'

'This isn't in the vicinity of anywhere,' she commented, turning to face the bitter wind. It buffeted her hair back from her face.

'The crime scene's not so far away,' he explained, following her into the cottage. 'I want to talk to Thomas Rønningen.'

Line unhooked her camera bag from her shoulder. 'Have you released the crime scene?'

'Yes, we finished there yesterday evening. I can't get hold of him by phone, so I thought I'd take a trip out to see if he's at his cottage.'

'Has he not made a statement?'

'Oh yes, but I've a few supplementary questions. A few details need to be set straight.'

Line wanted to ask more, but decided to let it drop.

'I haven't been here for years,' her father remarked as he surveyed the room. 'It's very pleasant.'

'I'm happy with it.' She crossed to the kitchen worktop to fill the kettle. 'Would you like a cup?'

'Yes, please,' he replied.

Her father made a tour of the house, checking room after

room, before sitting at the table in front of the large window. 'You shouldn't leave your computer like that,' he said. 'It's easily seen from outside. Tempting for burglars.'

'You're right,' she answered. 'I'm relieved I wasn't here on Friday night, when everything happened.'

Her father picked up the business card Benjamin Fjeld had left. 'Did you go straight home after dinner on Friday?'

'Yes, I did some shopping before going home to watch Rønningen on TV.'

'Did you have your car?'

'No, I took the tram. It's much easier.' She sat down to wait for the water to boil. 'Tommy had the car.'

'Why didn't he come and eat with us?'

'I don't know. He said something about a meeting with some Danes who were going to open a restaurant. I wasn't really interested. It suited me just as well that he didn't come. I'd already decided to finish with him.'

Her father replaced the young policeman's card on the table. 'When did you tell him?'

'When he came home. I sat up waiting but he didn't arrive until almost four in the morning. By that time I had fallen asleep on the settee. We had a brief conversation and he disappeared again. I went to bed.'

'Did he go out in the middle of the night?'

Line did not understand her father's intense interest in Tommy. There was concern in the tone of his voice, but his questions seemed to be heading towards a definite goal. He was weaving an invisible web.

The kettle was boiling, so she rose from her seat. 'He went out. That was after I told him I was coming home for a few days, and he'd to pack his belongings and find another place to live before I returned.'

'Do you think he's met someone else?' her father asked, accepting the cup she handed him.

Line sat down again. She hadn't wanted to think about that since it involved betrayal and deception, but it was an obvious conclusion. Many of Tommy's explanations about why he could not be at home or with her were just too blatant.

'That may turn out to be the case,' she said, tucking her feet underneath herself on the chair. 'But at the moment I couldn't care less. I'm just glad it's over.'

She wanted to change the subject and was going to tell him about the little hiding place someone had built on the steep outcrop, but her father spoke first. 'Is there a lot needing done here? It looks as though some of the timber is pretty dry.'

'Yes, it will probably have to be treated this summer,' she replied. 'I was thinking I could do some painting inside as well. Brighten the place up.'

'I can take care of the outside. You can fix things up inside, if you like,' her father suggested.

They sat talking about the things needing done, and how wonderful the summer was going to be at the mouth of the fjord, before her father stood up. He had to move on.

31

A sizeable bonfire was ablaze on the muddy, well-trodden area in front of Thomas Rønningen's cottage. Two men in joiners' overalls each carried a bundle of wooden planks in their arms that they threw on the flames. Wisting could feel the heat all the way to the walls of the cottage. All the bloody flooring in the outer hallway had been removed, as well as the walls, front door and splintered doorframe.

Wisting asked for Rønningen, but neither of the joiners had seen him. He dialled the number he had stored on his mobile, and this time received an immediate answer. 'Is there any news?' the TV host asked.

'I'm at your cottage,' Wisting explained. 'The joiners are keeping busy.'

'That's good. The insurance company agreed I could rip it all out.'

'Are you back in Oslo?'

'Why do you ask?'

'I've a few more questions, and we need to take your fingerprints.'

'I see. I'll be able to come down, but it will be late this afternoon,' Thomas Rønningen said, suggesting a time.

They made an appointment and Wisting replaced his phone in his jacket pocket. A flock of black birds wheeled above a plateau in the dense woodland. Like him, he thought, they were searching.

Instead of walking up to his car, he followed the path eastwards to the nearest cottage. Thick black smoke rose

144

from the chimney, where it was dispersed by the wind.

Wisting had read Jostein Hammersnes's statement to Benjamin Fjeld, describing how he travelled to his cottage on Friday evening, as he had done every weekend since the summer. Until the divorce settlement was finalised, he still lived under the same roof as his wife and two daughters, aged seven and nine, in a villa in Bærum. The weekends had become long and difficult, and he preferred to spend them on his own at the cottage.

The written statement did not contain any information about his short visit to the petrol station at the exit road for Larvik. It was probably a detail he considered insignificant, as indeed it was. The receipt found on the path below the parking place had turned out to be a dead end.

Wisting recognised the man from the CCTV footage when he opened the door to invite him in. He was wearing different clothes now: a loose-fitting pair of jogging trousers and chunky sweater. The cottage had probably belonged to Jostein Hammersnes' family for generations and never been modernised. The living room was decorated in rustic style with bell pulls and old copper kitchen utensils hanging on the walls. The damp air was filled with a strange, pungent odour, which Wisting could not identify.

Jostein Hammersnes crossed to the open fireplace where he rummaged in the embers, reinvigorating the flames before putting on two logs.

Wisting sat down at a long pine table with newspapers from the past few days spread over its surface, one of them opened at an article illustrated by a photograph of Christine Thiis. 'Haven't you gone back to work?' he enquired.

Jostein Hammersnes sat opposite. 'I would have liked to be somewhere else, but it's autumn half-term holiday and my wife, or former wife, is a teacher. We've just separated but are still living under the same roof. It's unbearable to be

145

bumping into each other all the time. Anyway, I can get most things done from here using broadband. I usually like being out here, but the enjoyment has gone.'

'Why is that?'

'The physical damage from the burglary is not too great, but the thought that there's been somebody here is almost intolerable. It overshadows all the happy memories I have of Else here with the children, and from the time when I was little. Now I'm not bothered that the cottage has to be sold to finalise the divorce settlement.'

Jostein Hammersnes avoided Wisting's gaze by lowering his eyes and staring at the tabletop. When he looked up again, they were shining. 'It's empty here,' he said wearily. He glanced past Wisting, towards a shelf on the panel wall, where a pale area revealed that something had been on display.

'They even took my glass ornament,' he said, crossing to the bare spot. 'I got it from my father the summer of my eighth birthday, after I succeeded in swimming across the inlet.' He moved his head in the direction of the sea.

'It's the only prize I ever won. I was a good swimmer, but I've never been involved in any kind of sport. My father was a glass craftsman. He had his own workshop at home in Høvik. I could sit for hours watching how he transformed molten, red-hot glass into the most beautiful shapes. That ornament was one of the loveliest things he ever made. He treated glass as if it were a precious metal, melted it, shaped, ground and polished it with love and care. When he gave it to me, he said that I could collect all my dreams in it. Fill it with my thoughts and hopes, without it ever becoming full or running over. Now it's gone.'

Wisting allowed the owner of the cottage to express the feelings he was nursing before making a start. 'Did you stop anywhere before you arrived at the cottage?'

146

'I dropped into the *Meny* shop at Holmen and did some shopping. I'd done my packing in the morning and worked a few hours overtime before I set out.'

'Did you make any other stops? At a petrol station for instance?'

'Yes. I stopped at an Esso station when I left the motorway.'

'Why was that?'

'I usually stop and buy some takeaway food. That way I avoid having to make anything myself.'

'What did you buy?'

'A hotdog, and a box of pastilles. Is this important? The policeman who spoke to me on Saturday didn't go into so much detail.'

'It wasn't important in the beginning, but we found an Esso receipt on the path out here,' Wisting said. 'There was a possibility it had been dropped by either the perpetrator or the victim, or there could be a third, simple explanation.'

He went through the rest of the man's statement, trying to make him recall whether he had passed any vehicles along the road or heard any sounds that might be connected to the burglaries or the murder. In the end he had to admit that Hammersnes had nothing to contribute. When they concluded their conversation, the flames in the hearth had died. Wisting rose to his feet and thanked the man for his time.

'I'll come out with you,' Hammersnes said. 'I need some air.'

Two pairs of girls' light summer shoes were lined up beside Hammersnes' big Wellington boots in the hallway. Wisting thought of how the girls would no longer be able to run over the rocks or paddle at the edge of the sea once the cottage was sold. A stroke of the pen by their intransigent parents wiped out future summer memories.

Hammersnes pulled on his boots and followed Wisting out. They trudged together partway along the path without uttering a word, until Wisting broke away and ascended to his car.

32

A magazine lay open in the conference room. Someone had acquired the summer edition of *Se og Hør* with the report about Thomas Rønningen's cottage. In the largest photograph, Thomas Rønningen was sitting closest to the camera, at the end of a long table laden with prawns and crabs. His guests were drinking white wine against a backdrop of blue sky. *Summer Idyll in Vestfold* was the caption.

Thomas Rønningen showed the readers around his cottage, room by room. In one of the pictures, he sat in a deep armchair in front of an abundantly filled bookcase, flicking through a crime novel. The article related that Rønningen was engaged in a book project, the theme and contents of which were secret.

The famous TV host enjoyed having visitors at his summer paradise, the report explained, rattling off a list of names almost identical to the list he had given Wisting.

Wisting read through half the report before being interrupted by his phone. It was Leif Malm from the intelligence section of Oslo Police. 'The surveillance team has lost Rudi Muller,' Malm said. 'He left home half an hour ago, much earlier than usual, and so we were short staffed. He called into *Deli de Luca* in Bogstadveien before continuing towards the centre. They lost him at the National Theatre.'

'Do you know where he was going?'

'No, we haven't picked up anything in particular on the *KK*, so he hasn't talked about it on the phone.'

KK was the abbreviation in use for *Kommunikasjons-kontroll*, meaning that the police listened in to all forms of communication a person had either by phone or via the Internet. One of the hidden methods of investigation, it was used mostly in the fight against serious organised crime, but was not as effective as they wished. The real candidates for this form of surveillance were aware of the interest and spoke in pre-arranged codes using keywords, and then only to arrange times and places.

'It's possible he has a mobile number and phone we don't know about,' Leif Malm continued. 'We're covering both his flat and *Shazam Station*.'

'What about the internet?'

'He's reading more or less everything the online newspapers have written about the case. There's one thing that supports our suspicion that he was involved in the incident with the hearse. He's spent a long time looking at pages dealing with fires and incineration. The one he has spent most time on describes fires and arson and the injuries caused by the effects of heat. The search words indicate he is interested in how lengthy and intense the heat must be in order to incinerate an entire body, and what possibilities exist to identify a charred body from dental records and DNA.'

'That's interesting.'

'Yes, it could be valuable evidence if we eventually reveal the communications surveillance,' Leif Malm agreed.

'Has the informant come up with anything else?'

'No. There was no meeting between him and Rudi yesterday. It may be that he's getting cold feet and wants to pull out.'

'That mustn't happen,' Wisting said. 'We need him.'

'Petter is encouraging him.'

'What's his motivation, really? Why has he put himself in such a dangerous position?'

For a moment there was silence. The use of police informants was demanding and could eventually turn out to be a game in which the police were simply pawns. The person who gave the police information often had his own personal motives: possibly revenge, possibly ambition within the criminal circle. It was a dangerous game, where the stakes were life-threateningly high. Therefore only an extremely restricted number of investigators knew the identity of any source.

'That's our business.'

Wisting considered asking whether they had taken into account that the source might have an interest in shifting their focus, that giving information to the police might involve moving suspicion away from himself and onto a trustworthy third person. He decided to let it lie, reassuring himself that Leif Malm and his officers were specially schooled in handling informants.

'I see the pilots of the police helicopters are denying their responsibility for the deaths of the birds,' Malm said. 'They're even writing about it in American newspapers. Rudi Muller is preoccupied by that as well. He's reading everything that appears about it on the net.'

'I'm relying on you to keep me informed,' Wisting said, returning to the point. He rounded off the conversation with a feeling that Malm was holding something back.

He stood by the window. The rain had started again, an impenetrable fine drizzle that made the town and landscape even greyer than before.

A broad-winged bird flew from a crack in the chimney on the old factory building beside the police station. It circled and squawked hoarsely before gliding in soundless flight over the rooftops and out of sight. At once Wisting felt an internal chill, as though the temperature in the room had fallen by several degrees. The unpleasant

151

sensation crept down his spine and across his fingers. His hands became clammy, his heart was racing and his mouth became dry.

The cold is not inside the room, but inside me, he thought, and shrugged it off.

33

Espen Mortensen placed a photograph on the desk in front of Wisting. It showed a slight, naked male body on the dissecting table. The missing eyes showed it to be the dead man Line found. Now the clothes had been removed and the body washed clean, it was not difficult to see what had been the cause of death. Two dark holes at the lower edge of his skinny ribcage indicated where the bullets had pierced his body.

'We know who he is,' Mortensen said. Lifting the photograph, Wisting waited to hear the name. 'Darius Plater.'

'East European?'

Mortensen leafed through his papers and read aloud. 'He comes from Vilnius in Lithuania. Twenty-three years old. Car mechanic.'

'How did we find that out?'

'Fingerprints. He was arrested for theft in a marina in Østfold last summer and registered in our records. Served thirty days' imprisonment in Halden Prison and was deported afterwards. Obviously he came back.'

Wisting replaced the photo. Crime committed by criminals from Eastern Europe had increased since the enlargement of the EU, mainly theft, but more frequently their lawbreaking also involved other types of serious crime, and the threshold for exercising violence was lowering. 'I can't quite get it to fit,' he said. 'This man's an itinerant burglar, but what took place was a drugs deal.'

'The Lithuanians are big in narcotics,' Mortensen

reminded him. 'It could have been a combined job. Drugs in, stolen goods out. We've seen that before.'

'That was amphetamines,' Wisting said. 'Cocaine comes from South America, via Spain and Portugal, sometimes via West Africa. Not from the east.'

'It fits with the information from Oslo intelligence that one of the men who arrived by boat from Denmark is missing.'

Wisting picked up the photo again. 'Did the pathologist find any bullets?'

'That's where it starts to get interesting. They've found two bullets, of different diameters.'

'Do you mean he was shot by two different guns?'

Mortensen handed him the report. 'That's what the numbers indicate. 10.4 millimetre and an ordinary 9 millimetre.'

'How big was the revolver we found beside him?'

'That's a much smaller weapon, a 22 calibre. The serial number's been filed off. We may be able to retrieve it but, before we place it in an acid bath, we must make some test shots to see what kind of marks are made by the firing pin and ejector.'

Wisting cast his mind back. 'Nine millimetre corresponds with the cartridge cases that were found on the path?'

'10.4 millimetre corresponds with 41 calibre. It could be from a revolver that doesn't discharge empty cartridges.'

Wisting looked at the photograph again. If they were right, something had happened in the darkness last Friday that turned the perpetrator into a victim.

'Two shooters,' Mortensen concluded.

'Or one shooter with two guns. Do we have any information on Darius Plater?'

Mortensen leafed through the pages again. 'Not much. He was stopped with several others travelling in a delivery van outside Grimstad this summer. Plater was driving, and only his name was entered. The van was searched. There were a lot of tools onboard, but nothing that allowed the police patrolmen to arrest them.'

'Have you been in touch with *Grenseløs*?'

'No, I thought you would do that.'

Wisting nodded. The flood of mobile thieves from Eastern Europe had become so overwhelming that the police district had established its own investigative group. The project had been given the name *Grenseløs* – without boundaries – for obvious reasons. The group comprised dedicated investigators who conducted enquiries directed at specific individuals across the boundaries of police districts.

Their innovative work had brought excellent results. Some of this success was due to a fairly informal cooperation with police in a number of East European countries. The group possessed skills that might be invaluable in the murder enquiry, but there was a long way to go.

Wisting sat deep in thought. These developments brought forebodings of a level of criminality he had rarely encountered: totally pragmatic, unscrupulous and cynical. We're falling short here, he mused. We need to redraw the map when the landscape changes.

34

The leader of the *Grenseløs* section was Martin Ahlberg, a bald man with a small beard, whose big dark eyes stared across the conference table at Wisting. He held a folder in his hand. 'I was expecting you to phone earlier,' he said. 'Serial thefts from holiday cottages are the pattern of activity we've come to expect.'

Wisting thanked Ahlberg before introducing him to Christine Thiis, Espen Mortensen and Nils Hammer. 'We have information that points in a different direction from Eastern Europe,' he explained, giving a brief presentation of the information they had received from the Oslo Police.

'Are you certain that cocaine is involved?' Ahlberg asked. Wisting admitted that they only had the whistle-blower's word.

'I have a hard time entertaining the idea that Lithuanians are involved in trafficking cocaine,' Ahlberg said. 'On the other hand, most of the amphetamines on the market in Norway come from illegal laboratories in Eastern Europe, and Lithuania has assumed the role of main supplier. Poland is still the most important country of origin, but most of the people who are arrested come from Lithuania.'

Martin Ahlberg helped himself to coffee from the thermos flask on the table but continued to speak with authority.

'Increasingly the drugs are transported by ferry across the Baltic Sea, but the most established route goes from Lithuania and Poland up through Germany and Denmark, across the Øresund Bridge and through Sweden to Norway. One place in Northern Europe is a point of intersection for cocaine coming up from Spain. The Lithuanians are prominent operators in the narcotics market and could have taken over the final stage. You must remember that we're talking about well-organised criminal gangs. They know how to make use of economies of scale the same as any other organisation.'

'What do you know about Darius Plater?' Wisting asked.

'Quite a lot.' Martin Ahlberg opened his folder and produced a photocopy of a Lithuanian passport. It was the slightly built man from the rowing boat. His name was printed in capital letters.

'Darius Plater belongs to a group of thieves from the out-skirts of Vilnius. They've been in Norway at least six times in the past three years. Last year he was captured in Østfold together with this man.' Ahlberg placed a copy of another passport on the table. The man in this photograph was called Teodor Milosz. He was a powerfully built man with a bull neck, flat nose and tiny eyes. 'They had prepared five large outboard motors for collection out at Hvaler. They were sentenced to thirty days each, and were deported after they'd served their sentences. They've been back twice since then.'

Wisting nodded.

'You must remember that the thefts vary according to the season,' Ahlberg said. 'The summer is high season for stealing large outboard motors. The autumn is the time for burglary from cottages closed for winter. Winter and spring it's houses and vehicles.'

'When did they last come to Norway?'

Martin Ahlberg produced a bundle of papers, but did not reply immediately. 'This is organised crime,' he repeated. 'The men behind this are former army officers and soldiers and they fear nothing, neither punishment nor prison condi-tions. They are a greater danger to society than most people imagine.'

157

Wisting glanced at the photograph of Darius Plater. The slim man was listed as a car mechanic. The picture contrasted starkly with the description provided by the section leader from *Grenseløs*, but he resisted pointing that out.

'Darius Plater and Teodor Milosz belong to a group we have christened the Paneriai Quartet,' Ahlberg said, 'four men from the same suburb of Vilnius, about ten kilometres south-west of the centre.'

'Have you been there?'

'We were invited by the consul in the spring. The local authority has a joint project on education, health, culture and industrial development that has been extended to incorporate cooperation in the fight against crime.' He paused while he drank his coffee. 'The thieves' market is located in Paneriai. You can buy anything there.'

'Who else is part of the quartet?' Hammer asked.

Martin Ahlberg gave two names with practised pronunciation and placed two more passport photos on the table. The sight of one of the men provoked a tingling sensation in Wisting's chest.

'That's him,' Wisting said, pulling the photograph towards him. 'That's the man who stole my car.'

'Are you sure?'

Wisting had only caught a glimpse of his assailant, but he was sure. He recognised the coarse facial features and deep-set eyes.

'Valdas Muravjev,' Ahlberg said. 'He's the oldest. Sentenced for robbery and violence in his home country.'

'Do you know where he is now?'

'He's at home in Lithuania.' Ahlberg lifted a printout marked DFDS Seaways. 'The entire quartet arrived by ferry in Karlshamn in Southern Sweden on the 18th September. They were driving a VW Transporter. Three returned by ferry at six o'clock yesterday evening.'

158

'What do you suggest we do now?'

'What is absolutely crystal clear,' Ahlberg replied, 'is that you have a case in which a Lithuanian citizen was shot and killed. The Lithuanian authorities must, of course, be informed. At some point too, the nearest relatives must be informed and an arrangement has to be made to transport the dead man home. At the same time, we know who he was with when he was killed. We could send over a legal request letter and have them interviewed, but if I were you, I'd travel over and do it myself.'

Wisting had reasoned similarly. Returning the photo of his assailant across the conference table, he leaned forward. 'Can you order tickets for us?'

35

At 17.07 Thomas Rønningen parked his black Audi S5 in the square outside the police station, seven minutes late for his appointment.

Wisting stood at the window watching him. His car was newly washed and he could see from a distance how the raindrops formed beads on the bonnet before sliding off. At the top of the windscreen was the outline of the subscription chip from the toll company.

Slamming the car door behind him, Rønningen threw a glance up at the façade of the police station building. He waved a greeting as their eyes met and he jogged through the rain to the entrance.

Two minutes later he was sitting in Wisting's office. He put down his mobile phone and car keys on the edge of the desk and used his hand to wipe the rain from his shoulders.

'Nice car,' Wisting said.

'I'm happy with it.'

'Is it yours?'

'Yes, why do you ask?'

'No, I was thinking it might be a company car or a car used by several people.'

Rønningen continued to smile, but now it seemed indulgent rather than sincere. 'It's a kind of company car, but I don't let anybody else behind the wheel.'

'So you're the only person who drives it?'

A slight grimace crossed Rønningen's face. His smile vanished.

The TV star was about to become of less interest, Wisting thought. The clues were pointing in every direction other than his, but there was something he was hiding and now he was about to be trapped by his own falsehood.

'It's possible somebody else has used it,' Rønningen said.

'Who would that be?'

'It's so long ago that I can't remember.' His irritated voice was very different from the tones he employed on TV. 'But I'm sure you haven't asked me to come here to talk about my car?'

'Yes indeed, I have,' Wisting said, 'because it was here in Larvik on Friday.'

'It hasn't got anything to do with the case,' Rønningen said.

'It has everything to do with the case. You no longer have an alibi. On the contrary, it puts you in the vicinity of the crime scene, and the fact that you have lied about it places you in an extremely bad light.'

'It's not as you think,' Rønningen stuttered. 'Am I suspected of something?'

'We can charge you with making a false statement,' Wisting informed him calmly, producing the printouts from the toll company. He placed them in front of him and pointed to the column showing the time and name of the car owner: *20.17, Thomas Rønningen.*

Despite years of research into how body language can expose liars, no one hundred percent certain method existed to distinguish between falsehoods and truth. In Wisting's experience, liars did not have shifty eyes, their bodies were not more restless, and they did not touch their noses or clear their throats more often than people who were telling the truth. The only thing that could expose them was proof, such as the printouts. For Rønningen there was no way out.

Although the physical signs of telling a lie could not be

161

interpreted with certainty, the body's resignation, as a signal that the lie had been uncovered, was easier to discern.

Rønningen subsided into his chair, shaking his head. 'I can explain,' he said.

Wisting had heard those three words from many others sitting in that same chair. He did not say anything, but waited for Rønningen to continue.

'I was in Larvik, but I wasn't at the cottage.'

'What were you doing here?'

Thomas Ronningen stood up and stepped over to the window before turning around and returning to his seat. 'Her name is Iselin Archer,' he said, remaining on his feet.

Wisting knew the name. She was a young painter who had received more attention for her marriage to Johannes Archer, a much older property investor and multimillionaire with a high media profile, than for her artistic endeavours. The ill-matched pair lived in Nevlunghavn where they had renovated the disused prawn factory into a combined residence and studio, where Iselin Archer regularly held private viewings and other functions duly reported in newspapers and magazines.

'She's been a guest on your programme,' Wisting recalled.

Thomas Rønningen nodded. 'Twice. That was how it began. I phoned her from the cottage the day after the first programme, to ask if she was happy with it. Johannes wasn't at home and she was alone in that vast house. He hadn't even seen it. When she heard I was sitting on my own in my cottage nearby, she invited me to her house for lunch. She served champagne and strawberries, and I stayed with her until the following day.'

Wisting listened vigilantly. When respect for the truth had been broken or impaired, everything became doubtful, but the story about how a relationship developed sounded convincing. Thomas Rønningen spoke with sensitivity and commitment once he started, somehow relaxed after admitting the secret relationship.

'We usually met at the cottage,' he said. 'But Johannes was away on business, so we were at Iselin's for the entire weekend. I daren't think about what might have happened otherwise.'

Wisting sat in silence for a while before asking: 'Where is Johannes Archer?'

'In France,' Rønningen replied. 'He's looking at some vineyards.'

'Do you think he suspected you were meeting at your cottage?'

'I think he suspected Iselin, but not that it was me she was meeting.'

'Does he know where your cottage is?'

'He's been there. Iselin was a guest on the final programme of the spring season. Johannes was present in the studio. I don't know how it came about, but I invited them both to a shellfish party.'

'Is he on his own in France?'

'As far as I know. Why do you ask?'

Wisting shook his head without answering. An absurd thought was forming in his mind, but he dropped it. 'I need to talk to her,' he said.

Rønningen nodded. 'She's prepared for that. All the same, I hope this part of the investigation won't become public.'

Wisting made no promises. As the case now stood, they had to determine the people about whom they had no grounds for suspicion, and he was not yet sure that Thomas Rønningen could be struck from the list.

He rose and accompanied the TV host as he left. The rain had increased in intensity and was now falling in torrents. Wisting remained standing under the roof as Thomas Rønningen dashed, neck bowed, towards his car, a liar making his way to his incriminating evidence.

163

36

Two messages awaited Wisting in his office. One was from Martin Ahlberg, informing him there was a direct flight from Oslo Gardermoen airport to Vilnius the next day at 10.45 and that he would meet him at the airport with their tickets. The other was from Leif Malm asking Wisting to phone him.

'We've located Rudi Muller,' Malm explained. 'He arrived at *Shazam Station* half an hour ago. I'll switch on the loudspeaker so you can hear the status report.'

A crackling sound and pressing of keys preceded an increased humming on the line. 'Charlie 0-5,' Malm announced. 'Do you have a situation report?'

The head of the surveillance operation responded: '*Muller is sitting at a window table with two other people, position 2-4. The vehicle is in Grensen. A black BMW 730, BR-registered.*'

Wisting saw the restaurant building in his mind's eye. 2-4 was the dimensional information, placing Rudi Muller on the second floor, fourth window from the left. This meant he was sitting beside the table where he and Suzanne had eaten with Line three days earlier.

'*Muller has taken off his grey jacket and is wearing a red T-shirt,*' the surveillance operator continued. '*Directly opposite him Tage Larsen is sitting dressed in a green hooded jacket. They're in the company of a third man we don't know. Dark, but Norwegian, black leather jacket, black cap. We have a photo.*'

Wisting transferred his mobile phone to his other ear. It

164

was a vague description, but could fit Tommy. 'We have identified the man who was found in the rowing boat,' he said loudly.

'And?'

'It's a Lithuanian called Darius Plater.'

Another unit broke in: '*Charlie 0-5; did you hear that?*'

'*Negative. What are you referring to?*'

'*We're listening to channel three. 01 has just reported a fire at Teppaveien 5 in Grorud. Isn't that Trond Holmberg's address?*'

Silence followed, until the surveillance leader spoke to Leif Malm: '*Charlie?*'

'I'm in now,' Malm replied. Wisting could hear him working on a computer keyboard. 'The report came via the emergency number 110 switchboard three minutes ago and states that the gable end apartment in a block of flats at number 5 Teppaveien is an inferno. The registered resident is Trond Holmberg.'

'*This is Charlie 3-1 interrupting. There's movement here now. Are we ready to tail him?*'

'*Charlie 3-2 in Akersgata,*' the first patrol acknowledged.

'*Charlie 3-3, Pilestredet.*'

'*Charlie 3-4, Møllergata at Stortorvet Square.*'

'*Muller's making a phone call. Are we covering him at KK?*'

Leif Malm answered: 'There are no personnel on duty there. We'll get a printout later.'

'*They're in a hurry. All three heading for the car.*'

There was silence on the line as they waited for the next message. '*They're getting in. Muller's driving.*'

'*Direction?*'

'*They're going up into Akersgata.*'

'*Charlie 3-2. We've got him.*'

The radio messages came thick and fast.

'Charlie 3-3 in position for the Vaterland Tunnel.'

'Charlie 3-4 driving parallel in Grubbegata.'

'3-2 under control. Following behind as third vehicle. They're in a rush, but there's a hold up in the traffic.'

'Charlie 3-1 following on.'

'They're driving along Ullevålsveien, along past Vår Frelsers graveyard.'

The leader of the surveillance team gave directions: *'Charlie 3-3 – Drive to Bislett and be ready to pick him up at St. Hanshaugen.'*

'Received.'

'Stopping at red light in Waldemar Thranes gate. He's turning right.'

'3-1 driving along Bjerregaards gate. We can pick him up further ahead.'

'Charlie 3-4, be ready for Sinsenkrysset!'

'Received.'

Wisting listened to the messages ricocheting at top speed. Surveillance was a special skill. It was important to remain three steps behind the object, but also one step ahead. The people who chose this type of work were, as a rule, not particularly enamoured of paperwork but had a well-developed hunting instinct. Many thought it exciting, although it mainly consisted of waiting. They could sit for hours staring at a door, but when something happened, it happened fast.

'It's taking Trondheimsveien,' Wisting heard a scratching on the police radio. *'Repeat: Trondheimsveien. I'm losing him, can someone take over?'*

'Charlie 3-1 has him. He's probably going to Grorud. I'll bet he's heard about the fire at Holmberg's.'

'Oh fuck, we can see the smoke all the way down here at Bjerke.'

Leif Malm broke in. 'You can let him go. He's going to

Teppaveien. He got a phone call from his lady friend a few minutes ago with news about the fire.'

'*Received.*'

'Charlie 0-5 can drive to Grorudveien, the others get yourselves into position. Be ready to follow when he takes off again.'

The various units acknowledged the order and Malm switched off the loudspeaker. 'What the fuck does that mean?' he asked. 'The flat's empty, of course.'

'I think you're going to find Trond Holmberg,' Wisting predicted.

'Whereabouts?'

'If Rudi Muller is as calculating as we think, then there is only one thing he can do.'

'Oh fuck,' Leif Malm commented at the other end as he realised what Wisting meant. 'He's put Holmberg's dead body in the flat and set it alight.'

'It's a rational course of action. He has to get rid of it without it being connected to him or to the case. Every dumped body with shotgun wounds is going to be linked to the murder enquiry.'

'He could have simply buried him or made sure that his body was never found,' Malm said, but he had already accepted Wisting's theory.

'Despite everything, we are talking about his girlfriend's young brother, whose disappearance would also lead to investigation. If he's lucky, there will only be teeth left to identify. If it hadn't been for the informant we wouldn't have seen the connection, and concluded that it was death by fire.'

'Fuck,' Malm swore again. 'We thought he was reading about fires and physical injuries on the net to find out how things had gone with the driver in the hearse, but it was research he was conducting.'

Wisting pressed ahead with information about the

167

identification of the corpse Line had discovered in the rowing boat. 'It sheds light on a great deal of what we had visualised,' he said. Leif Malm agreed. 'Are you sure that this is all about cocaine?'

'Absolutely certain,' Malm said. 'We seized some earlier deliveries.'

'Could the Lithuanians be behind it?'

'There could be a smuggling connection. We have very little intelligence, but we know that South American narcotics cartels are trying to build a network of transport routes via the Eastern European states. Many of the routes to Western Europe have been charted and broken by European police work. In the East European market, they see possibilities to avoid alert police officers, or think they'll be open to bribery.'

'I'm travelling to Lithuania tomorrow morning,' Wisting said. 'Could we meet before then?'

'Whenever you like,' Malm said. 'We'll try to get our source into position this evening. Hopefully we'll have news for you by then.'

37

The rain was too torrential for Line to venture out. More-over, the temperature had dropped as darkness set in. The logs in the hearth refused to burn and lay smouldering. Instead of trying to light the fire again, she had put on a thick sweater. She had attempted to write, but was stuck on the same sentence. Restless, she had to admit she felt lonely.

On the first evenings at the cottage she had not even tried to use the old portable television that was perched on a stool. Now she had managed to bring it to life but there was nothing onscreen but interference. It dawned on her that the analogue signal was defunct and she needed a decoder.

Thinking she might phone some old girlfriends from when she lived in Stavern, she ticked off some names in her head from school and the handball team, but understood they would be busy on a Monday evening.

It wasn't too late to drive into town. She enjoyed sitting on her own at a café table reading a newspaper or book, or working on her notes. Being surrounded by people gave her a sense of having company, while she carried on with her work, but it was not an appealing prospect. Pleasant enough with someone waiting at home, but not now.

At the window she folded her arms for warmth; the wall lamp outside cast a semi-circle of illumination on the veran-dah. At the far edge of the cone of light lay another dead bird, the fifth, which must have fallen in the last hour. She thought about throwing it into the bushes, but instead left it lying. Probably some hungry animal would carry it off during the night.

Behind the yellow shimmering light, the evening lay opaque and oppressive. It was impossible to see what lay out there, and the only sound was the ceaseless crashing of waves on the shore. Her mobile phone rang, wresting her away from her gloomy thoughts. It was her father. Her voice sounded hollow, even to herself, when she answered.

'How are you doing?' he asked.

'Fine,' she replied, sitting down. 'You have to stop worrying. I'm managing okay.'

'Are you sure?'

'Yes, of course, but it was good of you to call.'

'I'm going away for a few days, work related,' he said. 'I'm sure Suzanne would appreciate some company in the house.'

Line smiled at her father's concern. 'She's used to being alone. She lived on her own for many years before she met you, you know.'

'The offer's there, all the same.'

'Thanks anyway. Where are you going?'

'Not far. I can be reached by phone.'

She understood he was afraid she would pass on the information and that someone at the newspaper would guess that the case was about to turn a corner. It must be important, since he was leaving town.

'What have you been doing?' he asked, changing the subject.

Line tucked her feet underneath herself on the settee, selecting a book from the chaotic bookcase. 'Reading,' she answered.

'What exactly?'

'An old crime novel from the bookcase here.'

'Okay. I won't disturb you. Phone if there's anything you want.'

She promised before disconnecting the call and turning to the first chapter. She liked the opening sentence. *Immediately after midnight he stopped thinking.* Suddenly the flames in the hearth leapt into life and she smiled as she snuggled up on the sofa.

Wisting put down the phone. On the television, a newsreader announced that someone was missing after a fire in an apartment block in Grorud, Oslo. The following report showed images of fire fighters running to and fro in the barricaded street. The flat where the blaze had started was already burnt out and the fire crew was battling the flames as they licked their way towards the neighbouring apartments, flames billowing as streams of water played across them.

Picking up the remote control, Wisting waited until the end of the report before switching off. 'I don't know how long I'll be away,' he said to Suzanne. 'Do you think you could go out to see Line tomorrow?'

'Why are you the one who has to travel to Lithuania?' she protested. 'As leader of the investigation, shouldn't you stay here?'

'Right now I think it's best that I keep my distance,' he replied.

'What do you mean?'

Running his hand through his hair, Wisting fixed his eyes on a spot on the wall. 'I think Tommy may be mixed up in this somehow.'

Suzanne sat up. 'How can that be?'

Seldom did Wisting confide details of cases. The duty of confidentiality, and obligation to protect personal data, often constrained their conversations, but this time he needed to talk. 'We have information that the case revolves around a narcotics delivery that went wrong,' he said, going on to give an account of the smuggling route across the Skagerrak. 'The main man in Norway is called Rudi Muller, one of the owners of *Shazam Station*. The Oslo Police believe the whole restaurant business is about laundering drugs money, and that the restaurant is a focal point for criminals.'

Suzanne's eyes filled with concern. 'It doesn't have to mean that Tommy is involved.'

'He was jailed for narcotics before.'

'That was long before he met Line,' Suzanne said, but he could see the doubt in her face.

'There's more to it. The evening he was supposed to meet us, he was here in Larvik.'

'The evening of the murder?'

Wisting nodded.

'How do you know that?'

'We've surveyed all the traffic through the toll stations between Oslo and Larvik. Line's car passed the tollbooths at the optimum time relating to the murder. Tommy had the car then.'

Suzanne sat in silence.

'I discovered it by accident,' Wisting said, 'but haven't spoken to any of the others yet.'

'Have you told Line?'

'Not directly. I can't, as long as the enquiry is in progress.'

'Then you don't really know if the situation is as you believe. There could be quite a simple explanation.'

'In any case, I ought to tell the others.'

'What if you're wrong?'

'There's nothing to be wrong about. Tommy and the car were here on the day of the murder. Only he can answer for what he was doing.'

'Can't it wait until you come back?'

Biting his bottom lip, Wisting considered the compromise. 'I'll take the documents with me and read them on the plane,' he said. 'If nothing makes me see it differently, I'll phone Nils Hammer from Vilnius.'

38

Sometime during the night the rain stopped, but it was still misty when Wisting left home early on Tuesday morning. The police station remained deserted, and he was undisturbed as he walked to his office.

They had two systems for dealing with new documents in any case. In one all the reports were allocated successive numbers. In the other they were given special document numbers in accordance with a fixed system, depending on what type of information each document contained: witness interviews, technical reports, crime scene documents or information pertaining to the victim. The former was a practical work tool that was always kept up to date, while the latter was redrafted so that it could be presented to the state prosecutor and defence counsel when charges were brought.

Wisting took a set of copies filed in successive numbers. They had already collected so much information it was divided into two ring binders marked I and II. He found room for them both in his hand luggage, but was afraid his suitcase would be heavier than his cabin allowance permitted. Before leaving, he checked his emails without finding anything of interest. He then switched off the light and let himself out.

At nine o'clock, he drove into Grorudveien and, in a side street, saw the skeleton of the burnt out apartment building towering against the leaden sky. The street was still closed to through traffic. Driving up to one of the posts supporting the crime scene tape, Wisting climbed out of his car. A miasma of ash floated in the damp air.

The firemen had gone away, leaving behind an eerie silence that had settled like a shroud. Crime scene examiners in white hooded overalls wore masks to protect them from the gases they stirred from the ashes as they worked. Another car pulled to a halt. The superintendent from the intelligence section at Oslo police district finished a telephone conversation before joining him. They shook hands briefly, silently, before crossing to the site of the blaze.

Leif Malm waved one of the crime scene examiners across. As he approached, he tilted his particle mask onto his forehead. 'Have you found anything?' Malm enquired.

'It takes time,' the examiner replied. 'We're working our way down, layer by layer.'

Wisting had not expected anything else. Fire examination was time consuming work in which the crime scene examiners excavated the remains of the fire, keeping their eyes peeled for patterns imprinted on what was left of the walls and floor. Everything gradually uncovered was photographed and recorded in sketches. Every soot deposit could provide information about the fire burning rapidly or slowly, whether it had burned high or low in a room, and whether the flames had leapt up or down. In certain circumstances, they could also work out the direction in which the fire had spread – upwards from where it had begun, downwards only when everything above had been consumed. This was a job that would take not hours, but days.

'Any indication of the cause?' Malm asked.

'Given the intensity, it's easy to conclude that it was started deliberately.'

'If someone was inside, how much will be left of him?' Wisting asked.

'Not much.'

'Enough to tell us something about the cause or time of death?' Malm asked.

The examiner shook his head. 'It depends on how much is left. Certain things can be deduced even from the most charred bodies, but the precise time of death is not usually one of them. That requires an investigation of the rotting process in muscle proteins, amino acids and fluid fatty acids, all of which are normally destroyed in a fire.'

'What about ID?'

'Identification of teeth is probably the simplest method. That gives us a swift answer as well. If we can locate the missing person's dental records, it can be accomplished in a few hours, but first of all we need to find the body.'

'What about DNA?'

'That takes up to a fortnight. What's more, we have to collect reference samples from the family.'

'Will there be enough material to create a DNA profile?'

'I would think so, but the easiest and quickest method is the teeth. If the heat was intense enough it's not certain that there will be sufficient cellular tissue for DNA.'

Wisting knew what heat could do to the human body. Rudi Muller knew it too. Some of what the crime scene examiner related was almost identical, word for word, to the contents of the internet pages he had perused. 'Regardless, we need to have a DNA profile,' he said. 'It will give a direct link to our case and prove that Trond Holmberg was the person who was found murdered in Thomas Rønningen's cottage. We need it to move the enquiry forward.'

The man in white overalls gave him a nod before replacing the particle mask over his nose and mouth and returning to the site of the fire.

'Let's sit down,' Leif Malm suggested, heading for his car.

Wisting entered at the passenger side. 'Any news?' he asked, slamming the door behind him.

Leif Malm lifted his folder from the rear seat. 'Our source had a meeting with Rudi Muller late yesterday. He got the

175

impression that Rudi himself had gone to Larvik on Friday with Trond Holmberg, and that Rudi himself drew the gun.'

Wisting stared directly ahead. A gossamer veil of condensation had formed on the interior of the windscreen. 'His car is not registered at any of the toll stations,' he said.

Leif Malm started the engine, fumbling in his efforts to locate the heating switch. 'He may have used another car,' he suggested, turning on the fan. 'Send the material to us, and I'll get one of the boys in the analysis team to cross check the lists with known vehicles in Muller's criminal fraternity.'

Wisting nodded. The condensation on the glass disappeared and he could see clearly. Dark smoke still rose from the ashes of the fire. 'If he was with Trond Holmberg when he was killed I'd have a better understanding of the risks he's taken. If we could have put Trond Holmberg on the dissecting table, then the searchlight would have been focused directly at Rudi Muller.'

Leif Malm agreed and handed him a bundle of photographs. 'Surveillance photographs from yesterday's meeting at *Shazam Station*.'

Wisting accepted the photos and leafed through them. The pictures were taken from a distance, but were sharp nevertheless. He recognised Rudi Muller, but not the two others.

'That's Tage Larsen,' Malm said, pointing to a plump man with thick, curly hair sitting opposite Muller. 'We don't know the other guy.'

Wisting squinted at the third man in the photo. He could not discern who it was, but at least it was not Tommy Kvanter. Returning the photographs, he realised that possibilities existed other than those he had imagined. All the same, if Malm and his surveillance team did not know him and his connection to Line, then their intelligence was useless.

'My daughter's former boyfriend works there,' he said with a nod at the photos. 'He's one of the owners. Tommy Kvanter.'

Leif Malm looked at him for a long time before speaking. 'Isn't their relationship over?'

'Yes, it's been limping along for a long time, but now it's over. They've been living together in Line's flat. She's staying at the cottage now in the expectation that he'll find himself somewhere else.'

'I only understood it was some kind of break,' Malm remarked.

Wisting swallowed. It was obvious that the intelligence service was effective. There would certainly be surveillance photographs somewhere or other of Line and Tommy as well. 'Is he involved?' he asked bluntly.

Leif Malm packed away the folder to signal that the meeting was over. 'We don't have any information suggesting that. But if their relationship is finished I think you should be glad. This environment's not something you would want her to be part of.'

Wisting opened the car door.

'One more thing,' Leif Malm said. Wisting remained seated with the door slightly ajar. 'This is probably developing in a dangerous direction.' Wisting closed the door again. 'Muller is subject to extreme financial pressure. The European backers are holding him responsible for their loss and for the death of one of the couriers. They're demanding five million kroner.'

'What action is Muller thinking of taking?'

'He's mounting a robbery attempt. That was how he built himself up, with several robberies from security transport vehicles towards the end of the nineties. During the last decade he's benefited to a greater extent from the proceeds of narcotics traffic, but he still has a network of contacts.'

'What's the target of the robbery?'

Leif Muller shrugged his shoulders. 'We don't know yet. Our informant is working on it, but there have been rumours circulating for a long time about plans for a major heist, something like the *NOKAS* security firm.'

Wisting shut his eyes. It was a vicious circle. The criminals were sucked into a spiral of increasingly serious activities and, the deeper they went, the more difficult it became for the police to stop them.

39

The direct flight to Vilnius took off precisely on time. Wisting and Martin Ahlberg sat in the tenth row with a vacant seat between them.

The plane was no more than half full. Most of the passengers were Lithuanian guest workers on their way home, but there were also a handful of Norwegian businessmen in suits and with financial newspapers on their laps.

On the row of seats diagonally opposite, a young woman flicked through the latest edition of *Se og Hør* magazine. She stopped at a large photograph of Thomas Rønningen. Wisting could read the headline from where he was sitting. *Unknown man found MURDERED AT COTTAGE.* Some of the photographs used were archive images from the summer article about Rønningen in company with well-known colleagues from *NRK* television.

He leaned back and contemplated what he knew about Lithuania. Only a few days ago he couldn't have placed it on the map. He was shamefully ignorant of the country, although it was less than two hours by air from Oslo. The previous evening, he had leafed through the encyclopedia and read that it bordered Latvia in the north, Belarus in the east and Poland in the south. Once it had possessed an impressive empire stretching from the Baltic to the Black Sea, but now the former superpower was smaller than the area of Østland county in Norway.

It had surprised him to learn that there were no more than 3.6 million inhabitants, since Lithuanians comprised a disproportionately large proportion of the total number of foreigners in Norwegian crime statistics. Poland, with almost 40 million inhabitants, provided only half the number of criminals in Norway. The extent of criminality in Lithuania became even clearer. Unemployment of almost twenty per cent and a large number of people living under the poverty level had to take a great deal of the blame.

The capital city, Vilnius, with 580,000 residents, possessed a wealth of history, but he had never heard so much as a mention of the Lithuanian president. He had skimmed over the encyclopedia's information about the system of government and the country's economy, but had taken a particular interest in how the police force was organised. It was not especially different from Norway.

'We have an appointment with the Chief of Police at two o'clock,' Martin Ahlberg said, when they reached cruising height. 'We'll check in at our hotel afterwards.'

'How will we go about this?' Wisting asked.

'I've sent them information on the case and explained that, in connection with a murder enquiry, we wish to speak to the family of Darius Plater and three other Lithuanian citizens: Teodor Milosz, Valdas Muravjev and Algirdas Skvernelis. I've already received a list of addresses and information from the official records.' He produced a bundle of printouts with photographs of the three surviving members of the Paneriai Quartet.

'You said that Valdas was sentenced for robbery,' Wisting remarked, pointing at the man who had attacked him.

Ahlberg let his finger slide along the text underneath the picture. 'Assault and robbery in 2006,' he read. 'Six months' jail time.'

'What about the others?'

Martin Ahlberg traced his finger along the page before

shaking his head. 'No convictions,' he said, handing over the printed pages.

Wisting put on his glasses to read. Darius Plater was the eldest of five siblings and his address was listed as at his mother's home in Šešeʻliu gatve. There was no father listed. 'Has the family been informed about his death?' he asked.

'I've asked them to wait until we've spoken to the men he came to Norway with. It's not a problem as long as we don't have any more formal identification than the Norwegian fingerprint register.'

Wisting nodded and continued to study the printouts. One of the other men lived in the same street as Darius, also with close family. His assailant lived on his own, but had the same postcode, as did the fourth man. 'How do we manage with the language?' he asked.

'The Lithuanians will provide an English interpreter.'

Wisting stacked the papers so that his attacker's photograph was on top. 'I'd like to start with him,' he said. 'Valdas Muravyev.'

Ahlberg agreed. 'Just remember these are only witness interviews. If we're thinking of accusing them of house-breaking or theft we have to initiate completely different formalities.'

The flight stewardess arrived with coffee. Wisting handed back the papers and lowered his flight tray. Martin Ahlberg exchanged the papers for a laminated collection of documents which he handed to Wisting.

'What's this?'

'It's a comparative case analysis of the aggravated thefts in Eastern Norway we suspect the Paneriai Quartet of committing,' Ahlberg explained. 'Each individual crime scene is described.'

He thumbed forward to one of the last pages where a row of red dots was drawn on a map of Østland county, mostly concentrated in clusters along the Oslo fjord. 'Sixty-eight cottages,' he said.

On the next page there was a fine blue line drawn through the red dots along the same stretch of coastline. 'We've tracked Teodor Milosz' mobile phone on the Norwegian telephone network.' Martin Ahlberg indicated with his finger how the blue line started at the Swedish border and reached as far as Larvik before traversing in a loop to return by the fastest route along the E18 to Oslo and the E6 back to Sweden.

'It was his phone number they gave when they booked their ferry tickets. We received the telephone information yesterday and plotted the locations on the map.' Self-explanatory, the map showed how the group of Lithuanian travellers had left behind them dozens of burgled crime scenes.

'That's how we work,' Ahlberg continued. 'It's what's led to our success. We don't investigate the crimes, but the people, and see what pops up. If we find DNA or fingerprints at any of these crime scenes, then all the other cases with the same *modus operandi* fall like dominoes.'

'Do you have the telephone information for Friday evening?' Wisting asked.

Martin Ahlberg flicked to one of the final pages. A detailed printout showed an overview of incoming and outgoing telephone numbers, with date and time of day, duration of call and the location of the phone apparatus. 'They arrived in Larvik on Thursday afternoon. There's little phone activity until late on Friday evening. Then all hell breaks loose, but you know all about that, of course. We're carrying out a closer analysis of the phone numbers Teodor Milosz has been contacting.'

Wisting noted that the same numbers recurred time after time. He commented that several were Norwegian.

'They obtain Norwegian pay-as-you-go subscriptions

and use them to communicate with each other for as long as they're in Norway,' Ahlberg said. 'So far it doesn't look as though they're in touch with any external Norwegian numbers.'

'What about Spanish or Danish?'

'I don't think so. There are calls to and from Lithuania and among the quartet themselves.'

Wisting riffled through the analysis material while he drank his coffee, realizing this was an important case document that pursued the Lithuanian men through place and time. After reading the papers, he laid the folder aside and produced one of the two ring binders he had packed into his hand luggage.

The regular humming of the aeroplane engines made him feel sleepy, and he had not browsed through many pages before he leaned his forehead on the window. Outside, the clouds were grey and impenetrable.

40

The arrivals hall at Vilnius airport was more modern than Wisting had anticipated, with enormous glass facades and inviting restaurants. After twenty minutes, they had collected their luggage and were strolling to a queue of waiting taxis, without having to show either passport or any other ID papers. After the Schengen agreement, the strict border controls in and out of the former Soviet state had come down. Passengers from other Schengen member countries travelling by car, boat, rail or air had no need to identify themselves by means of passport or visa when crossing the borders.

This same agreement had imported crime to the Nordic countries. The extension of the EU in 2004 provided criminals with a huge market, and after the East European countries joined the Schengen cooperation in 2007, there had been a dramatic increase in crimes against property.

The driver of an ancient but spacious Opel took their luggage and welcomed them to Lithuania. Martin Ahlberg sat in the front passenger seat beside the driver and showed him a note with the address of the main police station. The driver bowed, thanking him for the directions, before heading out of the terminal precincts and keeping scrupulously just below the speed limit on the motorway leading to Vilnius.

The airport was located only a few kilometres from the city centre. The landscape outside the car windows managed all the same to change from thick forest and black ploughed fields to industrial areas and tall, drab blocks of flats. The sun broke through the monotonous carpet of grey covering the skies, and was reflected in the glass facades of the soaring buildings and new office blocks in the city centre. Tall cranes towered above the concrete carapaces of buildings under construction.

The police station was a sombre four-storey building on the northern bank of the river which divided the city. White police patrol cars with green stripes along their sides were parked outside. Martin Ahlberg paid the taxi driver and led the way in. He introduced them to a uniformed man sitting at the desk inside and produced a printout of the email with the appointment details.

They were half an hour early, but a young man dressed in an iron-grey shirt and maroon tie appeared immediately and waved them through a door. Depositing their luggage in a separate room, he accompanied them further into the police station, footsteps echoing as they followed him to the top floor. Halfway along the empty corridor he stopped outside a door marked *Sigitas Lancinskas – Policijos Viršininkas*. He seemed apprehensive about knocking. A young woman opened the door, letting them into an anteroom and thanking the man who had brought them up.

The woman asked them to wait before disappearing behind double wooden doors that led into the next room. Almost at once, she returned with a pale-faced man in his fifties with short silver hair, dressed in a thick green uniform jacket with three stars twinkling on the epaulettes. His chest was decorated with medals.

'Welcome to Lithuania,' he said in English, stretching out his arms before shaking with both hands. 'My name is Sigitas Lancinskas. I am Chief of Vilnius County Police Headquarters,' he said, translating the title on the doorplate..

His office was large and warm, but poorly lit. Deep-pile carpets covered the parquet flooring and the windows were

185

obscured by venetian blinds and heavy curtains. An oval conference table with its green felt cover, surrounded by twelve chairs, was the dominant item of furniture. In the centre of the green felt sat a carafe of water and several glasses.

Lancinskas suggested that they sit at the top of the table. As soon as they were seated, there was a knock at the door and a man in a dark suit entered. 'This is Head of CID, Antoni Mikulskis. He has been given responsibility for assisting you.'

The new arrival shook hands with them and handed each a business card with his contact details printed in English. 'Did your journey go well?' he asked as he sat down.

'No problems at all,' Wisting assured him.

The head of the crime department nodded, as though pleased, before opening a folder containing a number of documents and selecting one with a Norwegian police logo.

'Let me hear if I have understood this correctly,' he said in eloquent English. 'One of our countrymen has been shot and killed in southern Norway. You have come here to conduct interviews with three named persons who travelled with him, as well as with the family of the victim.'

Both Wisting and Ahlberg nodded in confirmation.

Antoni Mikulskis reached for the carafe of water. 'Has anyone been charged with this crime?' he asked, filling four glasses.

'No.'

'I understand your request to mean that the people who were travelling with him left Norway without talking to any officials. Is it the situation that some of our countrymen may be suspected of having something to do with the actual crime?'

'The enquiry is more comprehensive than you are aware of, and extremely complicated,' Wisting replied, producing the

186

ring binders and documents. For over an hour he explained the case in detail, lingering on the photographs and illustrations. As his report progressed the two officers contributed comments, suggestions and advice.

'Very interesting, and very strange,' the Chief of Police said. 'I hope your trip to Vilnius can provide the answers to all of your questions. Now, let's discuss the practical aspects. The case is of such a type that you want to make simple informal preliminary enquiries before later conducting formal interviews. Am I right?'

'Yes.'

'Then there is no point in bringing these people here. Instead we'll visit them unannounced. I'll accompany you personally. We can collect you in an unmarked police car from your hotel at nine o'clock tomorrow morning, if that suits.'

Wisting would have preferred to start that evening, but agreed anyway. The two Lithuanian police officers exchanged a few words in their own language before standing up. Wisting thanked them for their helpful attitude, and the Chief of CID promised to arrange transport for them to their hotel.

This is where the answers lie, Wisting reflected outside the police station. At the same time he was conscious of an indefinable anxiety. This must be what Suzanne meant when she spoke about the unknown. The thought that something unforeseen and dramatic could happen at any time in this foreign country frightened him.

41

From the rear seat of the police car they watched the young generation which had transformed Lithuania from a Soviet republic into a modern society. Vilnius was a contemporary, cosmopolitan capital city, reminiscent in many ways of Copenhagen or Paris, with busy city streets and picturesque squares and alleyways. Exclusive shopping centres, chain stores, pavement cafés and designer boutiques were everywhere spotless and spruce. It was not as Wisting had expected.

Martin Ahlberg pointed to a cathedral with a freestanding clock tower and a fortress on the crest of the hill behind the city, landmarks he had visited. Their driver nodded and smiled without seeming to understand what they were saying.

The Astoria Hotel was situated in the city's old quarter. As they neared their destination, the streets became cobbled, the gaps between buildings narrowed, and many of the old houses looked recently renovated. This part of the city had character and charm.

They were allocated adjacent rooms on the third floor, overlooking the main street of the old town. Wisting stepped onto his tiny balcony and took a firm hold of the cast iron railing. A biting wind gusted between the buildings and the sky was slate grey. Customers sat in the pavement cafés below, leaning back with cups of coffee and glasses of wine. Souvenir stalls offered amber jewellery, knitwear and babushka dolls. From here he could count eleven church spires, which contrasted with his view of Lithuanians as itinerant criminals.

Before dinner, Wisting phoned Nils Hammer who had no further news about the investigation. Wisting could tell from his voice that he was puzzled about something, and guessed that he had completed his analysis of the traffic through the toll stations. He should have spotted Line's car. His work colleagues were very familiar with her relationship to Tommy Kvanter, and Tommy's past. Only a few years earlier, his name had figured in several intelligence reports.

'There's one thing we haven't talked about,' Wisting said. 'Tommy Kvanter is one of the owners and proprietors of *Shazam Station*.'

'I know that,' Hammer answered. 'I thought it was over between them?'

'It's over,' Wisting confirmed. 'But I want you to tell me if his name crops up.'

'Is there any reason to believe it will?'

'No,' Wisting said, mentioning his meeting with Leif Malm. 'The informant thinks that Rudi Muller was in Larvik to collect the cocaine.'

'Do they know what car was used?'

'No, but they want you to send them all the material from the toll stations so they can check the vehicles.'

'I'll get it sent it over right away.'

Wisting refrained from saying that he had gone through the lists himself and spotted Line's car. He could not hear anything in Hammer's tone to suggest that he had made the same discovery and said nothing. After concluding their conversation, he felt that it had been wrong of him and was about to phone Hammer when he was interrupted by a knock at the door.

It seemed that Martin Ahlberg knew of a basement restaurant in one of the side streets where they served roast wild pork and a fantastic local beer.

189

42

Line looked up from her computer screen, rubbing her eyes. Late afternoon twilight settled on the cottage walls. She had read of an author who wrote five pages daily, and then finished for the day, regardless of whether it took one hour or ten, and of whether it had gone well or badly. The next day he read what he had written, deleting half and embarking on five new pages. She had decided to do the same, and eventually discovered that what she wrote assumed a deeper and more complex meaning. Her characters began to soften and become living beings.

She glanced through the window, where a black bird stood the windowsill, staring in with shining, glittering pinpoint eyes. While she sat staring back, another bird joined it. She stood up quietly to avoid startling them and a third bird landed, jostling between the first pair. In the background she saw an entire flock sitting in a row on the banisters and the branches of nearby trees.

As if at a signal they all took flight at once, joining in the air, swooping in an arc, and disappearing over the cottage roof. Line crossed to the window to see what might have scared them, but saw nothing. She drew the curtains and returned to her seat. The fabric was too narrow to cover the whole window and a narrow gap was left between them.

She turned her attention to the screen, scrolling through her text to read the last three paragraphs, but stopped before she was halfway through. Rising from her chair again, she stepped to the door and turned the latch before taking a pace back to stand and listen, her body filled with a peculiar sensation she had experienced before in the evenings, when the darkness was filled with strange sounds. Never, though, as intensely as this.

She had a horrible, creeping feeling that she was not alone, that someone outside was watching her and waiting. It was an irrational thought, but she felt vulnerable and exposed all the same. She fastened the curtains shut with clothes pegs while, outside, darkness descended. She lit a fire in the open fireplace and, this time, the logs burned easily, the blaze sending a congenial, flickering light into the room. She watched the flames until the yellow shafts of light stung her eyes.

Her laptop was in sleep mode, but sprang to life when she stroked the touchpad. Reading rapidly through the text she soon regained her focus. Rain was falling outside, but there was no wind.

She did not know how much time had passed when she was startled by a hollow sound from just outside the wall where she was sitting. It sounded as if someone was thumping on the grass. Then it stopped. She sat uneasily, straining to hear more, but could not catch anything other than the rain.

On the desk facing her she spotted the business card left by the policeman who had interviewed her, telling her to phone if anything turned up. *Benjamin Fjeld*, she read. She sat fingering it, but left the phone undisturbed. Then she heard the noise again, followed by a scraping sound along the wall.

A wild animal from the forest behind the cottage, she thought. At the kitchen worktop she filled a glass with water and stepped across to the front door to make sure it was locked.

The hands on the kitchen clock showed half past ten. She

191

was not tired, but decided to go to bed and read. She saved her work on the computer before brushing her teeth and checking that all the windows were closed. She took out a torch in case of a power cut and, before undressing, switched off the lights. She was searching for a T-shirt to wear in bed when a shadow fell on the living room curtains.

She froze and listened tensely, but could only hear the sound of her own breathing and raindrops dripping on the roof. There! A creak of timber on the verandah outside.

Her heart raced at murderous speed, pumping all the strength out of her. She trembled as though she felt cold and sweated as though she felt hot. There was someone outside the door, casting a shadow in the lamplight.

43

The wet cobbles shimmered in the street. It must have rained while they were eating. Feeling that the beer and strong liqueur they had consumed with dessert had gone to his head, Wisting told Martin Ahlberg he would take a breath of fresh air before returning to the hotel.

Evening gave the Old Quarter a different character. The streets were filled with upbeat laughter and pulsating music pouring from restaurant doors flung wide. He regretted being allocated a room facing the busy street.

Well-dressed men and heavily made-up women in flimsy, loose-fitting clothes hurried past beggars sitting on the ground. A man with no hands or feet, tied to something resembling a skateboard, propped himself up with the aid of two sticks. 'Help me, sir!' he begged. 'Help me! No food! No home!'

Shaking his head, Wisting thrust his hands deep inside his pockets, hurrying past with a twinge of conscience. When he took refuge in a narrow side street a young woman shot him an appraising glance. Alone under a lamp she was pretty in an alarming kind of way, in leather jacket, skin-tight jeans and high leather lace-up boots. She was nineteen or twenty years old.

'I might help you,' she said in stuttering English, placing her hand on his arm.

'I don't think so,' Wisting said.

'Are you not alone?' Her hand stroked his face and his body quivered. Never before had such a young, presumptuous woman touched him like this.

'Where are you from?' she asked.

'Norway.'

'I can come to your hotel room with you.'

'Sorry, no.' Clearing his throat, Wisting emphasised that he was not interested and strolled on.

A ten-year-old boy in filthy clothes approached him, holding out a tray of amber jewellery. 'Present for your lady at home,' he said. The selection comprised necklaces, bracelets and earrings made of solidified resin. A chain with a finely wrought, heart-shaped pendant of transparent burgundy drew Wisting's eye.

Noticing his hesitation, the boy grabbed his arm. 'Very nice price,' he said.

'How much?'

'Two hundred litas.' Four hundred and fifty Norwegian kroner, Wisting calculated. He shook his head and tried to move on. 'Please, mister! Tell me your price.'

As far as Wisting could judge, it was a good piece of craftsmanship. 'One hundred,' he offered.

The boy looked insulted, but reduced the price to 150 litas. Wisting stood his ground, but capitulated at 120.

He had only a large denomination banknote, which the boy couldn't change. Another street vendor joined the discussion and Wisting began to wonder if he would receive any money back at all. In the end, the boy handed over a bundle of banknotes, which Wisting accepted without counting. At the same time, he noticed a little girl emerging from the shadows. Encouraged by the jewellery seller's success, she held up a bowl of knitted dolls.

About eight years of age, her features were appealing. The time was now almost half past eleven. Wisting waved her towards him, and she offered him the bowl while speaking a few words of Lithuanian in a reedy voice.

He had a number of small denomination notes in his hand,

194

but instead produced another high-value note and handed it to her before selecting one of the dolls. The girl searched through her pocket for change, but Wisting signalled that she could keep the money. It was a useless form of benevolence, but he sacrificed his principles to brighten this late hour for the little mite. Perhaps she would remember it even though the money would soon be gone.

He found his way back to the hotel with no more stops. Placing the jewellery in his suitcase, he set the knitted doll down on his bedside table and, before retiring for the night, stepped onto the balcony again. Europe's new playground for the rich was spread before him. However, the new economy did not benefit everyone. The contrasts in wealth were more noticeable after nightfall. Open prostitution and poverty existed side by side with rich men emerging from expensive cars in the company of long-legged blondes. He understood how those who saw no future for themselves in this city would choose to steal in other countries.

44

Line's breath came in stiff, staccato jerks as the male silhouette raised his hands to his head and leaned forward against the living room window to peer inside.

She fumbled for a sweater hanging over the chair and pulled it on, lifted the poker from the hearth and stood still, holding it by her side, her sweaty hands sticking to the hard steel. She was on the point of lifting her mobile phone when a fist knocked on the windowpane.

'Line?' someone called. Another knock on the window, and her name was repeated.

It took some time for her to realise whose voice it was: Tommy. Laying the poker aside, she unlocked the door.

His hair plastered to his scalp by the rain, Tommy smiled warmly at her. She opened the door to let him in. 'What are you doing here?'

He ran his hand through his abundant hair. 'I had to see you.'

Line folded her arms across her chest. 'How did you find your way?'

'It wasn't easy,' he said. His training shoes left muddy footprints on the floor. 'There are a lot of cottages out here.'

'You're soaked through. Wait here.'

Tommy glanced down at his clothes while Line fetched a towel. 'Here,' she said, throwing it to him. 'Have you any dry clothes with you?' Shaking his head, he rubbed his hair vigorously.

'You're going to catch a fever.'

'I can dry my clothes at the fire,' he said, nodding towards the glowing embers.

Line was about to protest when he removed his shoes and pulled off his sweater and trousers. She sat on the settee, drawing a blanket around her shoulders, as he hung his garments on the chairs and around the fireplace, keeping on only his T-shirt. 'What do you want, actually?' she asked.

'I want to sort things out,' he said, sitting opposite her. In the room's semi-darkness, the flames from the fire reflected on his wet face.

'I don't know, Tommy,' she said. 'It's too late.'

'It's never too late. Not if this is the real thing, Line, and for me it is. I know what I want. The question is: what do you want?'

She was clear about that. 'I want stability. Security. Peace and quiet and a certain predictability. And, in fact, I want a man who has time to spend with me.'

'I can sell myself out of the restaurant business,' he said.

'You'll lose a lot of money.'

'I'll lose more if I don't.'

Confused, Line struggled for the right words as Tommy crossed to the chairs facing the hearth where steam rose from his trousers.

'What do you think about Mauritius?' he asked abruptly, but he knew what she thought. It was not so long since they had lain in bed talking about exotic destinations they could visit. The little group of African islands in the Indian Ocean was one such place, lush and fertile, fields overflowing with waves of sugarcanes and splendid waterfalls cascading down the mountainsides, lagoons and coral reefs and beautiful beaches encircled by palm trees.

Tommy took a sheet of paper from his back pocket and placed it in front of her. 'I'd like us to go there. Just the two of us.'

Line glanced at the ticket without picking it up. 'How …'

'I got them cheap.'

'All the same, you can't afford it.'

'It'll be all right,' he sat beside her. 'I'm going to get a lot of money from the restaurant. Everything's going to work out. I have a number of things to tidy up, and then we'll be on our way.'

She glanced at the departure date, only eight days off, and gazed at him without uttering a word. It was impossible to say what was going on behind those feline eyes. He rested his hand on her lap. 'It'll be wonderful.'

Her eyes went to the ticket again. Tommy had not paid for cancellation insurance.

When he rested his head in the hollow of her neck, she breathed in his satisfying scent, a pleasant, familiar and masculine fragrance. 'I've missed you,' he whispered.

His was the only safety and warmth she had right now and she felt a sudden impulse to embrace him. Her hand stroked across his cheek, explored his ears, found the warm nape of his neck. His skin felt good. He looked at her, examined her, placed his mouth against her neck and kissed it. She had thought she would never feel like this for him again. She gripped the back of his head, where his hair grew thickest.

'Is it okay?' he asked, looking deep into her eyes. When she did not reply, he leaned forward and kissed her mouth. She moved her tongue against his teeth. Her fingers coiled around his hair, stroked his back, and found their way inside his T-shirt. She let him pull her sweater over her head and throw it halfway across the room, laid her forehead on his chest, slightly shyly, listening to the hammering of his heart. He kissed her again.

Flinging her arms around his neck, she responded eagerly, teasing his tongue, nibbling his lips, sharing his breath and wanting only more. Soon afterwards, they were both naked.

She gasped as he slid inside her. Tears ran down her cheeks as he moved in his gratifying, familiar rhythm.

A tidal wave of emotions grew in her until she closed her eyes, biting her bottom lip, and reached climax with a little sigh, slowing down, almost unwilling to stop and afterwards lay breathless, her heart racing as Tommy stroked her hair. She sat up, drawing the blanket around her as he borrowed a corner to cover himself.

'How did you locate me? she asked.

'It wasn't so easy,' he said, 'but I knew roughly where you were so I drove around until I found your car. Then it was simply a matter of going from one cottage to the next. I visited almost all of them before I found you.'

'Whose car do you have?'

Tommy crossed to the window where he stood, naked, looking out. 'I borrowed a car from one of the waitresses,' he said. 'There was another car parked over there,' he added, pointing with his head. 'A muddy van.'

Line was glad she was not alone.

45

William Wisting and Martin Ahlberg each carried a coffee cup from the breakfast room to one of the small tables in the reception area. Wisting had slept badly. The impressions left by the city had pursued him in his dreams and he had wakened before his alarm rang.

At nine o'clock precisely, CID Chief Antoni Mikulskis entered through the swing doors. Wearing an unbuttoned dark overcoat, he stood with his hands in his pockets. He caught sight of them when they stood up, and came over to greet them, shaking with both hands. 'Have you slept well, gentlemen?'

'Very well,' they both said.

'Excellent,' he said. 'Excellent. Your car awaits.' He turned on his heel and led them out of the hotel. A silver Opel was parked at the kerb, waiting with the engine running. The Lithuanian policeman opened the rear door for them, and Wisting caught a glimpse of the carrying strap on the service revolver he wore concealed inside his coat. Behind the wheel of the unmarked police car sat a bullnecked man with cropped hair. Turning around, he uttered a polite comment in Lithuanian.

'Where are we going?' Mikulskis asked.

Wisting opened the folder of case documents. 'We'll make a start with this man,' he said, handing over the printout with the photograph and personal details of the man who had assaulted him. 'Valdas Muravjev.'

Antoni Mikulskis took the document, repeating the name

aloud. 'Vilkišk˙es gatv˙e 22,' he said to the driver. The man with the broad neck nodded and the car moved off.

The city centre streets were well maintained, but only a few blocks from the hotel the impression deteriorated when they passed through what reminded him of an old, Soviet suburb. The contrast with the wealthy and successful people around the hotel during daylight hours increased sharply the farther they travelled. After ten minutes, the buildings became more scattered.

They drove past weather-beaten timber frame houses and farmyards littered with wrecked cars, makeshift shacks, rusting septic tanks and hens pecking at the ground. In one place, a pig was rooting in a dunghill. They saw handwritten signs dotted around, offering vegetables.

After several kilometres, the driver swung off the asphalt road onto a gravel track bordered by moss-covered oak trees, and water stained by green algae pouring into a ditch.

Mikulskis pointed towards a cluster of houses on the other side of a field. 'Over there,' he said. The driver swung the car around, continuing to the end of the track and five buildings surrounded by a tangle of trees, bushes and ankle-high weeds. The largest was a once-white, two-storey house, its paintwork now faded and peeling. The place was strangely silent and gloomy. Foul smelling smoke from one of the smaller houses drifted down from a chimney, hanging like fog in the air.

Behind the houses, an old woman was hanging washing on a line. Antoni Mikulskis shouted her over and asked something. She pointed to a low timber house, its windows opaque with dust and dirt. Steps were missing as well as parts of the banisters. The Lithuanian policeman positioned himself in front of the door, shoulder to shoulder with the driver, while Wisting and Ahlberg waited on the wet grass. A flock of black birds took flight from a tree when they

201

knocked at the door. Wisting thought he could hear a baby crying inside, but there was no response.

The CID Chief knocked again. At once they heard a footstep, and a buxom woman appeared, her face pale and blonde hair lank. As the two Lithuanians explained they were from *Policijos*, they displayed their ID cards. Wisting understood only the name *Valdas Muravjev* in the deluge of words that followed.

The woman shook her head, looking behind her into the house where the squalling baby was crying loudly, and gave an explanation as she pointed to a handwritten sign in the window, the words *Kambariu nuoma*.

Mikulskis took a notebook from his coat pocket and asked a series of questions the woman seemed unable to answer. Her voice rose and she became angry, flinging out her arms expressively. The police chief responded sharply before the conversation was concluded with determined nods from the Lithuanian officers. The woman vented her annoyance with a few more exclamations before going inside, slamming the door behind her.

'He's moved away,' Antoni Mikulskis said. 'She's living here on her own and lets out a little room.'

The policeman pointed to the sign in the window to support the woman's explanation. *Kambariu nuoma*. Room to let. 'He moved out just over a week ago, owing her a hundred litas for a fortnight's rent. All she knows is that he was to travel somewhere to try to get work. Now she doesn't know how she'll manage to get food for the child. The room is difficult to let because there's no bus to the city.'

One hundred litas, Wisting mused. The woman let out a room in her house to a stranger for less than five hundred kroner a month, the same amount he paid for the knitted doll.

'Shall we press on?' Ahlberg suggested. Mikulskis asked

to see the list of addresses they were to visit. Wisting handed him the sheet of paper. 'Teodor Milosz is the one who lives nearest. Only five minutes away.'

Wisting sat in the back seat of the police car, studying the photo of the shorthaired man with the wide neck. Teodor Milosz was twenty-four years old and the next oldest of the Lithuanian men who had been given the name *Paneriai Quartet* in the Norwegian police intelligence files. It seemed he was some kind of leader. He owned the grey delivery van and had also booked the tickets for their journey across the Baltic Sea. They also had telephone data pinning him to the time and date of the incidents out at Nevlunghavn.

The address was in a more densely populated area, but here too the decay was apparent. The driver twice drove in the wrong direction before stopping in front of a low brick building, almost hidden between two gigantic trees. Several of the windows were nailed shut. The roof had subsided and was mottled with moss. An abandoned wheel-less lorry was supported on stone blocks and left to rot. Children's toys scattered on a pile of earth nevertheless suggested that the house was occupied.

Wisting stepped out of the car, inhaling the stench of mud and rotting leaves, and the less pungent scent of a bonfire. Roughcast flaked off the grey, liver-spotted façade at the corners and windowsills, and the gutters hung loose from the gable end. One of the two cast iron railings along the wide staircase had partly collapsed. Stepping over piles of rubbish bags, they arrived at the door.

Mikulskis knocked loudly and a young woman arrived almost immediately, a small child in her arms. Her hair hung straight at the sides of her face and she wore an olive green sweater.

The policemen introduced themselves and Wisting heard the word *Norvegija* when Mikulskis pointed to him with

203

his arm. The woman nodded when they asked for Teodor Milosz but her voice took on a quizzical tone. Antoni Mikulskis replied, and they exchanged words to and fro until the policeman turned to face Wisting.

'She's his sister,' he said. 'Teodor Milosz is not at home. She says he has been to Norway for work, but came home sooner than expected. Yesterday he went away again.'

'Where does she think he might be?'

The police officer translated the question. 'She doesn't know, but he may be at the market in Gariunai.'

'The thieves' market,' Martin Ahlberg said.

'Who is he with?' Wisting asked.

The question was again relayed and the answer came back quickly. 'She does not know.'

The child began to whimper and the officers rounded off the conversation without Wisting detecting any polite leave-taking.

'What now?' Mikuskis asked as the car reversed out of the farmyard.

'It won't take long for them to realise we're looking for them,' Wisting said.

'She's probably phoning her brother now,' Mikulskis said, taking a cigarette packet from his coat pocket. 'Shall we go to the last place on the list as fast as we can?'

Assenting, Wisting removed the printout with details pertaining to Algirdas Skvernelis from the bundle on his lap, passing it to the front passenger seat. The policeman put a cigarette in his mouth and lit up before accepting the paper.

'We know this man's brother very well,' he said, tapping the photograph with his finger. 'He's in Lukiskes Prison awaiting sentence for robbery on a shop.' He held the cigarette firmly between his lips as he talked, half closing his eyes to avoid the smoke. 'Algirdas is only a petty thief. He'll talk.'

204

On the main road they found themselves behind a horse-drawn cart. It was heavily laden with a high, wide stack of bales of straw, and they could not drive past until it turned onto a farm track. Noticing that none of the houses they passed were numbered, and only few of the streets had name plates, Wisting wondered how the driver could find his way at all.

Ten minutes later they stopped beside a modern, grey stone house with ploughs, old engines and lorry parts scattered around the yard. An ancient bicycle was firmly attached to a rusty gate with an enormous chain. A couple of windows were lit, and a woman of Wisting's age looked out as they parked. Small and slender, she had a narrow, pale face with a short, straight nose. She opened the door before they reached it.

The police officers introduced themselves, and the woman stared at them with glassy, blue eyes. She spoke a few words in Lithuanian before returning inside. Wisting followed Antoni Mikulskis through a cool hallway where dark wall panels and wallpaper brown with age created a bleak ambience. Tiles were missing here and there on the floor, but the house was clean and well cared for. The living room was adorned by orange, fringed lampshades with brown scorch marks. Yellow, faded curtains hung on either side of a window, and the only view was towards another grey stone building. On the top shelf of an empty bookcase sat a stuffed bird that someone had attempted to revive by opening its beak slightly, spreading its wings and inserting glass beads to replace its missing eyes.

On a shelf below the bookcase stood a huge flat-screen television, in contrast to the other old, sad furnishings. The woman sat on a settee covered by a blanket that matched the curtains. The two Lithuanian police officers sat opposite. As

205

there were no more chairs in the small living room, Wisting fetched two stools from the kitchen.

'She is Algirdas' mother,' Mikulskis explained. 'Her son has not been home for more than a week. He is in Norway, working.'

'Does she know when he'll be back?' Wisting asked.

The policeman asked again but the woman shook her head determinedly. 'She believes he is still working in Norway. He was to be there for three months. He has been there before, and is a good carpenter.'

'Tell her about the ferry tickets,' Martin Ahlberg suggested.

Wisting again found the conversation impossible to follow.

'She thinks he would have come home if he returned on the ferry. She washes his clothes and prepares his food. Otherwise he's not at home much.' The woman continued speaking as she rocked back and forth, rubbing her hands together. 'She can't understand what he has done wrong in Norway. He's a good boy, and she doesn't understand what the Norwegian police are doing here.' The woman rattled on, with the policeman translating. 'She's worried about him. He usually phones home a couple of times a week, but she hasn't heard from him since he called to say he had arrived in Norway.'

Martin Ahlberg stood up. 'Ask her where she got that huge television set.'

The policeman looked bewildered. Wisting raised his hand and told him to let it be. 'We're finished here,' he said.

Antoni Mikulskis was clearly in agreement. He rounded off the conversation with what Wisting assumed was encouragement to persuade her son to make contact with the police.

'Now we must eat,' the Chief of CID declared when they

returned to their vehicle. 'I know of a restaurant not far from here where they make excellent *kugelis*. We can eat and discuss our strategy,' he said.

'Potato pudding,' Martin Ahlberg elucidated.

That didn't sound too good, but Wisting had started to feel the first pangs of hunger.

46

Line woke slowly, her head dulled by the wine. The space beside her in bed was empty, but she was aware of sounds from the kitchen. There was no clock in the bedroom. Usually, she kept her mobile phone beside her on the bedside table, but last night she left it in the living room. Stretching, she reached across and tugged the curtain aside.

It had to be about nine o'clock. The weather had cleared. Although the sun had not yet risen, it was getting lighter and was going to be a brighter day than they had experienced in ages. She lay down again and pondered what had happened, in two minds about regret. At the time she thought she was making a choice; now she was not so sure.

Tommy appeared at the door, smiling to see her awake. 'Tea? Coffee?'

'Coffee.'

'Good choice,' he said. 'It's ready. There's not much in the kitchen. Breakfast is crispbread with cheese.'

'Yellow or brown?'

'Yellow.'

Line sat up, pulling the quilt around herself. When Tommy left the room she put on a jogging suit and a pair of thick socks. Before she joined him she glanced in the mirror. She really ought to do something with her face, but let it be.

Steam rose from the cup he placed in front of her. 'I have to go soon,' he said.

She did not know whether to be pleased or annoyed. In a way it made her feel used and exploited but, at the same time, there were so many emotions churning inside her that she welcomed being alone for a while.

'I have to be in Oslo before eleven. Pia needs the car.' She nodded. 'There's so much happening just now. It seems that Rudi's girlfriend's brother has been burned to death.'

Line frowned. She knew who Rudi was: one of the people who had bought a share in *Shazam Station* after one of the original investors had been forced to pull out. She had said hello to him only a few times, but had taken a dislike to him. He had a huge ego, but little self-awareness. His girlfriend was blonde and tanned with whitened teeth, the kind of woman it was impossible to hold a sensible conversation with. She had distanced herself from them both.

'Burned to death?'

'No one had heard from him for a few days, and on Monday his flat in Grorud burned down. They haven't finished examining the site of the fire yet.'

She had heard about the fire on the news. 'How did it happen?'

'I don't know, but the flat was totally destroyed. I went up and had a look yesterday. It will be a job well done if they find the cause.'

He emptied his cup before getting to his feet. 'When are you coming home?' he asked.

She didn't answer. She had told Tommy to pack his belongings and find somewhere else to stay before she returned, but now everything had been turned upside down. Now she understood that she regretted what had taken place. The relationship was not worth building on. A passionate night and a trip to the sun did not change that. 'We'll see,' was her only response.

Tommy did not seem happy, but said nothing. Placing his cup in the sink, he stopped at the door and pulled on his trainers. 'I need to get going,' he said.

'I'll come with you to the car.' Line finished her coffee standing up.

Tommy had arrived in a blue Peugeot. The silver van, a VW Caravelle, sat beside Line's car, the inside of the windscreen clouded with condensation. She glanced into the driving compartment as Tommy opened his car door. It was tidy, apart from a pair of training shoes on the passenger seat. The rear door was locked. She mentally noted the registration number and crossed her arms in front of her chest while she waited for Tommy to leave.

When he tried to kiss her she turned her cheek and threw her arms around him so that it became a hug instead. 'I'll phone you,' he said when she released him.

She watched Tommy's car drive away, feeling empty and drained. The decisiveness she had been so proud of only a few days before had vanished and now she was simply confused, and alone. Again.

47

The restaurant was close to a park where the trees were bright with autumn leaves. Wisting followed Antoni Mikulskis's recommendation and ordered the potato pudding. While they waited, they were served *Kvas*, a sweet, light beer that was a paler version of the kind Wisting's mother used to make at Christmas.

'All that remains is to speak to Darius Plater's mother,' Mikulskis said. 'Perhaps she'll be able to tell us where the other three are.'

'We have a practical problem,' Wisting said. 'We don't know with certainty that the dead man is Darius Plater. Identification is based on fingerprints from last year when he was arrested in Norway. He identified himself with a passport which we have no guarantee was genuine. We can't visit his family until we're sure.'

'When will you be sure?'

Martin Ahlberg replied: 'He is registered in the Lithuanian fingerprint records as well. Interpol is dealing with the prints from both countries as we speak. It's a merry bureaucratic dance, but we should get an answer today or tomorrow.'

'What do we do while we're waiting?' Mikulskis asked.

'Can we go to the Gariunai market?' Wisting suggested. He wanted to see how stolen goods from Norway were traded. 'Maybe we'll find the men there.'

Mikulskis drank as he considered this suggestion. 'There are seven thousand stalls. It'll be a hopeless task, but we can drive you there. I have admin work waiting at the office.'

Martin Ahlberg nodded. 'We can take a taxi back to the hotel, and meet again tomorrow.'

'Good,' Mikulskis said. 'You have my card. Phone me and we'll try again to make contact with these men.'

It took almost half an hour for the food to arrive. The traditional dish smelled faintly of oregano or some other culinary herb. Reminiscent of creamy potato gratin, it consisted of bacon and sliced potato layered in the casserole from which it was served. The top was decorated with lingonberry jam and *crème fraiche*. Afterwards, Wisting insisted on paying the bill, and brushed aside all protests by mentioning a government travel budget. He calculated that the entire meal had cost him less than one hundred and fifty Norwegian kroner.

Antoni Mikulskis lit another cigarette as they clambered into the car. The trip to Gariunai took fifteen minutes, a gigantic market place situated behind a wooden fence several hundred metres long, beside the motorway to Kaunas. The driver stopped in front of a police presence at the entrance gate and Mikulskis stepped from the car to speak.

Wisting stared at rows of sales booths, tin shacks and workmen's sheds with tarpaulins stretched across. Car tyres, stones and other heavy objects had been placed on the makeshift roofs to prevent the wind from blowing them away. He had visited markets in Turkey and Spain, but had never seen anything as colossal as this, with long stretches of shelves with car stereos, mobile phones, power saws, loudspeakers, vacuum cleaners, lawnmowers, car parts, music systems, refrigerators and a dozen or so white bridal gowns on display. It looked like multiple outdoor branches of *Clas Ohlson*, *Biltema* and *IKEA*, wrapped into one. 'What sort of place is this?' he asked.

'This is the centre for people who can't afford to buy clothes or food in ordinary shops,' Mikulskis said. 'Most of

212

what you buy here is second hand, and the prices are low.'

'Stolen goods?' Wisting enquired.

The policeman shrugged. 'Probably small quantities. We have bigger problems with pickpockets,' he said, pointing to a CCTV camera.

'But you don't have any guarantee that the goods aren't stolen?' Ahlberg asked.

'Having a certain amount of crime in a market such as this can't be avoided.'

'Why don't you just close down the whole place?' Wisting asked. 'There must be an enormous turnover that's never reported to the tax authorities.'

'There are too many people working here,' Mikulskis said. 'Nearly seventy thousand people live off that turnover. If we were to close Gariunai, there would be a social catastrophe. It's cheaper for Lithuania to battle crime at the market than get rid of it entirely.'

Wisting was speechless. An entire economy was based on the trading of smuggled goods and stolen property.

'What a bloody cheek,' Martin Ahlberg said.

The CID Chief, having no wish to discuss the topic, returned to the car. 'Let me hear from you tomorrow,' he said, signalling to the driver.

Wisting and Ahlberg wandered among the stalls and a cacophony of noisy haggling.

'No matter what they say,' Ahlberg said, stopping in front of a display of razor blades, deodorants and other cosmetics, 'this is a thieves' market.' He picked up a tin of shaving foam and showed Wisting the price ticket from *Rimi*, the Norwegian supermarket chain. 'The world's largest commercial centre for stolen property; it's a disgrace to both the country and the local police.'

Much of what was on offer was obviously stolen but, eventually, as they advanced, the market increasingly resembled

213

a recycling station for the gently used surfeit of the western world's consumer goods. Most were discarded white goods repaired for re-use, and outmoded home appliances.

'It's not so very different from eBay,' Wisting suggested. 'Here, everything is physically gathered into a single location while, in Norway, we offer stolen goods digitally and call it *a market full of opportunities*.'

'It's not quite the same,' Ahlberg said.

Wisting dropped the subject. When he started in the police force, the street was the most usual place for selling stolen goods. Now the internet had taken over. In the second hand market in electronics, at any time there would be 300,000 appliances for sale. The turnover was reckoned to be three quarters of a million kroner every year. Cautious estimates suggested that one tenth involved the resale of stolen property.

When a fine drizzle started, the vendors carefully placed transparent covers over the front of their booths.

Wisting halted at a jewellery table, with mostly gold rings, bracelets and necklaces. He lifted a broad ring while the man behind the table glowered suspiciously at him. *Your Kari*, he read. *12ᵗʰ August 1966*. A wedding ring, probably a precious memento lost forever.

'One hundred litas,' the man behind the counter offered.

Shaking his head, Wisting replaced the ring.

Outside a steel container, a man stood with legs straddled and arms folded across his chest, watching everyone who went in and out. One person heading for the exit carried a huge box with a picture of a flat-screen television. *LG – Life's Good*, the box proclaimed.

Wisting and Martin Ahlberg entered to find the container stacked with television sets, DVD players, home cinema systems, computers and games consoles. Some were in their original cardboard boxes, but most lacked any kind of packaging. Two men haggled over a thirty-two-inch Samsung flat-screen TV, identical to the one stolen from Thomas Rønningen's cottage. The price was in the region of five hundred litas, or twelve hundred kroner.

'I'm not enjoying this,' Ahlberg said. 'It upsets me.'

As the rain drummed more heavily on the roof of the container, the guard at the door huddled inside the opening. Standing at the entrance, they waited for the weather to ease. A man hurried along the row of stalls using a newspaper for protection and, as he passed them, raised his head, snatching a glimpse of the two policemen. His eyes widened but remained on Wisting. As his mouth dropped open, he lost his footing, stumbled and fell.

'That's him!' Wisting exclaimed, pushing past the doorman.

Scrambling to his feet, the man started to run, with Wisting ten metres behind. Valdas Muravjev had recognised him, just as Wisting had recognised him. Their previous encounter had been brief – five days earlier, the Lithuanian had fallen down at the road verge outside Nevlunghavn in a dramatic performance that had ended with him felling Wisting and stealing his car.

'I want to talk,' Wisting shouted, chasing after him between booths and rows of seats, casting aside flapping clothes, scarves and shawls on display along the pathway.

Muravjev ran through a narrow passageway into a more crowded street, twisting and turning through swarms of people who stepped aside, but closed again when he had passed.

Wisting ploughed on, angry cries ringing in his ears. Halfway down an alleyway he caught sight of Muravjev's broad back as he dodged down the next side street. Wisting forced his way through a sales booth overflowing with clocks, spectacles and belts, almost managing to intercept him. He grabbed hold of his jacket sleeve, but the other man tore free, staring furiously at him.

'I want to talk about Darius,' Wisting shouted.

The man took to his heels again, and Wisting thought he spotted a gleam of metal in his hand, a knife or some other weapon. He hesitated momentarily, but continued the pursuit, zigzagging through the market place, until they were stopped by a grey brick wall. On the left several containers were stacked one on another; to the right, a man was selling jeans from a shed.

Valdas Muravjev stopped, and Wisting stopped with him. 'I want to talk to you about Darius Plater,' he said.

Muravjev eyed the wall calculatingly before taking a couple of backward paces to gain momentum and haul himself up. Wisting did not manage to reach him before his feet disappeared over the top.

Rain cascaded down the side of his face, and his breath heaved in laboured, staccato gasps. He rested his hands on his knees.

His mobile phone rang. It was Martin Ahlberg. 'Where the hell are you?' he asked.

Wisting looked around. 'I'm not sure,' he replied, and described the chase.

'Madness,' Ahlberg said. 'I'm waiting for you at the entrance – we can take a taxi back to the hotel.'

Wisting headed in the direction of their arrival point. On the way, he stopped underneath a parasol where an old woman was selling vegetables and beverages from a fridge with glass doors. Purchasing a bottle of water, he drank half while waiting for his change, and felt his heartbeat return to its normal pace.

Martin Ahlberg shook his head when he arrived at the entrance to the car park. 'What on earth were you thinking?' he asked. 'These are dangerous men.'

216

In the course of the day, Wisting had formed a different impression. They now appeared more like confused young men with no hope for the future, than an organised criminal gang.

'You're right,' he said. 'I'm too old for this.'

Running his hand through his wet hair, he looked back at the countless sales booths. He had the feeling that many of the people were staring back, checking him up and down, before he turned his back and crossed over to one of the waiting taxis.

48

The grimy silver van belonged to Gunnar B. Hystad from Sandefjord. The text message from the Roads Department did not contain any information other than that his road tax had been paid. Taking out the Yellow Pages, Line found that he was listed with a landline and a mobile subscription, at an address in what she knew was an established residential area west of the town centre. A woman was listed at the same address and number.

She found him again in the tax lists and noticed he was born in 1950. There was no indication of what the B in his name stood for. He had a small amount of capital and an annual income of just under half a million kroner.

A simple internet search produced no hits. The newspaper's text archive did not contain any information either. A search with only the words *gunnar* and *hystad* produced too many results, making it impossible to sort through them.

Gunnar B. Hystad might be the mysterious man with the binoculars.

She wondered whether she should phone Benjamin Fjeld and give him the registration number, but from what she had discovered online, Hystad did not seem particularly interesting.

Sunlight shone diagonally through the smudged cottage windows, causing glittering dust to dance in the air. Closing the lid of her laptop, Line concluded that it had provided no answers. Nevertheless, there was something about Gunnar B. that titillated her curiosity. The vehicle had been parked overnight. Of course, he could be staying at one of the other cottages, but she had a growing conviction that he had spent the night in the makeshift shelter she had discovered.

She fetched her camera and looked through the photos she had taken a day or two earlier before putting on her outdoor clothes and going out. The sea lapped gently and softly on the shore and the air was crystal clear. Two fishing boats were heading towards the Skagerrak, their masts in sharp silhouette against the horizon.

Line followed the path westward, through the dense woodland. The waterlogged forest floor softened beneath her feet and, with each step she took, her Wellington boots sank deeper into the mud.

She reached the sea at the same spot as before; waves were beating rhythmically on the beach below. Windswept, crooked pine trees hung over the stony outcrop, and wild flowers grew in the clefts between the rocks. Raising her camera, she located the hidden shelter with her lens. For a long time she waited, hoping to catch a movement. Eventually her arms became tired, and then she caught sight of him.

He was standing on a plateau beside the sea, scanning in an oblique line along the pebbly coastal edge. His back was half turned towards her, so she could not see what he looked like other than he had stubble covering his cheeks, chin and throat.

Line took a couple of photographs before squatting again in the undergrowth. Several black crows took off from the treetops, screeching and fluttering through the foliage before coming to rest a short distance away.

A trail across the springy carpet of moss led her closer to the man. She halted just before the woodland met the hillside to prevent him from spotting her and looked again, but could no longer see him.

Leaving the woodland behind, she scared several more

birds. The sun's rays were intense now, and steam rose from the glistening rocks on the shore.

A narrow crevice led down from where she stood. Holding her camera to her chest with one hand, and supporting herself on the slope with the other, she followed the path downwards until she reached the plateau. She could find no trace of him, but looked in the direction he had been facing.

Breakers rolled in from the sea, crashing onto the pebbled beach. Further inland lay the woodland, almost grey in its bleakness. The wind had wrenched the autumn leaves from the trees, leaving only fragile branches.

While she stood there, a flock of black birds, probably a hundred times larger than the one she had seen several days earlier, took flight, gathered into a huge oval ball and soared into the sky like a dark cloud. The roar created by the flapping of their many thousand wings drowned out the sound of the waves, and a fluttering shadow from the massive flock slid across the landscape. It was like an enormous flying carpet as it veered and writhed through the air.

When the flock moved out to sea, the temperature dropped as the birds covered the sun.

The flock then divided into two pointed groups heading back inland. The sun reappeared, and just as suddenly as the birds had materialised they vanished, descending into the woodland. She was left with only the sound of their flapping wings in her ears. Not until then did she lift her camera, but it was too late to capture the spectacular sight.

'Did you see that?' a voice behind her asked.

Line wheeled round. The man was standing two metres away. He must have been sheltering in a cleft at the outer edge of the hillside and had climbed unnoticed to where she stood. His binoculars were hanging from his neck, and he carried a camera. He seemed delighted to have someone to share the experience with.

220

Line nodded. 'Yes, it was fantastic.'

The man was still peering in the direction the birds had disappeared. 'I've been waiting for something like that for days, but that was even better than I expected.' Letting the camera rest, he lifted the binoculars to his eyes. 'There it is,' he said suddenly, letting go the binoculars to point out a huge falcon or eagle flapping its wings to catch the air currents. 'They gather here to search for food before they journey on. Then they're especially vulnerable to attacks by birds of prey. That's why they fly in flocks, just like a shoal of herring in flight. They change direction hither and thither to fool the enemy.'

'Amazing how they manage to do it,' Line said.

'Birds have large hearts in relation to their body size,' he explained. 'The distance between their eyes and brain is short, and the electrical impulses that are sent out travel at lightning speed. To us, it looks as though the entire flock turns instantaneously when a bird reacts to its neighbour's movement.'

Line studied the man, obviously an extremely enthusiastic ornithologist, before extending her hand to introduce herself. 'Yes indeed,' he said, confirming that he was the owner of the dirty van. 'Gunnar Hystad.'

'You're interested in birds?'

He smiled at her. 'It's always been a hobby, but this summer I took early retirement and that has given me more time. During this past week, I've practically lived out here.'

'Do you have a cottage nearby?'

'Unfortunately not. I would like to, especially now at the migration season. The flyways go directly over this area.'

'But you stayed the night out here?'

'Sometimes I sleep in the back of the van, but otherwise I have built myself a lean-to. I arrived here yesterday afternoon. The weather forecast predicted high pressure and wind from the west-northwest, optimal conditions for migration, and I was ready from first light. Now I'm just waiting for the woodpigeons. Tens of thousands of them can pass in the course of a few morning hours.'

Line looked at the sky, where a number of seagulls were circling. Excepting them, the heavens were empty.

Gunnar B. lifted the binoculars to his eyes again, scanning the skies before lowering them again. 'What about you?' he asked. 'What brings you out in the autumn chill?'

'I'm staying at a cottage here,' she said. 'I'm trying to write a book.'

Together they made their way down from the plateau.

'Then it's a good idea to be fairly isolated,' the man said, hopping from one boulder to the next. 'There aren't many people to be seen out here.'

'I noticed you the first day I arrived, but apart from that, I haven't seen anyone.'

'When did you arrive?'

'On Saturday.'

Nodding, Gunnar B. rubbed his hand over the stubble on his chin. 'That was after all the commotion at Gusland. Did you hear about that?'

Acknowledging that she had, Line wondered whether she should tell him that she was the one who found the second body. She decided against.

'There was quite a lot of traffic along the coast then, of course. One of the boats was busy all day Saturday, going back and forth all day long, scaring the birds out at the Måkesjæra rock. I don't know what they were searching for.' Keeping his head cocked as he spoke, the man abruptly raised his camera to point it at something he had spotted, but too late to capture the image with his lens.

'There's a sea eagle around here,' he said. 'They're rare. They don't usually nest so far south. It's a mature female. Her wingspan is almost two point five metres.' He came to a

222

standstill. 'I can show you,' he said, tilting his camera screen upwards. Various birds glided rapidly over the display until he stopped at an eagle soaring majestically towards a leaden sky. 'I have a series showing it catching a fish too,' he said, flicking further on.

A self-bailing inflatable dinghy with a man onboard occupied the display before the sea eagle returned.

'What was that?' Line asked.

'What do you mean?'

'The boat.'

The man flipped back through the images. 'That was the boat I was talking about. It was going to and fro here all weekend. The pilot was scouting the land along the coast the whole time, obviously searching for something or someone.'

Line took hold of the camera, scrutinising the picture. The boat was large, battleship grey with an aluminium hull and enormous inflatable pontoons along the gunwales. She knew the police had been searching with helicopters and dogs after the body had been found at Thomas Rønningen's cottage, but not that they had used a boat. If they had, then they would probably have found the boat that had drifted ashore near her cottage with a corpse on board. This boat was not marked with a registration number or nationality either.

She tried to study the face of the man behind the steering controls, but the details were too minuscule on the display. 'I don't think this is a policeman,' she said.

'No? Who is it then?'

Line shrugged. 'My father works in the police. I can send him the photo.' The man retrieved his camera, as though reluctant to let go of something so valuable. 'You can come with me to the cottage,' she said. 'Then I can offer you a cup of hot coffee while I transfer the photos to my computer.'

Stroking his hand over his stubbly chin, the man smiled and nodded.

223

49

'In Denmark they call it the black sun,' Gunnar B. called to her from beside the window.

Line counted five spoonfuls into the coffee filter. 'What's that?' she asked, filling the container with water.

'When thousands of birds fly in a flock and cover the sky like an eclipse, it's a tourist attraction every autumn and spring in western Jutland.'

'Have you been there?'

'Many times.'

Crossing the room, Line opened the lid of her computer on the low coffee table.

'Can I borrow your memory card?' she asked.

Opening his camera, Gunnar B. removed the card and handed it to her. She inserted it in her computer, selected eleven images of the boat and copied them across. By the time she removed the card, coffee was ready.

Generously filling two mugs, she handed one to her visitor who had taken a seat on the settee. 'What do you think about the dead birds?' she asked, curling her hands around her mug.

Gunnar B. peered through the steam rising from his cup. 'Dead birds will fall from the sky,' he laughed. 'Isn't that what the doomsday prophets say? It's the first sign that the end is nigh? There were a hundred thousand birds in that flock we saw today. That makes a few hundred dead birds nothing more than a small percentage. Birds die all the time.'

'But what can have killed them?' Line persisted.

'If the sea eagle dives into the flock in pursuit of prey, it can kill a dozen just with the flapping of its wings. Others may have become terrified and flown into trees or quite simply died of exhaustion. Birds are easily stressed.'

'I've found two on the doorstep,' Line said. 'Before that, I think it's been a decade since I found a dead bird, and that one flew into a window at home.'

'There could be some kind of illness or poisoning. A group of them may have eaten something that did not agree with them. People are so thoughtless. A lot of the stuff they put on bird-trays is downright dangerous, leftover fatty food that causes diarrhoea and leads to the birds being unable to accept nourishment. They die within a day or two.'

They talked about birds for almost half an hour before Gunnar B. stood up, thanking her for the coffee. As soon as he was gone, Line sat at the computer, allowing one of the photos from the birdwatcher's camera to fill the screen.

The resolution was excellent. She could zoom onto the face at the controls without the quality degrading. Leaning slightly forward with a stern expression on his face, his eyes were hidden behind dark pilot's glasses and his hair ruffled by the wind. He was not wearing any kind of uniform and did not appear to be a policeman or from any of the rescue services. Moreover, police officers always work in pairs.

She zoomed out a couple of notches to see him full length, searching for details. He was wearing a dark windcheater with a large red *R* emblazoned on the chest and the name *Sailwear*. She googled it and discovered a Danish clothing company.

She then went through the same procedure with the dinghy. Behind one of the pontoons the name *RaveRib* was printed in white letters. A search on that took her to the webpage of a Danish boat manufacturer.

Zooming all the way out, she leaned back in her seat.

The boat was large enough to have crossed the sea from Denmark, but what was it doing here?

It struck Line that she was hungry. She got to her feet and crossed to the refrigerator. Butter and cheese, that was all. Before she sat down again, she refilled her cup. Regardless of what the man in the picture was searching for it must have something to do with the murder case.

Opening her email program, she typed her father's name into the address field, noting the words *Observation of suspicious boat* in the subject field. She then wrote a short summary, giving the name, address and phone number of Gunnar B. Hystad and attaching three of the photographs.

Just as she was about to send it, it struck her that her father was away. She deleted his address and picked up the business card belonging to the policeman who had interviewed her, adding his email address before clicking *Send*. With that, she stood up and went to do some shopping.

50

Wisting emerged from the shower in his hotel room. His mobile phone was ringing.

Wrapping the towel around his waist, he stepped out of the bathroom. The caller's number was not shown in the display. He raised the phone to his ear, announced himself, and immediately recognised Leif Malm's husky voice.

'Any news?' Wisting asked.

'There's a few things, but I waited until now to phone you. I expect you've had plenty to do today.'

Wisting ran his hand through his wet hair. 'Let me hear anyway.'

'Rudi Muller was in Larvik last night.'

'In Larvik?'

'We followed him down from Oslo yesterday evening. He booked into that new hotel, the *Ferris Bad*.'

'On his own?'

'Yes.'

'What was he doing there?'

'We don't know. Nobody known to us has gone in or out of the hotel, and there are no interesting calls on the phone number we're monitoring.'

'Is he still there?'

'No, he drove back early.'

Wiping the condensation from the mirror, Wisting leaned towards his reflection. The wound had healed into a bright pink mark. He ran his hand over his chin, realising he ought to have shaved before his shower. 'What does that mean?' he asked.

'It's possibly some kind of reconnaissance trip. He went out for a drive last night around all the side roads in the area for almost three hours. It was hopeless trying to follow, so we let him go and waited for him at the hotel.'

'Could he have met someone?'

'No, we mounted a tracker on his car after he'd checked in, and he was on the move the entire time.'

'You said he might have been reconnoitring. Do you mean the target for the robbery may be in Larvik?'

The reply came rather more swiftly and with slightly more assurance than Wisting had anticipated: 'Yes.' He waited for his colleague to continue.

'*NOKAS*, the Norwegian cash handling service, has five cash centres, one of which is located in Larvik. We know that plans for a raid have been circulating for a long time. The plans seem to be worked out down to the finest details, but so far no one has seized the opportunity. The risks are too high, but from the New Year, the centre in Larvik will be moving to Oslo. If the plan is to be carried out, it has to be done sometime in the autumn.'

Wisting knew that, at one point, plans had circulated for a raid on one of the town's *Norges Bank* branches, but this was before the Stavanger premises were raided. Nevertheless, it did not surprise him that plans existed for a robbery on the cash.

'Do you think Rudi Muller has bought the plans?'

'Some things suggest that he is interested in taking them over for a share of the proceeds. An hour ago, we got hold of the list of guests from the hotel. One of the other guests last night was Svein Brandt.'

The name was familiar to Wisting, but he allowed the intelligence chief to continue.

'Svein Brandt is a central player in criminal circles in the Østland area, but always operates in the shadow of others. His name is included in previous intelligence material dealing with possible robbery plans for the cash handling service in Larvik. He lives in Spain, but it seems he's paying a visit to Norway.'

Wisting let the information sink in. 'What does the informant say about it?'

'He hasn't been in touch, but we're hoping to arrange a meeting for this evening.'

'How imminent do you think the robbery might be?'

'We're probably talking about days rather than weeks. Rudi is really under the cosh.'

Wisting rubbed his hand over the stubble on his face. 'I have a return ticket for the day after tomorrow, but I'm not sure whether that will be possible. We haven't actually achieved anything at all.'

'Take whatever time you need,' Malm said. 'We'll take care of this.'

'What's your plan?'

'Rudi will need three or four men to carry out the plan. What's more, he needs vehicles and weapons. Usually we get signals when something like this is going on. We reckon also that the informant's involvement will continue.'

'What do we do if we find out when and where they're going to strike?'

'At the end of the day, that's a decision for your Chief of Police to make, but I would recommend that we grab them there and then. The alternative is to take preventive action by being conspicuous in the vicinity, but that would just postpone the raid.'

Wisting agreed. Besides, everything that turned up in the wake of such events would help to clear up the murder case. 'Have you found Trond Holmberg?' he asked.

'He was removed from the scene of the fire four hours ago, or at least what was left of him. We have the skull and teeth. It was obviously a simple matter for the forensic odontologist to confirm it was him. It will take longer for us to find out whether we have DNA, but the crime scene technicians are optimistic.'

Wisting gripped the phone underneath his chin as he looked for clean underwear in his suitcase. 'Cause of fire?'

'That's not so good. The idiot was a motocross fanatic and had two motorbikes in his living room, ditto petrol tanks. Inflammable liquid has been detected in several places, but it will be difficult to establish whether it has anything to do with the cause of the fire.'

They exchanged a few more words, and Leif Malm promised to keep him informed about developments.

Wisting dressed before going into the corridor to knock on the door of Martin Ahlberg's room. They had to discuss their return journey. In his present location, he felt far too distant from the centre of forthcoming events.

51

Martin Ahlberg's hotel room was slightly smaller than Wisting's, but just as elegantly furnished with a crimson carpet on the floor and paintings of the Old Town hanging on the walls. 'We've verified the ID,' Ahlberg said, sitting at the computer on the massive desk. 'Interpol confirms it was Darius Plater who was found on board the rowing boat.'

Wisting leaned towards the screen where an open email with the logo of the Organisation for International Police Cooperation was visible. 'At last,' he said. 'We'll make an early start tomorrow. Things are happening at home that make it difficult to postpone our departure.'

Ahlberg placed a ballpoint pen between his teeth and looked at him.

Wisting gave a brief outline of how the parallel enquiry was developing. 'Can I borrow your computer?'

'Of course.'

Martin Ahlberg logged himself out and relinquished the chair to Wisting. His computer was equipped with software that allowed him to access the police systems via an encrypted mobile broadband connection. As it was an expensive arrangement Wisting had never requested one for himself. He was usually at his office when anything happened, and had no wish to take the electronic aspects of his work home. Emails rolled in as soon as he entered the system. Sorting according to relevance, he read rapidly through mostly formalities and banal information.

'How about dinner tonight?' Ahlberg asked. 'We could try somewhere different?'

Wisting agreed just as a new email arrived. The sender was Benjamin Fjeld, and the subject *Danish narcotics supplier in Norwegian waters*. The message was marked as extremely important. *Have tried to phone you*, were the young policeman's opening words.

Patting his trouser pocket, it dawned on Wisting that he had left his mobile phone in his hotel room.

The email was a short summary of how an elderly birdwatcher had taken photographs of a fast boat that had been scouring the coastline at the Gusland fjord, travelling to and fro as though searching for something, the day after the discovery of the first body. Investigation had revealed that the boat was of Danish manufacture. The photograph had been sent to the Danish Police in Copenhagen and they had identified the man on board as Klaus Bang, known to them for repeated drugs violations.

Wisting clicked on the file attachment: the photograph of the boat with a man surveying the coastline. His eyes were concealed behind dark glasses, but he would be easily recognised.

He composed a quick response, confirming that he had received the email and telling Benjamin Fjeld to pass the information to the others in the group. He forwarded the message to Leif Malm, requesting him to assess it in relation to his information.

This fresh information was a huge leap forward in establishing a complete picture. It corresponded well with the case involving a drugs delivery to Rudi Muller that had gone awry. At the same time, there was something that did not add up.

The source had informed the police that one of the couriers who had crossed the Skagerrak was assumed to have

232

been killed in a confrontation, and that people in Muller's circles believed he was the man found in the rowing boat. However, now that he had been identified as Darius Plater from Lithuania, there were no grounds for thinking he had arrived from Denmark. Who, then, was the man in the large inflatable boat looking for along the coastline?

As the photo on the screen provided no answers, he logged himself out of the system and stood up.

Ahlberg was flicking through the channels on the television. 'Shall we go and eat?' he asked.

Wisting did not see any reason to inform him of these new developments, working on a need to know basis. 'I must make a phone call first,' he replied, heading towards the door. 'Let's meet in reception in a quarter of an hour.'

52

Wisting dialled Nils Hammer's number, and received an immediate answer. 'Have you spoken to Benjamin Fjeld?' Hammer asked.

'I've got an email from him,' Wisting replied. 'It's extremely interesting, and excellent work. How did he get hold of that witness?'

'It was Line who came across him at the cottage.'

Wisting frowned out of the window. Night was falling. 'Line?' It was strange that she had chosen to share the information with Benjamin Fjeld without first contacting him.

'Fjeld interviewed her,' Hammer explained, reading Wisting's thoughts. 'She had noticed a man and a parked van the day she arrived there, who turned out to be a birdwatcher.'

Wisting did not pursue the subject. 'Have you spoken to Leif Malm?'

'Less than five minutes ago. Plans for a robbery on the cash service premises in Elveveien correspond with reports from their security that their cash transports have been under surveillance. Six months ago they reported that a car had parked several times across from the vehicle access route into the centre. That would be a good vantage point for observation. The registration plates were stolen, so there was something going on.'

'I can be home on Friday at the earliest,' Wisting said.

'It looks as though Oslo's monitoring this. We'll take care of the local angle. There are a number of weak spots in the cash centre's security that make it a likely target. Mainly,

234

the building wasn't constructed for the purpose of storing money. There are several other tenants in the same building, and the arrangements are not optimal. That's probably one of the reasons they're centralising and relocating the whole shebang.'

'How much money are we talking about?'

'They have seven vehicles that uplift and deliver cash the length and breadth of the Østland area. Each vehicle carries an estimated fifteen million kroner, but that's continually exceeded. At the most, they can have eighty million stored overnight, but it's not likely to be such a large amount these days. It entirely depends on cash sales in the shops.'

'When do we warn the company's management?'

'There'll be a meeting with the Chief of Police tomorrow. Leif Malm and a few colleagues from Oslo will be coming too.'

Wisting nodded to himself, appreciating that Hammer was on top of things. 'Any other news?'

'Mortensen has traced the revolver that was lying in the boat with the dead Lithuanian. It was stolen from a cottage in Tjøme two days before our murder. The same gang has obviously been on the prowl out there. They broke into nine cottages in one night.'

They discussed a number of practical problems relating to staffing and resources, but the entire time they were talking, Wisting's thoughts returned to Nevlunghavn on the Friday evening almost a week earlier. 'How well have we searched the territory out there?' he asked.

'We used dogs and helicopters on the night of the murder, but it hasn't been finely combed. The roughest terrain was given low priority in the assumption that a killer on the run would choose the easiest paths. With the passing of time, it's fallen off the radar.'

'So there may be places we haven't looked?'

235

'I don't think the crime scene technicians have been in the scrub and woodland. A search like that would take weeks, without having anything in particular to look for.'

'I want you to organise a fresh search out there,' Wisting said. 'Make sure every square metre is examined.'

'Okay, but what are we looking for?'

Wisting took a deep breath before replying. It was only a theory, but it hadn't simply been snatched out of thin air. 'Something went seriously wrong that night. I think we're looking for another body.'

53

After stowing her purchases on the kitchen shelves, Line took an apple, a blanket and her newspaper onto the porch. Folding the blanket, she placed it on the top step before sitting down, leaning against the pillar supporting the roof overhang. She closed her eyes and turned her face towards the low autumn sun. Somewhere close by, a woodpecker hammered on a tree.

Crunching into the apple, she delighted in the view across the fjord. She was already looking forward to spending summers out here. A mild breeze rustled the branches on the nearest trees, as one leaf after another fell to the ground.

The case no longer featured on the front pages, but the editor had allocated two pages further back. All of what was printed was already old news. The newspaper had been published ten hours earlier, and the online version had given her updated news since then.

She also came across a page heading about the fire in the block of flats in Grorud where the brother of Rudi Muller's girlfriend was missing. The blaze was described as intense and explosive. Twenty-seven people had been evacuated from the adjacent flats and surrounding residences, and an elderly woman had been hospitalised because of heart problems. In addition to the flat, which belonged to the missing twenty-three-year-old, two other apartments had been rendered uninhabitable by fire, smoke and water damage. The firefighting crew had battled the flames for well over an hour and a half before gaining control. The police officer

237

in charge of the operation was interviewed and explained it was too soon to ascertain the cause; crime scene technicians would start as soon as practically possible.

The report was written by one of the more experienced crime reporters in the news section. That was unusual. Normally, the news editor would allocate such a story to an ordinary reporter. This might mean there was more going on than was evident from the text.

She finished eating her apple and threw the core into the bushes. Her fingers turned blue with cold as she read the remainder of the newspaper and, as soon as she was done, she returned inside.

From a seat on the settee, she logged into the newspaper's computer system, an efficient and flexible platform facilitating cooperation among journalists working on a variety of projects and allowing the retrieval of information.

The case folder dealing with the fire had been altered since the newspaper hard copy had been published. There would probably be an updated report on the online version. The journalist had also logged a similar story at 12.32 about a fatality taken from the ruins of the fire. She postponed reading this, instead clicking into the case log for information and background material not used in the report. The missing person was twenty-three-year-old Trond Holmberg.

In the bullet-pointed list of keywords, she found that an unnamed source in the fire service thought the fire had been started deliberately. The police were of the same opinion. The number of crime scene technicians on site was unusually large, and police had conducted door-to-door enquiries. The officers on duty were unusually reticent.

Holmberg was well known to the police, and had a connection to Rudi Muller. One of the reporter's informants thought something was afoot around Muller. A job had gone wrong, landing him in enormous debt. This story might grow legs and require more column space. The suspicion that the fire had been staged to cover up another crime was unavoidable.

Rudi Muller was obviously a familiar name to the crime reporter. In his words, Muller appeared to be a 'not inconsiderable presence in the criminal world'. Line's mouth became dry.

Highlighting his name, she copied it into the search field, and the links came thick and fast. Rudi Muller was mentioned eleven times. One of the background memos was based on a police informant who gave a thorough description. He came from a petty criminal milieu in Sagene that had become more brutal towards the end of the nineties, breaking and entering jewellery and electronics shops. Their proceeds were invested in consignments of narcotics. He was known for his aggressive methods and nowadays had emerged as the leader of a criminal gang at the heart of the drugs trade in Oslo.

He had been sentenced to six months' immediate imprisonment for being in possession of a gun in a restaurant. The police had ransacked his flat and discovered a machine gun and explosives.

One of the latest notes was linked to an article about money laundering in the restaurant business. Line went cold inside as she read about how the police presumed that Muller's share of the proceeds of an unsolved robbery on a jewellery shop in Karl Johans gate the previous year had been invested in the restaurant *Shazam Station*.

Rudi had been an active criminal earlier, but seemed now to operate in the shadows, untouchable by the police.

54

An older woman smiled at them as they left the restaurant, extending a grubby hand. Wisting dropped her some loose change and she bowed gratefully. At the next corner, they encountered more beggars. Children sitting on their mothers' laps shouting *Prasom! Prasom!* with pleading eyes. Wisting had to walk past, his pockets empty. Farther along, a blind man sat in front of a Gucci store. The tin cup placed beside him contained next to nothing. At the wall of the building behind, another beggar lay sleeping off a vodka binge.

Returning to their hotel in silence, Wisting declined the offer of a glass or two in the bar. He ascended directly to his room where he kicked off his shoes, hung his jacket over a chair, and stretched out on the bed. He had a feeling that the case was heading for a catastrophic finale. One alternative he wanted to raise with Leif Malm before tomorrow's meeting was that they should arrest Rudi Muller on the basis of what they already knew. It would be a gamble, not least on the security of the informant.

The most important work undertaken by the police was the prevention and obstruction of crime. By doing so, they saved the public from criminal activities and the criminals from long sentences.

They had no proof that Rudi Muller was involved in murder. Again though, an arrest might produce fresh evidence. It was like throwing a stone into the water. In some of the spreading rings, information might surface, but they had no guarantee of success and there was a risk that Muller would go free.

Placing his hands behind his head, it struck him he had not spoken to Suzanne that day. He dialled her number.

'We had such fabulous weather here today,' she told him. 'I went for a long walk after work.'

'You haven't been out to see Line at the cottage?'

'I phoned her, but she was out shopping.'

'How was she?'

'Tommy had been there.'

'Why on earth …'

He heard Suzanne take a deep breath, pausing before she answered. 'He spent the night.'

Stunned into silence, Wisting rubbed his eyes. 'Are they back together?'

'He arrived late last night after getting soaked in the rain. She let him stay until the morning.'

'What did he want?'

'To talk. It's probably not easy for either of them. I said I would go out to see her tomorrow. I'm quite excited to see what the place looks like.'

The conversation changed to a different tack, with Suzanne telling him about the tradesmen at her home who would soon be finished and about a strategy meeting she had attended at her work, before asking how his day had been. Wisting told her about all the poverty he had witnessed, and about all the people who survived with no hope for the future.

'That's probably what makes them come here to commit burglary,' Suzanne remarked.

'What do you mean?'

'That's probably their opportunity to realise their dreams of a better life.'

Wisting did not reply. She was probably right, he had to

241

agree. Her thoughts echoed his own. 'What are you going to do now?' he asked. It was just past eleven o'clock, ten in Norway.

'There's a film just starting on TV2. I thought I'd watch it before going to bed.'

Wisting took hold of the remote control. 'We have nothing but Finnish and Swedish channels.'

'Finnish TV drama is good,' Suzanne chuckled. They said good night and disconnected the call.

On the television screen, Wisting read: *You have 1 message*. He clicked *OK* on the interactive menu and received a message telling him there was a letter for him at reception.

At the desk he gave his room number and received a brown envelope addressed to *Mr. Wisting*. He turned it over in his hand, but there was no indication of the sender. 'When did this arrive?' he asked.

The receptionist did not know exactly. 'Maybe three hours ago.'

'Who delivered it?'

'It came by taxi.'

He opened the envelope as he headed towards the lift. The contents were a short message written in clumsy handwriting.

Talk about Darius Plater.
Come to number 1 Birut̓es gatv̓e
Midnight. Alone.
Please.

242

55

Wisting looked over the hotel lobby with the letter in his hand. Subdued voices were buzzing in different languages. A woman in a knee-length black dress, sitting on her own in the bar, glanced at him without making eye contact. No one was watching.

The only possibility he saw was that his attacker, the man he had pursued through the sales booths at the Gariunai market earlier that day, had spoken to the taxi driver who had driven them to the hotel. He could have obtained his name from the internet. It was a small world these days. It would not be strange if they had made an effort to follow the news coverage of the case they were part of. He was featured in the majority of Norwegian media sources with his name and photograph. A few keystrokes would get them an automatic translation into Lithuanian.

He asked for a map. The woman found a tourist brochure and folded out the centre. She placed a cross approximately in the middle, explaining that this was the hotel where he was staying. 'Where are you going?'

Wisting peered down at the note he had in his hand. 'Birut'es gatv'e.'

She repeated the street name with the correct pronunciation and moved her pen to the east side of the city, pointing along the bank of the river. Thanking her, Wisting folded the map. The clock on the wall behind her showed 23.26. It looked as though the trip to Birut'es gatv'e would take no more than ten minutes by taxi.

The elevator returned him to the third floor, where he paused outside Martin Ahlberg's door and raised his hand to knock, before lowering it again and letting himself into his own room.

When the clock showed half past eleven, he put on his outdoor clothes and went downstairs. Before leaving his hotel room, he unfolded the note with the message about the meeting place and appointed time, and left it in the middle of the desk.

Four taxis were parked outside the hotel. The driver in the first peered optimistically up at him. Drawing his jacket around himself he crossed the street, strolling for half a block before flagging down a taxi that happened to drive past.

Settling himself into the back seat, he gave the driver a note with the address. The man smiled and nodded, chattering away in his own language before setting off. Complex rhythms from some Slavic band of musicians drifted from the music system. Outside the car windows, darkened shops and warehouses with deserted car parks slipped past.

The journey ended at the perimeter fence of a football pitch. The driver pointed and posed a question. When Wisting could not answer, he drove in front of a darkened clubhouse and pointed at the meter. Wisting paid and stepped into a bitter wind that blasted from the river, carrying a rotten stench.

When the taxi disappeared, he stood alone in the empty square, surrounded by nothing but the glow of lights from the city on the opposite riverbank. A solitary lamp in a streetlight high above him cast a sparse glimmer on the grey asphalt and the peeling paint on the wall of the building behind him. A notice board was plastered with torn scraps of paper on which the word *futbolas* was repeated. Football was a language everyone understood.

He glanced at his watch: three minutes to twelve.

244

When his eyes had adjusted to the darkness, he stepped a few paces from the circle of light and caught sight of a delivery van in a narrow alleyway between two warehouse buildings almost sixty metres away. Its lights were out and its engine switched off. In front of the bonnet, he could see the glow of a cigarette.

'Mister Wisting?' a voice behind him asked.

He wheeled to face the man who had attacked him almost a week earlier. His square face was unkempt, with a beard and some kind of rash around his mouth. He wore a navy blue sports jacket that was too tight across the shoulders, and both hands were thrust into his side pockets. 'Mister Wisting from Norway?'

'Mister Muravjev.'

The lights on the delivery van were turned on and the vehicle rolled towards them. The driver jumped out and threw down his cigarette butt. Skirting around the van, he pushed open the side door.

Muravjev's hand curled around an object in his right jacket pocket, and he made a sign that Wisting should put his hands in the air. The driver patted his hands over his body, appropriating his mobile phone, wallet and passport. Wisting protested vehemently.

'English not good,' Muravjev said, but managed to explain that Wisting would have everything returned after they had talked. He gestured with his head towards the van. Wisting hesitated, but entered. Maravjev followed and pushed the door closed behind them.

There was a strong smell of grease, motor oil and rubber. A lamp on the wall near the driver's cabin helped him find a wheel arch to sit on.

They drove in silence, Wisting trying to concentrate on the route, memorising right and left turns, braking and acceleration, but quickly losing his bearings. At one point the tyre noise changed and it seemed that they were crossing a bridge.

After almost twenty minutes the vehicle came to a halt, the ignition was switched off and a door opened. A garage door was already drawn up beside them. A piercing light flooded the van interior, and he recognised the driver as one of the four members of the Paneriai Quartet. Algirdas Skvernelis.

Wisting stepped from the van. Swallowing, he wiped the sweat from his upper lip and tried not to show his fear.

They were in a disused warehouse. The air was cold and raw, but smelled of straw and hay. They were probably in the countryside.

Muravjev approached a steel door. The noise echoed in the immense space when he shoved the large bolts to one side, and fragments of rust fell onto the floor. They followed a maze of corridors and stairs before arriving in a cramped, brightly lit room with fluorescent lights on the ceiling. It was furnished as a sort of living room, with a worn out three-piece suite, a few broken chairs and a small table in front of a television set. Along the wall were rows of old wardrobes. The stink of sweat stung his nostrils.

A door opened at the back of the room, and a burly man with a thick neck, flat nose and tiny eyes entered, leaving the door open behind him. Wisting recognised him from Ahlberg's photographs as the third man in the group. Closing the door behind him, he came across, shaking hands and introducing himself. Teodor Milosz spoke good English and invited Wisting to sit.

'I'm sorry about all this,' he said, sitting opposite, but this situation we've landed in is making us feel insecure and unsafe.'

'I understand,' Wisting said. His nervousness had increased from the moment he arrived at the deserted sports ground.

'What has brought you to Vilnius?'

Wisting concentrated on his breathing. Calming down

246

allowed him to think more clearly. 'I'm investigating the murder of Darius Plater.'

Silence fell in the room. Somewhere in the building a fan hummed. 'Tell us how he died,' Teodor Milosz said.

'We found him in a boat. He had been shot twice in the stomach. We believe he was fleeing from something and hid on board. He died of blood loss.'

'Do you know who did it?'

'We don't know who or why.'

Muravjev interrupted in Lithuanian. Teodor Milosz exchanged a few words with him before addressing Wisting again. 'Why have you come here? What do you want from us?'

'You were there when he died. I want to know what happened.'

Teodor Milosz translated. Muravjev gestured with his arms as he spoke. 'What will happen to us?' Teodor Milosz interpreted once more.

'What do you mean?'

'Are we to be punished?'

'You are suspected of several instances of aggravated burglary from cottages in the area, but that's not why I'm here. That's not what this case is concerned with. It's about justice for Darius.'

This answer was translated and a fresh exchange of opinions followed.

'What are the Norwegian police intending to do about the theft cases?'

'I can't provide you with any kind of amnesty. If you come back to Norway, you risk being punished.'

Muravjev rose to his feet, placing both hands on his head. His voice was full of bewilderment as he spoke.

Teodor Milosz relayed: 'Will we have to go to Norway if there is a trial?'

'Yes you will, but I'm sure the state prosecutor will be kindly disposed if you contribute towards the solving of this case.'

Muravjev's voice was raised now. 'But we don't know anything!'

'You know more than we do. You were there when it happened. I need someone who can speak for Darius.'

The three men held a discussion in their own language until, finally, Muravjev shook his head and sat down. Teodor Milosz rested his forearms on his knees, leaning forward in his chair. 'I will tell you,' he said.

56

One of the filthy fluorescent light tubes on the ceiling flickered and hummed faintly before going out. Teodor Milosz' face fell into shadow. 'It's true that we stole from the cottages,' he began. 'We had been into six of them and were on our way to the last when we realised we were not alone in the woods.'

He straightened up before continuing. 'It was dark, with only a little light on the outside of the cottage wall. We sat among the trees, perhaps twenty metres away, and waited to be sure that there was nobody there. Besides, we were not entirely sure whether to break into that one. The cottage was old and looked as though it wasn't occupied.' He paused to clear his throat. 'We heard him before we saw him. He was careless and clumsy, breaking branches from the trees, even though he was walking along the path. When he approached the cottage, we saw that he was wearing a hood, and that he was carrying a bag.'

Teodor Milosz used his hands to indicate the size of the bag. 'He looked around before placing it on a box on the verandah. The kind of box lots of people have for storing the cushions they use with their outdoor furniture.'

Wisting nodded that he understood, although Milosz' English pronunciation was poor.

'We lay totally silent for ten minutes,' the Lithuanian continued, his voice lowered. 'Then Darius crept forward on his own. He opened the lid of the box, lifted out the bag and opened it.' The dusty light tube above him blinked a couple of times before coming to life again, giving his face sharp shadows and hollow cheeks. "*Piniga!*" he shouted up to us. "Money!"'

The two other Lithuanians in the room exchanged glances, as though the story brought back bad memories.

'He held up a whole fistful,' Milosz said, demonstrating with his hand. 'Then he stuffed it back and hoisted the bag over his shoulder.'

Wisting leaned back. The account was so obvious he ought to have thought of it himself. The Lithuanians had been on a thieving foray in the cottages and by chance had stumbled on Rudi Muller's showdown with the cocaine dealers. The cushion box was probably a prearranged delivery location.

'Then everything happened so fast, and in the dark,' Teodor Milosz said. 'Two masked men came running from the woods, shouting. Darius ran the other way, towards the sea.'

Rudi Muller and Trond Holmberg had been lying hidden in the woods, waiting for the bag to be exchanged for cocaine.

'We ran after them, but everything was in darkness. We had flashlights, of course, but they were of little use. They only lit up a small area in front of us, and after that you see even less than before. Also, it gives away your position.' Teodor Milosz brushed aside his digression with a hand gesture. 'Valdas ran first,' he said, nodding towards the man who had ambushed Wisting. 'Algirdas and I were right behind, but Algirdas tripped and fell, and Valdas disappeared into the darkness ahead of us.'

Valdas Muravjev made a remark that was not translated. Teodor Milosz stood up and took a few paces backwards and forwards across the floor before resuming. 'Then we heard shots,' he said. 'Many shots.'

'Did Darius have a gun?'

Milosz stared at Wisting without responding.

'The one you stole from one of the cottages at Tjøme two days before,' Wisting said. 'We've found it. It was in the boat with Darius.'

Teodor Milosz nodded wearily. 'It was Darius who found it. It was lying in the drawer of a bedside table, but he wasn't the only one who fired. The shots went back and forth, just ahead of us.' He waved his arms about to demonstrate how there had been an exchange of gunfire. 'Algirdas and I sought cover away from the path. We were not armed, so there was nothing we could do.'

Valdas Muravjev interrupted the conversation once more. Wisting's attacker obviously found it easier to understand what was said in English than to speak the language himself.

'Valdas thought he saw Darius in front of him on the path,' Teodor Milosz translated.

'A man with a bag,' Muravjev clarified. His wide-open eyes gave his features a confused, desperate expression.

Sitting down again, Milosz held up his hand, as if to say that he would tell the story at his own speed. 'Valdas crouched beside the path and came forward to meet him when the man was directly facing him, but it was not Darius. It was another man.'

Muravjev made another attempt: 'There was a fight. I was strongest, but the man ran into the forest. I did not follow him.'

'One of the men who chased Darius?'

Muravjev shook his head furiously. 'It was not either of them. He was wearing different clothes, and did not have a hood over his face.'

The details of this account could be woven into the existing information. The man on the path was probably the narcotics courier who was carrying ten kilos of cocaine.

'I was the one who had the keys for the van,' Teodor Milosz continued. 'Algirdas and I went back. We thought

251

that both Darius and Valdas might have done the same, and we were in a hurry to drive away, but they weren't there.'

'Was there any other vehicle there?'

The Lithuanian nodded. 'In a space a little further away, another car was parked. A Golf, I think.' He turned to Algirdas and asked him. The other man nodded. 'Yes, it was a black Volkswagen Golf.'

Wisting swallowed. That was Line's car.

'Darius' phone was lying in the van, so we couldn't call him,' Teodor Milosz said. 'But we spoke to Valdas. He said he would continue to search for Darius, and we should wait for them in the van on the main road.'

Muravjev made several more comments that were not translated.

'We had been waiting a long time, maybe an hour or so, when a police car arrived. We had to leave. The idea was that Valdas would hide in the woods and wait until we had emptied the van and could come back for him.'

Muravjev interjected several sentences in his mother tongue.

'He came up to the main road and waited beside a tree,' Milosz translated. 'But then more police cars turned up, this time with dogs and a helicopter. He couldn't wait any longer.'

Muravjev fixed his gaze on Wisting. 'I am sorry. I took your car.'

Wisting brushed this aside. Teodor Milosz' story was coming to its end.

'We have an agreement,' Milosz explained. 'If anything happens and we get separated, we have to phone and leave a message. All Darius had to do was get hold of a phone and call us.' He lowered his eyes. 'He never did.'

Wisting stretched out. The pieces had fallen into place, but there were still many unanswered questions. 'Where is the bag of money?'

252

'No idea,' Teodor Milosz replied. 'We thought perhaps you had found it when you found Darius.'

Wisting shook his head.

Algirdas spoke for the first time. 'Who is the dead man in the cottage?' Teodor Milosz translated.

'A Norwegian,' Wisting replied.

'Do you think Darius shot him?'

Wisting had to reflect for a moment before answering. It was likely that Darius Plater had shot and injured Trond Holmberg, and also that it was Holmberg and Muller who had inflicted the fatal gunshot wounds on Darius Plater before fleeing from the scene. If it was Rudi Muller there with Trond Holmberg.

'It's too early to come to a conclusion,' he said, without mentioning that the man in the cottage had probably died not from gunshot wounds, as had been reported, but from a blow to the head.

'Where are the items you stole from the cottages?' he asked.

Milosz threw out his arms expressively. 'You were at the market, weren't you?' he answered. 'Most of it has been sold.'

'Most of it?'

Teodor Milosz got to his feet and stepped across to one of the metal cupboards lining the wall. Opening it, he waved Wisting over.

A portable computer sat on a shelf beside a DVD player. Underneath were a couple of car stereos, and a number of MP3 players and mobile phones. At the bottom of the cupboard lay several candlesticks and other *bric-a-brac*. Light fell diagonally onto the shelves, and was reflected on coloured glass.

Wisting hunkered down and picked out a pendant-shaped glass object about the size and shape of a fist. The light played

253

on it as he held it up. The transitions of the different colours were almost imperceptible, changing according to the direction and intensity of the light. The colours and luminescence brought the glass to life, and it was easy to imagine it as a dewdrop filled with dreams, thoughts and hopes. 'I know the owner of this,' he said.

'It's beautiful,' Milosz nodded. 'It was Darius who wanted it, even though it's not worth much. At least, not here in Lithuania.' He shut the cupboard door. 'We waited another day for him to phone, but then we read on the internet that a dead man had been found in a boat. We thought it must be Darius and came home.'

Wisting tucked the glass droplet into his pocket. 'I'm grateful for all you have told me,' he said, 'but we must formalise it through an interview at the police station.'

'There is someone else here who wants to meet you,' Teodor Milosz interrupted him.

The Lithuanian strode to the door through which he had entered. 'Wait here,' he said.

57

The woman who appeared in the door opening was in her mid-twenties, with a round face and blonde curls. Her eyes, more grey than blue, were red around the edges. She wore a buttoned brown coat with sleeves that were too short. Wisting recognised her instantly as the woman whose photograph Darius Plater had been carrying.

'This is Anna,' Teodor Milosz explained.

Wisting rose to his feet. 'You're Darius' girlfriend,' he said, introducing himself as a police detective from Norway. 'My condolences.'

'Thanks,' the woman whispered.

'Anna has been listening to our conversation,' Teodor Milosz said. 'But she wanted to meet you.'

'I don't want you to think of Darius as a thief,' she said. 'He loved Norway. He talked about all his experiences there. He had seen mountains and waterfalls along the roadsides, and described all the buildings that were both practical and beautiful. Norwegians were clever at making beautiful things, he told me.'

'You speak good English,' Wisting said.

'Anna's a university student,' Milosz explained.

They sat down again, and Wisting listened to the woman. She had a great deal to tell him.

'We have the same sun and the same moon in Norway and Lithuania,' she said. 'We live on the same earth, but our world is split in two. We are poor. You are rich.'

Wisting could not do other than agree.

'Darius did not dream of being rich, but he did dream of a good life. For himself, for me and for the child we talked about creating. When people from poor countries like ours come to work or steal in your country, it's not to become rich, but to gain enough money to stand on our own two feet. Of course it's wrong, but poor people must always think of themselves. At one time, you Norwegians were poor as well. I think you have forgotten that, but you are so proud of your Vikings that you build museums for them. They were a hundred times worse than the Lithuanian people. They plundered, raped and killed, but now everyone thinks of them as heroes.'

'Why did you go to Norway?' Wisting asked, glancing across at Teodor Milosz. 'Why not travel to Germany, or stop in Sweden?'

'When you are going to do things that are wrong, it's important that what you do is as little wrong as possible,' Milosz said. 'It's better to steal from Norway, because it's a wealthy country, than a poor country where people don't have so much. Norway doesn't notice if a person steals a hundred thousand kroner.'

'What would you do if someone stole from you?' Wisting countered.

'I would be angry,' was the reply. 'But eventually I would think that the person who did it was desperate and needed money. People who have their belongings stolen must not take it personally. It's only chance that it happens to them.'

Wisting looked at the three pale men in turn. In the annual reports about trends and tendencies in crime developments they were described as cynical members of organised gangs of burglars from the east. There probably were such people, but from what these men had told him and what Wisting himself had witnessed in this country, they represented a type of criminality that arose from necessity rather than immorality. It was easy to understand where criminality came from, but it was not a justification.

After Wisting embarked on his career in the police, the Norwegian economy had grown enormously. With the development of the welfare state, there were fewer poor people in Norway but, at the same time, crime had increased dramatically. The causes of criminality were considerably more complex, with elements other than poverty and need. However, the crime statistics in Norway would certainly look very different if the economy of Eastern Europe showed improvement.

'When is he coming home?' the slightly built woman asked, rousing him from his thoughts.

'Sometime next week.'

Silence descended on the room once again. Teodor Milosz coughed. 'We'll drive you back,' he said, giving instructions in Lithuanian.

Algirdas handed Wisting's mobile phone, passport and wallet back to him.

'I can take a taxi,' Wisting said, as he stood up.

'There are no taxis out here. We'll take you back to your hotel.'

'Wait,' pleaded the woman who had been Darius Plater's girlfriend. Wisting waited for the difficult question. 'Will you get him?' Will you catch the man who killed Darius?'

'That's my job.'

58

The breakfast room was filled with the smells of newly baked bread and percolated coffee. Martin Ahlberg sat at a table by the window and had almost finished eating. Wisting helped himself to orange juice and a large portion of bacon, egg and toast before sitting opposite his colleague.

'I'm going home today,' he said. 'There's a SAS flight via Copenhagen as early as eleven o'clock.'

Ahlberg set his cup down on the table but, before he managed to say anything, Wisting continued: 'Teodor Milosz, Valdas Muravjev and Algirdas Skvernlis will come to the police station at twelve to provide formal statements. They'll bring the stolen goods that haven't already been sold.'

Prodding a rasher of bacon with his fork, he raised it to his mouth before explaining what had happened overnight.

Martin Ahlberg shook his head disapprovingly. 'You've no idea what kind of people they are,' he said.

Even when he left the hotel the previous evening, Wisting had been prepared for Ahlberg's criticism. If the outcome had been different, it would have been justified. 'I know now.'

Ahlberg sighed in resignation. 'Do you believe them?'

Wisting saw no reason not to believe the Lithuanians' version, although it did not provide a complete picture. They still knew only fragments of the story, with the most important parts missing. Before they left the breakfast table, they discussed some practical details about Ahlberg's continuing work on the case. Wisting then collected his suitcase and checked out of the hotel.

Ahlberg accompanied him to the queue of waiting taxis. 'It's been a pleasure,' he said, holding out his hand.

'Thanks, same to you,' Wisting replied.

He had come to know his colleague as a competent investigator. Methodical and thorough, but had to admit that they were very different in outlook.

He thought of Martin Ahlberg as a tired policeman, someone who had encountered too many people who had suffered from criminality, too many people whose security had been stolen. His everyday working life among East European criminals had rubbed away the nuances. You would think that the opposite would happen but, if you became weary enough, you lost the strength to absorb the complexities of the world. Then it was easier to see criminals and victims in black and white although, deep inside, you knew fine well that it wasn't always easy to decide where the moral blame lay.

The legal blame was, as a rule, easy to allocate, but everyone who worked with criminality knew that morality was considerably more complicated.

An hour later he sat on seat number 18F watching the city diminish below him until it vanished in the grey carpet of clouds. Momentarily he ruminated on the arbitrariness of having been born in Norway in peacetime, and whether any kind of justice truly existed. The plane broke through the clouds to reveal blue skies all around.

59

Darkness descended as Wisting approached Larvik. The sky was clear, a deep shade of blue and the opalescent moon, full and round, was wreathed in quivering light.

The phone rang as he swung the car off the motorway. 'Where are you?' Nils Hammer asked.

'Why are you asking?'

'I'm at Gusland,' Hammer explained. 'You should probably come straight here and see for yourself. You were right. There's another body.'

The conversation ended with no new information. Curling his fingers around the steering wheel, he took the road leading to Helgeroa. Ten minutes later he stopped at the parking area at the outer edge of the cluster of cottages that had been in the glare of media focus for the past week. The voluntary searchers were in the process of packing up, and the first journalist had arrived on the scene.

Some way along the path, he encountered a uniformed police officer who provided him with a flashlight and pointed him in the right direction. He followed a trail of broken branches. Ahead of him he heard the noise of generators and voices, and eventually took his bearings from the light shed by the newly erected floodlights.

Seven policemen huddled together on the discovery site, frosty mist swirling between them in the heat from the huge lamps. Hammer turned to meet Wisting as he crouched under the last branches and emerged onto the plateau. 'Welcome back.'

Wisting thanked him, staring into the distance. Only then did he notice that policemen were standing on either side of a crevice that divided the hillside in two. Espen Mortensen hauled himself out as Wisting strode past.

'He's been lying here for a week,' Mortensen said, adjusting his headlamp.

Wisting peered into the cleft, not at first understanding what he saw. It was a human body, lying approximately two metres below him. The head was positioned at an odd angle in relation to the neck, the mouth open and the eye sockets empty. On the right shoulder, a splinter of bone jutted from a decomposing wound, but there was something else down there too, that sent shivers through his body.

Around and across the dead body lay dead birds of different kinds, protected from foxes and other scavengers by the precipitous hillside. There were blackbirds, starlings, a couple of crows and several birds whose names Wisting did not know, enough to fill a sack.

'We're most probably dealing with an accident,' Mortensen said. 'He leapt right into the jaws of death.'

Rubbing his hand across his forehead, Wisting saw for himself what had happened after the unknown man Valdas Muravjev had met on the path stormed into the woodland. The drop had not been sheer, but in the darkness it must have been sudden and savage.

The corpse lay entangled in the branches of a birch tree, the roots of which protruded from the boulders at the foot of the chasm. Beside the dead birds lay the bag that Muravjev had told him about, its side ripped open and the contents spilled out.

Wisting jumped to the other side of the fissure. From this angle, it was easier to see. A number of brick-sized packages were scattered across the rocks, sealed in plastic and thick,

261

brown tape. One of them had burst open, and the white powder packed inside had turned into a glutinous mass.

'Cocaine?'

Nils Hammer nodded. 'We think his name is Malte Ancher,' he said, opening a folder he carried under his arm. 'We received information from the Danish Police this morning. He was reported missing on Tuesday by his girlfriend in Aalborg.'

Wisting accepted the papers, but continued to listen.

'He served a sentence at the same time as Klaus Bang in a prison in Horsens in 2006. It seems they've hung out together quite a lot since. Two years ago they were caught in a car with five thousand blue Valium tablets on the border between Germany and Denmark.'

'Professional narcotics couriers?'

'It's not exactly professional to put two men in a car full of smuggled drugs, but it does at least seem as though they're involved in that line of business. Klaus Bang was interviewed in connection with the missing person report. He says he was at home with a sore stomach all weekend and didn't have any contact with anyone. He didn't say a word about a boat trip.'

'Have the Danes confronted him with our photographs?'

'No.'

Wisting nodded in satisfaction. That gave them an excellent starting point for the investigation to follow. The photographs of the boat and the discovery in the rock crevice would be enough for a charge of aggravated importation of drugs. Klaus Bang risked more than ten years jail for that. The simplest course of action would be to put all the blame onto his dead friend. If he was smart enough, or managed to obtain a good defence lawyer, he could strengthen his credibility by giving the police details of their lines of connection with Norway. He could give them Rudi Muller.

As a light, cold mist began to settle over the landscape, Wisting pushed his hands into his pockets and drew his head down between his shoulders. 'How are you planning to get him up?'

'There's equipment coming,' Mortensen said. 'We'll rig up a tripod crane with a hand winch over the crevice, pull the body onto a canvas sheet and haul him out. That's the plan.'

'When can we have the ID verified?'

'I've already been down to secure fingerprints. I'll scan them as soon as I get back. Malte Ancher is on record in Denmark, but it's not certain we'll get an answer from them until their offices open in the morning.'

Wisting nodded in acknowledgement. Before leaving the discovery scene, he positioned himself so that he could look to the east. Now that most of the foliage was gone, the plateau made an excellent lookout point. A fine veil of mist drifted in the air, but he could make out the illumination from the lighthouse out at Tvistein and an island that must be Jomfruland. Further inland, he could distinguish the scattered outdoor lights of the cottages, closed for winter. Here and there, windows were illuminated.

The contours of what must be Thomas Rønningen's holiday cottage were outlined against the backdrop of the sea and, to his left, lights were on in the cottage belonging to Jostein Hammersnes. He tried to pinpoint the cottage where Line was staying, but by now the mist was thickening and eventually he had to desist, turning his back on the panorama.

60

Recognising that he needed rest, Wisting drove home without calling at the police station. He called Leif Malm from his car. The leader of the intelligence section in Oslo answered at once, and Wisting gave a brief account of the discovery of the third body.

'I'll see what I can find out about him through our channels,' Malm said. 'I don't know his name from our intelligence files, but there must be some connection to Rudi Muller.'

'Any news about the planned robbery?'

'It's probably fairly imminent.'

'What does that mean?'

'Days. We've informed the management of the cash service company, but as long as we don't know anything about where or when, there's little we can do. For the moment, they're withholding the information from their staff. The probability of them getting information from the inside is high, and we can't risk any leaks. The surveillance on Muller is tight, and we'll have warning when things start to move.'

Wisting restrained himself before picking up the thread of the conversation they'd had at the scene of the fire. 'At some point we need to interview Tommy Kvanter,' he said, telling him about the results of his visit to Lithuania. 'The Lithuanians confirm that the car he used that night was at the crime scene.'

There was such a long silence at the other end that Wisting wondered whether the connection had been broken. When he was about to ask if Malm was still there, he received his answer: 'I think it would be unwise to do that now. It would reveal how closely we're breathing down their necks. Before you do anything like that, we need to have Trond Holmberg's DNA confirmed. That would link him directly to your crime scene.'

Wisting had to agree with this tactical assessment. If they played their cards in the right order, they should also detain Klaus Bang before exposing themselves to the circle surrounding Rudi Muller. All the same, he could not wait to pass on the information to his investigation group, and he would do that at the meeting tomorrow morning.

He rounded off their discussion as he swung the car in front of his house in Herman Wildenveys gate. The huge birch tree in the garden had dropped many more leaves since Suzanne had raked away a wheelbarrow-load earlier in the week. He carried his suitcase inside, to be met by glowing candles and a warm embrace.

'Good to have you home again,' Suzanne said.

'Great to be back,' he said, smiling.

'Are you hungry?'

'No, I grabbed a bite at a petrol station.'

They sat in the living room. Suzanne turned down the volume on the television and demanded to know how his trip had gone.

He recollected Lithuania as grey and grim, but Vilnius as a city of contrasts. After the fall of the Soviet dictatorship, a great deal of freedom had been returned to the people and, with that, a greater opportunity to influence their own lives. The economy of the country was making visible progress, but the poverty still remaining had made the strongest impression on him.

'I've brought something for you,' he said, standing up.

He stepped out to the hallway, where he opened his

suitcase to produce the amber necklace. It dawned on him that this was the first time he had bought her a present.

Unwrapping it, she said, 'It's beautiful. You must put it on me.' She returned it to him and pulled her hair up.

'You don't need to wear it all the time,' he said, looking at the heart-shaped pendant. 'I bought it mostly as a charitable gesture.' He told her about the boy who had sold it to him in an alleyway in Vilnius.

Suzanne placed her hand on it. 'That just makes it even more beautiful. It says so much about you.'

'I have something else.' He took out the knitted doll he had bought for a hundred litas, thinking of the little girl's hopeful eyes, dirty hands and broad smile.

'What's that?' Suzanne asked, pointing towards the suit-case.

Wisting picked up the glass ornament. The reflection from the candles on the table made it almost incandescent. 'It's a dreamcatcher,' he said, handing it to her, 'to hold all your thoughts about the future. You should have been given something like this.'

'Who does it belong to?'

Wisting explained how the little glass figure was one of the most cherished objects that had been stolen from Jostein Hammersnes' cottage, and how he had found it in a secluded storeroom in Lithuania.

'He'll be pleased to get it back,' Suzanne said.

Wisting smiled, looking forward to delivering the glass pendant to the man who felt he had lost everything. 'Have you spoken to Line today?'

'I put together some food and had a leisurely lunch with her,' Suzanne replied, handing him back the glass ornament. 'She's writing a book.'

'A book?'

'A crime novel, and I think she'll manage to do it. She's

smart. If there's something she wants to do, she usually manages to accomplish it.'

'What's it about?'

'She didn't say.'

'Did you discuss Tommy?'

'Not much. I think she worries about what he's doing when he's not with her.'

'Like what?'

'I didn't like to ask, but she knows that some of the people he's working with are involved in shady dealings. That was one of the reasons she finished with him.'

'So it is all over?'

'I think she became even surer of that after his visit.'

Wisting nodded in satisfaction.

A familiar face appeared on the television screen, and Suzanne turned up the volume to listen to Thomas Rønningen's trailer for the next day's programme. Among the guests were a couple of actors who both appeared naked in a new film, a politician who felt naked and exposed, and a celebrity from the world of finance who wanted his guests to swim in the nude at his spa hotel.

That's what everything is about when push comes to shove, Wisting mused: money, power and sex.

61

Christine Thiis' office was as tidy as it had been on the morning they initiated the investigation. She was sitting behind her desk with a cup of tea and a selection of the day's newspapers when Wisting entered. The case was on the front pages again, with the discovery of the third body splashed. 'Welcome home,' she smiled.

'Well played,' said Wisting, nodding in the direction of the newspapers. That the police had not found the corpse earlier with dogs and helicopters could have prompted headlines about police deficiencies. Instead, Christine Thiis was quoted as saying that progress in the investigation had led to the decision to carry out a further search in extremely rugged woodland terrain.

Beyond confirming that the discovery of a dead man in his late twenties was being linked to the current enquiry, she had been extremely reticent with information and would not make further comment. The statement gave the impression that the police were on the offensive and close to a breakthrough, which was exactly how Wisting viewed the situation.

'How are the children?' he asked, leafing through one of the newspapers. The media had not dropped the story about the dead birds.

'Fine. My mother's staying until after the weekend.'

They discussed the main aspects of the case before leaving to join the others in the conference room.

The morning meeting was divided into five segments.

Wisting took the final segment first, asking Espen Mortensen to elaborate on what had been reported in the newspapers.

'I'll start with the most important information,' Mortensen said, opening a folder. He laid out several photographs illustrating the discovery site. 'The deceased has been identified by fingerprints as Malte Ancher, twenty-nine years old, from Aalborg in Denmark. His post mortem will take place today, and I would expect it to report that the cause of death is blunt trauma to the head, his injuries consistent with a fall. So we're talking about an accident.'

'We've interviewed Gunnar B. Hystad,' Torunn Borg interrupted.

'Who?'

'The birdwatcher who took the photographs of the other Dane, Klaus Bang.'

Wisting nodded. This was the witness Line had come across.

'It seems the boat was close to shore almost all day Saturday,' Torunn Borg said. 'As though waiting for someone or something.'

Wisting's mobile phone vibrated on the tabletop, Leif Malm's number on the display. Letting it ring, he asked Espen Mortensen to continue.

'We found a black bag in the crevice on the hillside. It had torn open and some of the contents had spilled out. A quick test we carried out yesterday was positive for cocaine. The weight is just under ten kilos.'

'As most of you know, we have verified the identity of the man in the rowing boat,' Wisting said. Moving to the second segment of the meeting he told them what he had learned in Lithuania. 'The formal statements are being translated and will arrive in the course of today.'

The third segment concerned information being dealt with on a need to know basis. Although most team members

269

understood that the case revolved around a drugs confrontation, limits had been set on the intelligence from the informant. Wisting also felt that the information received from Leif Malm had been filtered before it reached him. He peered at the keywords he had noted for the agenda before continuing.

'You know my daughter, Line,' he said. 'Some of you also know that she has been living with Tommy Kvanter in Oslo, and that a number of years ago he was sentenced for a drugs offence. I want you to know as well that he is an associate of Rudi Muller and they both have ownership interests in *Shazam Station*. The Oslo Police, who have contact with an informant and are conducting a surveillance operation on Muller, naturally know this too. His relationship with Line is over, actually, and as the case stands now, I don't feel that it creates any conflict of interest, but that's something I'll keep in mind as we progress.'

He looked down at his papers again. It had pained him to get that out, but at the same time it was a relief. As far as Line's car being linked to the case was concerned, he would take that up with Nils Hammer in private before the witness statements arrived from Lithuania.

He was about to continue when Benjamin Fjeld thrust his hand in the air. 'Is Tommy Kvanter not originally Danish?'

'Yes.' Wisting let a question hang in the air with this confirmation.

'There is obviously a Denmark connection here,' Benjamin Fjeld said. 'Do we know whether he has any association with Klaus Bang or Malte Ancher?'

Wisting was surprised that Benjamin Fjeld had such intimate knowledge of his daughter's private life, but the possible link was so obvious he could not comprehend why his own thoughts had not taken him in that direction. All the same, he managed to respond positively. 'The intelligence section in Oslo is following that line.'

270

He scanned the faces around the table without detecting any sign of discomfort, stood up and stepped forward to the whiteboard at one end of the room. 'So, now we know a great deal about what happened,' he said, introducing the fourth segment of the meeting. At that moment, his mobile phone vibrated again – another call from Leif Malm. 'The Danes travel across the Skagerrak to deliver ten kilos of cocaine,' he said, allowing it to ring out. 'It's a regular route, and they send a prearranged text message when they arrive.'

He illustrated his theory by using a blue marker pen to sketch a boat with two matchstick men.

'The recipients are Rudi Muller and his prospective brother-in-law, Trond Holmberg,' he continued, selecting a green marker pen before drawing a car with two men. 'The transfer occurs at a regular location.' This time he sketched a cottage. 'Chance circumstances cause the four itinerant burglars from Lithuania to be hidden witnesses to the transaction.'

Four red matchstick men were lined along the board.

'One of them takes the bag of money, but is chased by Muller and Holmberg. Both parties carry firearms, and both make use of them. Darius is hit by two bullets, but manages to hide from his pursuers in an old rowing boat. It drifts off to sea and he dies of his wounds.'

One of the red men now lies horizontal on the board.

'Trond Holmberg is also shot, and seeks refuge in the nearest cottage.' He drew another cottage and placed one of the green matchstick men lying prone inside. 'The three other Lithuanians search for Darius, and bump into one of the Danes.'

'Malte Ancher,' Mortensen said, and Wisting crossed out one of the blue men.

'He flees into the woodland with the bag of cocaine and plunges to his death.' He sketched the new position of Malte Ancher.

271

'Klaus Bang waits in the boat, but has to return to Denmark on his own. The three remaining Lithuanians retreat when the police start to appear. Rudi Muller must also leave the crime scene and, when he discovers from the media that Trond Holmberg is dead, he does all he can to avoid being drawn into the case that now involves not only aggravated drugs offences, but also murder. He steals Holmberg's body and places it in his flat before setting it on fire.'

Wisting replaced the lid of the marker pen. The board outlined a simple, intelligible chain of events. As he envisioned it, there were still two important questions remaining. He turned again to the board, this time with a black marker pen.

'Who killed Trond Holmberg?' He drew a question mark above the green matchstick man. 'And what's happened to the bag of money?'

Several people spoke at once. Wisting, making an effort to steer the discussion, invited one of the investigators drafted from another district to speak.

'Has Thomas Rønningen been eliminated?' he asked, pointing to the cottage Wisting had sketched on the board.

'His girlfriend has given him an alibi.'

'Does that check out? He might have been there and surprised the housebreaker.'

'It checks out until we know otherwise,' Wisting replied. 'Besides, Trond Holmberg wasn't the housebreaker. The Lithuanians confirm that they emptied the cottage before Holmberg and Muller turned up.'

Christine Thiis spoke without waiting to be asked. 'Do we actually know that it was Muller who was there with Holmberg?'

Wisting shook his head. 'We're basing that on the assumptions of the informant and the fact that Muller would hardly have hijacked the hearse, killed the driver and desecrated the

272

body of his girlfriend's little brother except to conceal his involvement in the case.'

'But do we know it was Muller who stole the hearse?'

'It's still just a theory,' Wisting said. 'If we could prove it, Rudi Muller would be under arrest.'

Several of the detectives wanted to voice opinions and questions. Wisting stood behind his chair, his hands resting on the back, like a captain firmly holding the helm aboard a vessel in choppy waters. He allowed everybody a chance to speak before moving to the last segment of the meeting.

'We have definite information that Rudi Muller is planning a robbery,' he said. 'The target has been chosen, the cash service centre in Elveveien here in Larvik.' He outlined the information from Oslo before giving the floor to Nils Hammer.

'The *NOKAS* cash service is Norway's third largest security company,' Hammer said when a photograph of the reddish-brown brick building appeared on the screen. The advertising sign on the façade proclaimed that there were five other companies in the same building. 'The centre is a depot and loading station for coins and banknotes from banks and commercial businesses in the counties of Vestfold and Telemark. The administration offices are situated on the upper floor, while the actual depot is located in the basement with the entrance at the rear.'

Hammer changed the image. The building was positioned on a gentle slope, with a road running around and down behind it, where there was an entrance through a drive-in gate and steel door. 'The perimeter of the building is fitted with an intruder alarm and, in addition, there's a robbery alarm and a threat alarm.'

'What do you mean by a threat alarm?' Christine Thiis asked.

'If an employee is forced to switch off the alarm system,

273

they're instructed to key in an extra digit that sets off a silent alarm at a twenty-four hour security centre in Oslo. There are internal CCTV cameras, as well as cameras in the basement. The footage is beamed directly to the security centre.'

He changed to a photograph of the interior. The first room resembled an ordinary garage with tools and stored winter tyres. There was a wide door on the side wall of the room.

'That leads into the cash room,' Hammer said before changing the image again to one of pallets stacked with steel boxes that must contain coins. Two pallet trucks stood in the middle of the picture. 'It's unsuitable as the target for a robbery, because the valuables are too heavy and cumbersome. The room containing banknotes is further inside.'

The next photograph showed a narrow room equipped with four large safes. 'This room is fitted with a smoke alarm that fills the space with a screen of artificial smoke when the alarm is sounded.'

'How are they thinking of managing it?'

Nils Hammer switched off the projector, but remained on his feet. 'The weak point is always, of course, when the money is loaded and unloaded from the security vans. There's a regular cash delivery from Oslo arriving between nine and ten o'clock this evening. In addition, there are two further weak spots. One is through a side door from the garage belonging to another tenant. The other is through the ceiling from a tool wholesaler's on the floor directly above the room where the banknotes are stored.'

'What's our plan?'

'This is an operation led by Oslo Police and the Emergency Squad. Right now, there are around forty million kroner stored at the depot. It will be emptied in the course of today, and we'll fill the building with our people. The cash transport is the most likely target. It will be crewed by officers from the Emergency Squad, and follow its usual route.'

'What's our assignment?'

Wisting took the floor again. 'Our department is not playing an active role in the operation. A plan has been drawn up for us to man individual civilian surveillance points. The nearest building to the cash centre is the fire station. We'll establish a base there and follow the action on video.'

'Weapons?'

'The Chief of Police has given orders for concealed weapons, including handguns for our officers. That applies from this moment, until fresh orders are received.'

His mobile phone vibrated for the third time. This time Wisting picked it up, but refrained from answering. 'Any questions?'

No one had anything to add; the meeting was over. Wisting observed his colleagues as they left the room: tough, stern and resolute faces, fists clenched. He was aware too of his own pulse beating in his temples. For one entire week they had lagged behind, chasing a solution. Now they would go into live action and, in only a few hours, would have the answers.

62

Leif Malm's voice was unsteady when Wisting phoned him back. 'We've lost sight of Rudi Muller,' he said.

Wisting sat behind his desk. 'How?' he asked.

'He went out early this morning, just after six o'clock; totally atypical for him. We're on reduced staffing until eight o'clock, and the two cars we had on duty didn't manage to follow him.'

'Don't you have electronic tracking on the vehicle?'

'Yes, and that's why we have fewer men. We lost the GPS signal when he drove into the Vaterland Tunnel, and never came out again. Now the boys have located the car in the car park underneath the Ibsen Kvartal office block.'

Wisting pictured in his mind's eye the car park in the middle of Oslo city centre, with a direct entrance built into the tunnel leading from the ring road.

'He could have changed vehicle or disappeared on foot,' Malm continued.

'What will you do now?'

'We have three surveillance posts. The car, his flat and *Shazam Station*.'

'What about the telephone monitoring?'

'It's giving us nothing. We're trying to identify other numbers he's using.'

'Does your informant have anything new?'

'There's been no contact with him for thirty-six hours. The last update was that Muller is stressed out. We'll see what he can come up with in the course of the day.'

'Do you have anything else on Svein Brandt, the man Muller presumably met at the hotel when he was in Larvik on Tuesday night?'

'He returned to Spain yesterday evening. He may have been here to sell the robbery plans.'

Wisting shuffled the papers on his desk in an attempt to bring order to the reports that had arrived while he was on his travels. 'What about the Danes? Have you looked more closely at them?'

'So far we haven't found any direct connection to Muller or his associates.'

There was a pause as Wisting collected his thoughts. 'What do we do now?' he asked. 'What on earth can it mean that Muller has disappeared?'

'I think it means things are about to take off,' Malm answered. Some of the assurance had returned to his voice. 'I'm coming down with the Emergency Squad. We'll be with you by twelve.'

63

Line stood at the window with her arms crossed. After two days of warm autumn sunshine, the fog had returned. The weather was bleaker and more cheerless than ever.

Tommy had not phoned, nor had he answered when she had tried to phone him. She needed to talk to him. He was not the man she wanted to share the rest of her life with, and she had to let him know that. Turning around, she crossed to the kitchen, where she rinsed a couple of plates before returning to the window. The fog was denser now and she could barely discern the sea.

Her mobile phone lay on the coffee table. She flopped down on the settee and tried again, but there was no response. The blank screen on her computer was glowing. In the past two days she had crossed out more of her novel than she had written.

'Fuck!' she shouted into the room.

It felt good to release some of her frustration. She called out again, slamming down the lid of the laptop before putting on her outdoor clothes.

As she inserted the key to lock the door, she was struck by a rational thought and went back inside. Packing the laptop computer and camera in a bag, she checked the room for anything else that might tempt an intruder, and carried the bag with her to the car.

An empty bottle Tommy must have left in the passenger foot-well rolled backwards and forwards as she manoeuvred along the bumpy gravel track. It lay beside empty doughnut bags and old parking receipts trampled into the rubber mat. Everything about him irritated her now.

The fog lifted as she headed inland, but a cold, misty drizzle made visibility poor and the windscreen wipers did nothing more than spread water across the screen, making the drive to Oslo an exhausting experience. By the time she arrived at her flat, a thumping headache was developing behind her right eye.

She slammed the car door behind her and peered at the façade of the building. The ceiling light in the kitchen was switched on but, if she knew Tommy, he would be in bed fast asleep.

Tommy's head appeared around the kitchen door when she let herself in. 'Line?'

She dropped her bag as she approached him. 'Why don't you answer the phone when I call?'

He glanced backwards, and she realised he was not alone. A longhaired man, leaning over the kitchen table, peered at her. Papers and photographs were spread out in front of him. Tommy stood in the doorway, blocking Line from entering. 'I'm a bit busy at the moment.'

The man swept the papers into a shoulder bag.

'What's going on?' she demanded.

The man with the shoulder bag slipped past Tommy. 'I have to go now,' he said, pushing past Line.

'Who was that?' she asked, watching the door as it closed behind him.

'I can't …,' Tommy began, breaking off abruptly. 'It's to do with *Shazam Station*.'

She entered the kitchen, positioning herself with her back to the worktop. 'What was all that about?' she asked, nodding towards the empty table.

'There's such a lot going on just now,' Tommy said. 'That's why I haven't phoned you. I can't explain all of it.'

'You can try.'

'Not now. There are a number of things I need to sort out.' He lifted the jacket hanging over the back of the chair. 'Are you staying? Have you finished at the cottage, I mean?'

She shook her head dejectedly. 'Do you know what? This here ...'

'I just need a few days,' Tommy interrupted. 'Everything will be okay. Can't you be patient with me?'

'My patience has run out,' she declared emphatically, stepping towards the door. 'I'm leaving, and when I come back, you'd better be gone. Gone and away!'

'But ...'

She held the palm of her hand up before whirling around, impetuously grabbing her jacket and rushing out. Her eyes were filling with tears, and she did not want him to see her cry.

64

Her hands trembled as she inserted the key in the ignition. She paused before turning it, allowing her emotions free rein, sobbing and gasping for breath, without really understanding why she was reacting like this. It felt like a terrible betrayal that he had dragged the part of his life she could not bear into her home.

She pressed her hand to her chest. Her breathing was noisy and rasping. It took time to regain control, but eventually she calmed down. She took out some napkins from the glove compartment to wipe her nose and dry her eyes and struggled to gather her thoughts.

She could pay a visit to the newspaper office to pass the time, but when she glanced at herself in the car mirror she realised her appearance would provoke too many questions.

Through the rain-spattered windscreen, she saw Tommy emerge from the building. Speaking on his mobile phone he did not look in her direction. Instead, he hurried across the street and into the little blue Peugeot he had borrowed to visit her at the cottage.

As the vehicle swung from the kerb, she turned on the ignition of her own car and, waiting until he was almost out of sight, depressed the accelerator and followed. She stayed three vehicles behind as they entered Ullevålsveien, without entirely knowing what she was doing.

Crisscrossing the city centre, Tommy found his way to Grønland, with Line following through the one-way streets, all the time careful to remain far enough behind to remain unseen. At the end of Tøyengata, the distance between them was so great that when he turned into the enormous car park in front of the Botanic Gardens, she was able to veer across to the Munch Museum, parking behind a container building where modern art was stored.

The distance between her and Tommy was almost two hundred metres. She observed that he had parked behind another car and stepped out, but not whether anyone was occupying the other vehicle.

Lifting her camera, she zoomed in. The door of the other car opened and a dark-skinned man emerged. Line pressed the shutter button by sheer force of habit.

The man skirted around the car and shook Tommy by the hand before opening the lid of his suitcase. He removed a bag and let it rest on the edge of the boot. The zip was open and Tommy leaned forward to check the contents before nodding. The man shut the bag again, and handed it to Tommy. It seemed heavy. Tommy placed it on the rear seat of his own car before resuming his place behind the steering wheel.

Line slid down in her seat. The containers partly concealed her car, but it was possible that he might spot her. After his car passed she waited for a moment or two before looking up, hurriedly turning to follow him.

After several hundred metres she caught sight of him again, three vehicles ahead, driving back the way he had come. At the roundabout at *Galleri Oslo* he continued across the marshalling yard at Oslo Central Station and drove out along the E18 highway travelling east towards Bispelokket. Two cars now separated them and she was afraid she would lose him in the heavy traffic.

Suddenly he turned into the harbour area. She let a couple of lorries and a cement vehicle go in front of her to avoid him seeing her, and eventually followed along the water's edge to Sørenga, the area that would soon become a new urban district. At Sjursøya he swung his car onto the quayside and drove into a colossal warehouse, right down by the sea, where cranes soared to the leaden skies.

Line halted behind a stack of steel pipes piled on a kind of frame so that she had a satisfactory view of the surrounding area.

Several East European construction workers were working with scrap iron directly in front of her, but appeared to have no interest in what she was doing. For several minutes she stared at the entrance to the warehouse Tommy had driven into. Container trucks and terminal tractors were driving here and there, but nothing else was going on.

She felt nauseous. The palms of her hands were sweaty and she felt slightly dizzy. She wanted to scream out loud, to hit out, to find some outlet for her despair.

Her camera lay on the seat beside her. She cradled it on her lap and glanced through the photos she had taken beside the Munch Museum. Using the zoom function she noticed that the legs of the unknown man partly screened the car registration number. She could try searching for a variety of combinations later.

When she zoomed a couple of notches closer to the bag sandwiched between the two men, she froze. She could not be certain, but thought she saw the barrel of a gun protruding from it.

65

Wisting hung his blazer over the gun cabinet door and removed his shoulder holster. Placing one strap over his shoulder, he fastened it so that it lay under his left breast, before taking out his service revolver, a Heckler & Koch P30. The metal felt cold in his hand.

Pulling the magazine from the stock, he placed both parts of the gun on the bench and opened a box of ammunition. He picked out nine brass cartridges, weighing them in his hand before pushing them into the magazine, the resistance in the spring increasing as he filled it. He then let the magazine slide into the stock again. A metallic click told him it was in place. Metal slid easily over well-oiled metal when he loaded a cartridge into the chamber before securing the firearm, shoving it into the shoulder holster and donning his blazer.

It had been a long time since he had worn the gun. He turned his lapel aside and abruptly pulled it out, his finger settling automatically along the trigger guard as he fixed on an imaginary target at the opposite end of the room. It was reassuring to feel the firmness of the revolver in his hand. He was still proficient.

Prior to his return, someone had left a closed cardboard box in the middle of his desk. Underneath, bundles of unread reports and notes were still stacked. He picked it up. There were no markings of any kind on the outside, and it weighed next to nothing. Something inside slid from one end to the other.

Putting it down, he opened the lid, grimacing at the contents. A dead bird with an angry yellow beak and lacklustre eyes, its black wings spread out from its body. He stepped back with the lid in his hand, and looked around as though looking for someone to explain why a dead bird had been left on his desk. He carried the box into the corridor and listened to voices from the conference room.

Espen Mortensen and Nils Hammer stood beside the coffee machine. 'Do you know what this is?' he asked, holding out the box.

'A dead bird?' Hammer suggested, grinning.

'What's it doing in my office?'

'I was the one who put it there,' Mortensen said. 'I came in with the report. You weren't there, so I left it while I got myself a cup of coffee.'

'What report?'

'From the Veterinary College. It just arrived by fax. Haven't you read it?'

Wisting shook his head.

'They've carried out post mortems on several of the dead birds,' Mortensen said. 'They died of cardiac arrest following multiple organ failure.'

'What the hell does that mean?'

'They were poisoned.'

Wisting glanced down at the bird in the box.

'Poisoned?'

'Cocaine.'

The logical connection dawned on him, like a child finally understanding a simple sum.

'Fatal overdose,' Hammer commented.

Espen Mortensen agreed: 'The physical effects are approximately the same. High pulse rate, high blood pressure, cardiac arrhythmia, heart attack and cerebral hemorrhage.'

Wisting rested the cardboard box on the young crime scene technician's chest.

'Give this to Christine Thiis,' he said. 'Ask her to issue a press release about it, and after that you can bury the evidence in the garden.'

66

Line looked up from the camera. For seconds she had forgotten to breathe, and now her breath came in short, sharp gulps as she glanced at the other photos. The first was the only one with any of the bag's contents visible.

A piercingly loud noise, followed by a furious outburst in a foreign language, made her start in her seat. Twenty metres away, three men in raincoats stood around a metal drum that had fallen from the back of a truck. Another man emerged from a workman's hut, waving his arms and shouting at them. Her heart pounded in her chest.

She started the car, driving until she found a spot where the containers formed a passageway and she could park under cover of an untidy stack of concrete panels. From here she could see the warehouse and parts of its interior. It appeared that the building contained huge steel structures, and there were vehicles inside, although she could not make out any activity. Through her camera lens she could see people moving about, although still indistinct shadows.

Lowering the camera, she looked for a better vantage point. There were sheds at the water's edge, but they would not give a better view. The skies above the sea darkened and the rain became heavier, hammering on the car roof. A deluge cascaded down the windscreen.

Putting aside the camera, she picked up her phone and, flipping to Tommy's number, sat with her thumb poised on the green button. The simplest thing would be to call him, launch into an innocent conversation but try to get something out of him about what he was up to. She was about to press the button when car headlights were switched on in the warehouse interior, followed by another vehicle starting up. Two large, dark cars with shaded windows rolled from the open storage hall, passing less than forty metres away. Muddy water splashed up from potholes in the gravel surface.

She waited until they were out of sight and reached for the ignition key. As she was about to start, the doors on both sides were snatched open. A man threw himself across the passenger seat and grabbed the bunch of keys, the long-haired man at her kitchen table. The other man placed his hand over her mouth and dragged her from the car.

67

The shoulder holster and revolver chafed uncomfortably against his ribs. Adjusting the strap, Wisting studied the video footage from inside the cash centre.

The fire officer's office on the top floor was fitted out as a control centre. From the window they had a direct view of the cash depot. Torrents of rain pelted the asphalt and turned into little streams that ran down the road to the rear of the terracotta-coloured building. The wide river below usually flowed slowly and quietly, but today churned wildly. The water almost reached the top of the poles on the old jetty.

Leif Malm arrived with the Emergency Squad, moving in and out of the side room, talking continuously on his mobile phone.

The Emergency Squad leader, installed in the same office as Wisting, was called Kurt Owesen. Tall and strong, with hair cropped short, his complexion was marred by open pores and scars. 'Excellent images,' he said. 'Razor sharp.'

It was true – the images were top quality. Wisting was pleased to be participating in the coming action via screens instead of from inside the heavily guarded room where the armed officers were gathered downstairs. The fire engines were lined up outside, and armoured police vehicles were concealed behind the doors, ready to go.

From the window, Wisting watched a flock of ducks flying low from the east. One of them broke away and landed on the murky waters of the river, where it was carried along by the current, momentarily caught before managing to struggle free.

He positioned the blinds so he could see through the slats, but was still uncomfortable with this situation: too much uncertainty, no knowing when the robbers planned to strike or whether the cash centre was the actual target. His whole body tingled with anxiety.

Malm entered and positioned himself beside him, scanning the array of monitors.

'Any news?' Wisting asked.

'The vehicle that's going to empty the depot will be here in twenty minutes. Once that's done, we'll lock our own personnel inside. Then it's a matter of waiting.'

He sat down, but stood up again when the phone rang. Wisting listened to his monosyllabic answers until he wrapped up the conversation. 'Klaus Bang is on his way to Norway.'

Wisting visualised the man in the boat who had been photographed by the birdwatcher. 'How is he travelling?'

'By Colorline from Hirsthals. He's booked tickets on the ferry docking in Larvik at two o'clock tonight.'

'We'll see he gets a warm welcome.'

Replacing his mobile phone in his pocket, Leif Malm surveyed the room. 'Any coffee here?'

'We have to use the fire crew's kitchen,' Wisting said, leading the way. The fire crew on duty had been given a brief resumé of the operation, with secrecy duly emphasised.

Each filled a cup in silence. The Emergency Squad leader took coffee to his colleagues, while Wisting and Leif Malm returned to the makeshift command centre. Malm stood in front of the map hanging on the wall. 'Are your people in position?' he asked.

Wisting glanced at his watch. It was almost three o'clock. 'I would think so.' He crossed over to the map. 'We have five surveillance posts,' he said, pointing to strategic points at the town's entrance and exit roads. Simultaneously, the police radio crackled into life.

'*Kilo 0-5, this is kilo 4-1.*'

It was Benjamin Fjeld's voice. He was in a car beside the motorway exit.

Grabbing the police radio, Wisting pressed the send button.

'*4-1: come in.*'

'*A NOKAS cash service security van has just turned off from the E18. It should be with you in a couple of minutes.*'

Leif Malm nodded. This was one of the vehicles that collected cash from commercial businesses and delivered it to the cash centre. Today the driver would be instructed to fill his cargo hold instead of emptying it.

'It's expected,' Wisting said.

'It will be escorted to Oslo by two unmarked police cars,' Malm clarified.

Wisting stood by the window, waiting for the security vehicle. Two minutes later, he spotted it in the downpour, swinging off the main road and driving behind the building. On one of the monitor screens, they saw it at the drive-in gate. The gate slid open and the van entered. Wisting reported his observations over the police radio.

'They'll take approximately half an hour,' Leif Malm said. 'Shall we order a pizza or something?'

Wisting did not feel hungry, but said yes thanks anyway. On the screen, two guards emerged from the cabin of the van. A man and a woman.

'Perhaps you could order it,' Malm suggested. 'You must know the restaurants around here?'

About to answer, Wisting's stood rooted to the spot. Two men in black overalls had suddenly appeared beside the guards.

291

'What the hell!' He knocked over his cup which fell to the floor and smashed. 'Where did they come from?' He tore the venetian blinds aside but saw no activity outside.

The men were wearing balaclavas. One was slightly taller and burlier than the other and had a machine gun hanging from a sling across his chest, while his companion pointed a revolver at the female guard's head.

'It's started!' Wisting shouted, grabbing the police radio.

68

Before the leader of the Emergency Squad was in position in the makeshift command centre, the robbers had intimidated their way into the bank note storage room. The male guard, held at bay by the man with the machine gun, stood beside the wall, while the woman keyed in the code on the first vault door. No alarms had sounded.

Wisting saw how Kurt Owesen's eyes flitted across the screens. They had not planned for this. The veins on his temples were swollen, and there was a distinct cracking from the muscles of his jaw.

Suddenly he moved, barking commands over the radio. 'We have a hostage situation. Two guards held at gunpoint in the cash centre. Adversaries are two men, one armed with a two-handed automatic weapon, the other with a handgun.'

On the CCTV screen, Wisting watched bundles of banknotes from the first strongroom being packed into a capacious bag while the female guard was forced to open storage vault number two. The raid would be over in minutes.

The Emergency Squad leader issued orders to launch a counter attack. They would strike as the robbers fled, provided they left the two guards behind. How the two masked men thought they could get away was incomprehensible. No other vehicles had appeared.

The second storage vault was emptied. Two full bags were already at the door. The taller of the two robbers spoke into a two-way radio and Kurt Owesen quickly relayed that the thieves must have accomplices outside.

Messages flashed on the screen. Attaching the radio to a clip on his chest, the masked raider stepped towards the CCTV camera and stared into it. Wisting gazed into a pair of dark eyes before his weapon was raised. The butt of the gun slammed hard against the lens and the screen went blank. Automatically, Wisting took a pace backwards, not knowing whether it was the blow against the camera or the glowering look that had frightened him.

He looked at the main road. Nothing. He lifted his eyes to the clouds, after a sudden thought that the robbers' help might come from there. He then spoke into the police radio to update his officers in their unmarked vehicles.

Benjamin Fjeld reported back from his observation post: '*A Chevrolet Suburban has just gone past. Impossible to see the number plate. That could be the getaway car.*'

Kurt Owesen relayed the message to his officers. Wisting heard a rasping sound in his earpiece as the action groups acknowledged the information.

One of the screens showed images from the garage interior. He could see what was going on through the open door of the banknote storage room. The third storage vault looked empty when it was opened.

The smaller of the two raiders pressed the barrel of his revolver against the female guard's neck as she tried to explain a practical problem. The two guards exchanged places. The man keyed in the combination and the heavy door swung open. Simultaneously, the message *Alarm #4 Alarm* appeared as a line of text at the top of the screen. None of the people in the picture reacted. The guard must have keyed in a combination of numbers to trigger the threat alarm as the vault door opened.

Half a minute later, it looked like it was over as the

four bags were carried from the depot by the robbers. The Emergency Squad leader relayed this to the officers waiting downstairs.

Wisting leaned his head on the window to see as much as possible of the main road. A lorry passed, followed by two delivery vans. Swearing out loud, he looked at the screen again. The raiders were heading for the exit with the female guard in front of them. Wisting still could not understand how they entered the building, and had no idea how they meant to escape.

It then dawned on him as absolutely obvious. He was not sure whether he understood or saw it first. A large rubber dinghy, a Zodiac, approached along the river, slightly less elaborate than the type that had arrived from Denmark with the cargo of drugs. A masked man stood behind the steering console. Slowing down, he manoeuvred towards the riverbank.

On screen, the door of the banknote storage vault slammed behind the robbers. In a matter of minutes, seconds, they would be gone. The Emergency Squad officers would never regroup in time.

Wisting stormed out of the room into the corridor, smashed open the emergency exit at the rear of the fire station, and clattered down the spiral fire stairs on the building's exterior. At the foot, he drew his gun, releasing the safety catch as he ran.

The two robbers pushed the female guard ahead of them. They must have left the man inside. The woman fell over, and the smaller of the raiders put down one of his bags to haul her to her feet again. None of them had spotted Wisting.

The speedboat was at the jetty, its distance from the robbers less than fifty metres. Wisting could cut them off, but paused as the female guard stumbled and fell for a second time.

'Armed police!' He shouted his routine warning, shielding himself behind a telegraph pole. 'Stand still!'

Twenty metres away, the two masked raiders froze. The woman lay for a moment before clambering to her feet and running to safety.

Wisting withdrew behind the pole, though it afforded him little cover. The man armed with the machine gun dropped the bags he was carrying and pointed the machine gun at him. Repeating his warning, Wisting curled his forefinger around the trigger, aiming at the man's chest. Rain streamed down his face. The pressure on the trigger increased. Wisting made eye contact and something he saw made him straighten his finger.

The man in the boat shouted and the raider grabbed the bags and raced towards the river. Plunging forward, Wisting fired a series of six shots. As the explosive noise hurt his eardrums, the stench of lead assaulted his nose. The shots entered the bow of the boat, piercing the left inflatable tube. He lowered his revolver, watching the masked man on board accelerate into the middle of the river. The boat tilted in the water.

'Armed police! Drop your weapon!' Wisting heard a rough command at his side.

The leader of the Emergency Squad stood legs apart with a revolver in his hand. The two robbers were at the jetty, and paid no attention to the warning. Wisting could hear one of the armoured cars approaching.

The boat, already low in the water, was heading back to the jetty. The Emergency Squad leader repeated his command, and the raider carrying the machine gun dropped the bags and raised his weapon. Kurt Owesen fired a shot from Wisting's flank, and the man fell to the ground.

Three armoured vehicles rushed forward, forming a barricade between Wisting and the river. Armed police officers spread themselves in fan formation, shouting commands.

The Zodiac keeled over, capsized and was carried off by the current, the man aboard clinging on desperately.

On the jetty, the smaller of the robbers let go of his bags and put his hands in the air.

69

The man who had played the more active part in the robbery was on his knees, his hands behind his neck. One of the Emergency Squad officers handcuffed him and pulled the balaclava from his head. It was Rudi Muller.

Blinking his wide eyes, he blew a raindrop from the tip of his nose. Wisting was amazed at how easily he had capitulated, until he looked at the wall of armed policemen.

Loud cries came from the riverbank when the wreck of the Zodiac drifted to land. A group of policemen dragged the drenched sailor ashore, where he was given the same treatment as Muller. A shock of curly hair was revealed when his mask was hauled off, and Wisting recognised him as the chubby man in the surveillance photographs from *Shazam Station*.

The raider who had pointed his machine gun at Wisting writhed on the ground in pain. Owesen's bullet had struck him in the left knee. His overalls were torn and splinters of shattered kneecap were visible in the open wound. One of the members of the Emergency Squad was administering first aid, while another held him covered.

Kurt Owesen approached the injured man, with Wisting a few steps behind, wiping his wet face with the back of his hand. The leader of the Emergency Squad pulled his hood off in one swift movement. His hair, saturated with sweat and rain, was plastered to his head. His eyes were evasive, and it was impossible to make eye contact with him.

'Name!' Owesen demanded.

The man responded by spitting. Owesen glanced at Wisting, who shook his head. He had never clapped eyes on him before.

'What's your name?' Owesen asked.

'He's called Frode Jessing,' Leif Malm said from behind them. 'They call him Yes-man,' he added.

The uninjured robbers were placed in two separate cars. Jessing would be transported by ambulance.

Wisting looked for the two guards. He wanted to speak to them, to provide some reassuring words after their ordeal. He did not see the man, but the woman stood outside an unmarked police car, talking to a uniformed officer. Something was clutched in her hand. The policeman waved him over.

The woman could not be much older than Line. She was shaking uncontrollably, pain and desperation in her tear-stained eyes.

'We have a new situation,' the policeman said, nodding towards a mobile phone the woman was cradling with both hands.

Placing one hand on her trembling fingers, Wisting took hold of the phone with the other. She was reluctant to let go, as though it were extremely valuable.

There was a photo message on the display, the screen divided into two. In the top section, a little girl was making her way up a climbing frame, smiling as the photo was taken. The lower section of the photograph showed a revolver held behind a newspaper, invisible to anyone other than the person holding the camera phone.

Don't phone anyone but me if you want her to live, was the message underneath the picture.

'Your daughter?'

The woman answered with a nod, covering her face with her hands.

299

This was how they had been able to accomplish the robbery, Wisting realised. They had threatened the female guard who let them hijack the security van, making a Trojan horse of it, to take them inside the cash depot.

Finance people had become smarter at securing their valuables these days, and less attractive to extortionists. More often now, it was guards or employees who were exposed to hostage taking or blackmail. Or police officers – he had heard how police officers in other countries had been forced to remove or delete evidence, or ensure that cases were dismissed.

'They've got Emma,' the woman sobbed. 'She's only five.'

Her narrow back was trembling. Wisting stroked the palm of his hand gently to and fro over her guard's uniform while the policeman told her story.

'She phoned the sender and was told the robbers were in a car behind them. She was ordered to stop and let them board the security van.'

Wisting curled his hand around the woman's shoulder. 'It'll be all right,' he reassured her. The conviction in his voice seemed to calm her. 'Where was the photograph taken?'

'In a playground near where we live. My mother is looking after her.'

Wisting pointed at the child's red and yellow raincoat in the photo. 'Was that what she was wearing today?'

'I think so. They were going to the playground.'

'Have you tried to phone your mother?'

The female guard shook her head. 'Then they would know, you see.' She broke down again.

Wisting shut his eyes in an effort to clear his head. He had to focus. The picture was genuine, without a doubt, and had been taken today. All the same, it was likely to be a bluff. If they had actually physically captured the girl, she would have been photographed in a closed environment, and kidnapping both the child and her grandmother would be extremely risky.

Muller sat in the back seat of a patrol car. The driver was about to sit inside when Wisting shouted over. He hurried to the vehicle and sat beside Rudi Muller. 'I'm William Wisting,' he said. 'I'm responsible for the investigation.'

Rudi Muller leaned forward, his hands cuffed at his back. He looked back but did not respond. Something about him suggested that he knew who Wisting was.

'We're going to have a lot to talk about in the days to come,' Wisting said, 'but right now the situation is that nothing you say is going to be used against you. At the moment I'm only concerned about one thing.' The man beside him remained silent.

'The little girl,' Wisting said. 'Is she safe?'

The other man's eyes narrowed. 'What little girl?'

'You have only this one opportunity to put right some of what you've started,' Wisting said. 'The daughter of the woman driver.'

Rudi Muller twisted to find a more comfortable position for his arms. 'There's no danger,' he said quietly. 'Nothing's going to happen without my say so.'

Wisting asked himself what Rudi Muller's words were worth. He decided to trust them. 'Thanks,' he said, and left the car, tapping a couple of times on the roof of the vehicle as a signal that the driver should leave.

70

Line was in an unused office of the police station, with old film posters pinned to the walls, and an internal phone list on the notice board. The desk had been stripped of phones and computers.

Outside, torrential rain fell across the dirty windows, running slowly down the pane in crooked rivulets. She was on the fourth or fifth floor, looking down on long rows of vehicles, too high to escape through the window, which could anyway be opened no more than a tiny crack. As she looked down, the streetlights came on.

Returning to the chair, she leafed restlessly through the pages of an old magazine she had now read several times. The door opened and the longhaired man entered, this time with an ID badge from *Politiet* around his neck. Behind him another policeman chewed energetically on a piece of gum.

'I'm sorry you've had to wait so long,' the first man said, 'but we had to go about things this way. We were in the middle of a surveillance operation which you were in the process of wrecking.'

The gum-chewing policeman introduced himself. 'I'm Petter Eikelid. Can you come with me for a minute?'

Line remained silent, but followed him into the corridor. The place was deserted, the offices in darkness, and the level of activity had reduced considerably since she arrived several hours earlier.

The longhaired detective had roughly explained what had been going on behind her back. Tommy had approached them months before with information about a group of drug dealers. His information confirmed much they already knew. Expressing willingness to help them, Tommy had infiltrated the group.

The road had been rocky, the central figures more reticent than they had anticipated, and unforeseen events had taken place. A delivery had gone wrong and people had been killed. Today had brought the end with the failed robbery leading to Rudi Muller's arrest.

Tommy was waiting for her in an empty room on the floor below, standing at the window with his back turned, his hand on his forehead. His solemn expression changed to a smile when she entered. He embraced her, and she threw her arms around him.

'I'll leave you alone together,' said the policeman.

They sat at the table, speaking almost like strangers, fumbling and hesitant.

'I discovered that all was not as it should be at *Shazam Station*,' Tommy said. 'In another life, I would have shrugged it off or become involved, but I couldn't let that happen now. I couldn't risk spoiling things with us. I wanted to do the right thing.'

She could not understand why he had chosen to keep her in the dark, but accepted and forgave his secrecy. Impulsive, passionate, carefree, thoughtless, that was Tommy. These differences had first attracted her, but she knew she could not endure them for the rest of her life.

He understood. 'I'm going to look at a flat in Sagene tomorrow,' he said. Something in his tone begged her to say it was not necessary.

Steeling herself, she nodded. 'That's fine,' she whispered.

71

Wisting read through the Tommy Kvanter interview that had just been conducted at Police headquarters in Oslo. It described how he had at his disposal a black Golf belonging to Line Wisting. On Friday 1st October he had loaned the car to Rudi Muller, who was alone when he drove from the restaurant at approximately half past six. Tommy Kvanter did not know any more until they were about to close the restaurant and one of the waiters told him the car was back and the keys lying in the office. He did not know where Muller had been or who he had been with. He himself had been at a business meeting with three named men who wanted him to join them in a new restaurant venture.

It was a thorough witness statement, with Tommy talking about several named people, but the interview was almost free of the sort of contradictions that could be expected. No critical questions had been asked. Nothing indicated that the policeman who had recorded the statement was fishing for particular answers or wanted more out of Tommy than the entirely superficial.

Leafing forward to the front page, Wisting read the name of the investigator: Petter Eikelid, the detective who had accompanied Leif Malm to their first meeting. One explanation for the interview shortcomings might be that the interviewer was unaccustomed to the task. As such, he might leave the tactical, critical questions to a follow-up interview.

Another explanation was that the interviewee was their informant. That had been Tommy's role in this case. That was why the questions were wrapped in cotton wool. There was nothing to rouse Rudi Muller's suspicions. The information that Muller had borrowed his car was going to be decisive, but it was innocent when viewed in isolation.

Wisting placed the report beside the other paperwork. The existence of an informant within Rudi Muller's inner circle would forever be concealed. Anything less would put the source's life in danger.

Although no meeting had been called, several of the investigators gathered in the conference room. The CCTV recording of the robbery was being shown on the large screen. Espen Mortensen stopped the footage when Wisting entered, rewinding a few seconds to the moment when the robbers emerged from the security van with the guards. The weak point had not been with the building, but the personnel.

'She's a single mother,' Mortensen explained, referring to the police statement the female guard had given. 'She has worked in the *NOKAS* cash service for almost two years, and for the past six months has driven regularly with the same guard.' He stopped the film and pointed at the screen. 'They were having a relationship, and when her little girl was threatened, they both chose to cooperate and take the robbers on board their van.'

'Are there no systems to guard against that kind of thing?' Benjamin Fjeld asked, 'a tracker or something that registers if they make a stop along the route – something like that?'

'The vehicles are monitored of course, but this would be a shorter stop than at a red light. Besides, the vehicle was empty. They were on their way to collect money. The van was not the robbery target.'

'Are they saying anything?' Christine Thiis asked.

Wisting shook his head. 'They're waiting for their defence lawyers.'

305

The police lawyer leaned back in her chair with a resigned expression. 'An indictment for robbery is unproblematic,' she said. 'We're going to be criticised for not taking preventive action when we knew what was happening, but we'll certainly obtain a conviction for all three men. The challenge will be to connect Rudi Muller to the deaths and the import of narcotics.'

'We'll manage it,' Wisting said, without mentioning Tommy Kvanter's statement. 'It's now our work begins. From here on, the case is going to unfold to our advantage.'

He let his gaze travel around the investigators sitting at the table, aware of how secure his experience made them feel. All cases reached a breaking point, and they had arrived at that point now. So far, their work had consisted of bringing the investigation onto the right track. From this point onwards, it involved securing evidence, building the case brick by brick.

He described this to the detectives as the moment the police put their foot down. Stamp on the ground! Something always swirls up that does not favour the suspect.

'Speaking of shoes,' Mortensen said. 'The guy they call the Yes-man wears the same size as the footprint in the blood at Thomas Rønningen's cottage. The Oslo police are searching his flat now for a pair of Nikes.'

Wisting frowned. Although this day had advanced them, there were still unanswered questions. What had actually happened inside Thomas Rønningen's cottage being one of them.

'Have we got hold of Klaus Bang?' he asked, glancing at the clock on the wall. The narcotics courier was one of the unknown elements that might tighten the net around Rudi Muller. He had given Nils Hammer responsibility for the arrest.

'The welcome committee is ready,' Hammer assured him.

306

'Who's that?'

Nils Hammer and two others put their hands up. 'It should be straightforward. The customs officers will take him aside for us.'

Wisting nodded in acknowledgement and the informal meeting broke up. He poured himself a cup of coffee before returning to his office. It was dark outside. Rain was beating against the window and trickling down the pipes from the gutter.

He had promised Suzanne to be home by ten o'clock, when exactly one week would have passed since the case began. Line was in Oslo so he had not had time to speak to her properly. She had told him she would come home and spend the night in her old room, but he had time to read through some of the last reports.

At quarter to ten, Nils Hammer came into his office, holding a blank DVD. 'You were right when you said that the pieces would now fall into place. Three days ago, I discovered that Line's car passed through the toll stations at the crucial time.' Hammer sat down. It was no longer a secret, but he had every reason to criticise Wisting for not admitting his discovery. 'I guessed you knew.'

It was obvious that criticism was not on the agenda. 'The car took almost seven minutes longer than the others between the toll stations,' Hammer said.

'You mean they stopped along the way?'

Hammer handed Wisting the DVD. 'I received that half an hour ago.'

Wisting inserted the disk into his computer and watched Line's car driving between the pumps at a petrol station.

'This is the Shell station at Grelland,' Hammer said. 'It's the only petrol station between the toll booths.' The passenger door opened and Trond Holmberg stepped out to fill the car with petrol. Then the door on the driver's side

307

opened. Wisting leaned forward as Rudi Muller emerged and disappeared into the petrol station building.

'Someone has a problem with his statement,' Hammer said.

72

A different policeman drove Line back to Sjursøya to collect her car. The terminal trucks were still operating a shuttle service in the docks area. Heavy strokes of falling rain carved through the yellow glow of the floodlights. Although it was still parked where she left it, something was different.

Stepping from the police car, she groaned as she approached, shaking her head. The passenger side window was smashed, and the seat where her camera and laptop bag had been lying was empty, apart from a little puddle of rain.

I do not deserve this, she thought. After everything that had happened, the last thing she needed was a break-in. She was always careful not to leave valuables in the car, but everything had happened so fast when the surveillance officers grabbed her and took her to the police station.

She had no backup copies. Neither of the photographs she had taken nor of what she had written during the week in the cottage. Everything was gone.

'Can I help you with anything?' asked the police driver. Line shook her head. 'Sure?' he asked, 'because in that case, I need to get back.' She could not summon the energy to fill in a whole pile of forms. She just wanted to go home.

Tears welled in her eyes when she was alone, but they eased the pressure in her chest and she let them flow. Somehow it felt good to stand in the rain, weeping. She drained herself completely before beginning to think practically. In the boot she found a roll of tape and a number of plastic carrier bags. She opened them and used them to cover the broken window. She also had some dry clothes in the boot. She removed her soaked sweater and changed before starting the car.

The fluttering of the plastic cover made her dizzy and she was frazzled by the time she reached the house in Stavern. The stony driveway was covered in brown leaves glued to the ground by the rain. As she slammed the car door, another car drove into the driveway. It was her father. He was obviously exhausted, but he smiled when he caught sight of her.

'Just arrived?' he asked, hugging her. She put her hand on his shoulder and pressed her cheek to his. 'How are you getting on?' he asked.

She shrugged her shoulders and he peered past her to her car. 'What happened?'

'Break-in,' she explained, as he examined the damage more closely. 'I left the car with my computer and camera lying on the seat. There were some East Europeans working nearby.'

'Where did it happen?'

'In Oslo, down at the docks.'

'Have you reported it?'

She shook her head. 'I'll do it online tomorrow. I think I can claim something on my insurance.'

Line wondered how much he knew about Tommy's double life. 'Let's go inside,' he said, interrupting her thoughts.

Line went directly to the bathroom, where she undressed and took a shower, standing in the hot spray for a long time, her thoughts meandering. She and her father had always spoken openly, so they had to be able to discuss Tommy.

When she finished in the bathroom she pulled on an old jogging suit and put her clothes into the washing machine. Afterwards, they gathered around the table in the living room to eat a casserole Suzanne had prepared. Her father had told her about the break-in.

'What about the book?' she asked. 'Do you have a back-up copy?'

Line shook her head. She had worked on her story for an entire week, and now it was all gone, but that was not the reason for her sadness. When all was said and done, it did not really bother her. The story was fragmentary and she could reconstruct and improve on it. The two years she had spent with Tommy were a different matter; they felt like two wasted years.

'Did you speak to Tommy today?' her father asked, as though he had read her mind.

'Yes, and we agreed how we'll go about things,' she said. 'He's going to view a flat tomorrow. Over the weekend, he'll move in with a friend and stay there until he finds his own place.'

Suzanne stood up, clearing the table and leaving the two of them to talk.

'I read his statement,' Wisting said, broaching the unavoidable subject.

'It's not quite as you think.'

Leaning back in his chair, Wisting gave her a long look. 'Do you know what I think?' I think Tommy did what he thought was right.'

When she opened her mouth to speak, it sounded like a sigh. 'I feel as though I've betrayed him. He wanted to do some good for once. He wanted to please us.'

Sitting with them again, Suzanne joined in. 'What he has done isn't the reason you're leaving him,' she said. 'It's because he is the person he is, and you can't change him.'

They talked for almost an hour, until Line decided to go to bed. On her way towards the staircase, she stopped at the hallway table, where a pendant-shaped glass ornament lay on top of a bundle of her father's papers.

'What's this?' she asked.

The light from the wall lamp played on its surface, casting strange patterns on the walls. Her father approached and stood by her side. 'It's hope,' he said.

'Hope?'

'The man who owns it calls it a dreamcatcher,' he explained, relating how he had found the glass droplet that had been stolen from one of the cottages out at Gusland. 'He'll get it back tomorrow.'

Line replaced it on the table. 'I don't think there's much hope for my belongings,' she said. She watched the dancing abstract patterns made by the coloured glass before shaking her head. You could have many hopes and dreams for the future, but you could never know what would become of them.

She switched off the lamp and went to bed.

73

The two women were asleep when Wisting left for the police station the next morning. It was Saturday, the rain had stopped and the clouds were breaking. The police station was quiet. There were no eager voices or rapid footsteps in the corridors.

Wisting was keen to learn where the night's events had taken them. Placing the glass ornament near the edge of his desk, he took hold of the pile of new documents, beginning with the arrest report for Klaus Bang, apprehended at the ferry terminal situated at number 8 Revet, at 02.27 hours.

The next document was more interesting. Bang's interview had commenced at three fifteen, and been recorded by Nils Hammer. Wisting skimmed through ten closely written pages, more than he had hoped for. Bang admitted his involvement in the import of ten kilos of cocaine and provided a detailed description of the narcotics network and Rudi Muller's position within it.

When he finished, Hammer appeared at the door, looking like he had not had more than a couple of hours' sleep. 'Really good,' Wisting said, waving the papers.

Nils Hammer took hold of the coloured glass ornament and sat down, cradling it in his lap. 'It didn't take much, actually. It was enough to let him know the public prosecutor's advice was that, if he provided a comprehensive statement, the earlier drugs runs wouldn't be prosecuted, and he could expect a reduction of four years in his sentence. When he also heard that his Norwegian partner in crime had been nailed for robbery and was only a few cells away, it wasn't difficult at all.'

'Did he say why he had come to Norway?'

Hammer tossed the glass ornament from one hand to the other. 'Haven't I written that down? He was to meet Rudi Muller to discuss payment and future business.' The burly detective leaned back in his seat. 'There are others behind Rudi Muller and Klaus Bang, you know.'

Wisting nodded. There were always backers. Behind every domino that fell, there was another, each and every time. The largest and most important dominoes generally remained upright. 'Be careful with that,' he said.

'Where did you get it?' Hammer asked. He was about to hold it up towards the light to study it more closely, when it slipped from his fingers and fell. Hammer drew his legs together so that it dropped softly onto his lap. Picking it up again, he returned it to Wisting.

'I brought it back from Lithuania,' Wisting said, placing it beyond Hammer's reach. 'It belongs to Jostein Hammersnes, stolen by Darius and the other Lithuanians.'

'Hammersnes?' Nils Hammer yawned, propping his feet on the edge of the desktop. 'The neighbour who ate the hotdog at the Esso station?'

'I'm going out to give it back to him now,' he said.

'He'll be delighted, I'm sure,' Hammer said. 'Will you be back by twelve? We were talking about having a review of the entire case.'

Wisting nodded. He looked forward to it. A multitude of thoughts were whirling around in his head.

Hammer dropped his feet from the desk, stood up and crossed to the door. Wisting remained seated, one single thought penetrating deeply into his consciousness. Oblivious to what his colleague was saying, he began to leaf through the bundle of papers, persuaded that an answer had been there all along.

74

A quarter of an hour later his inkling turned into a conviction. He could not find Nils Hammer in his office, but bumped into Benjamin Fjeld in the corridor. 'Come with me,' he said.

'Where to?'

Wisting dropped a pile of papers into his arms. 'Just come with me. We'll discuss it in the car.'

'Should I bring anything?'

'Do you have handcuffs?'

Benjamin Fjeld patted his thigh and nodded. 'Good,' Wisting said, leading the way to the car in the yard at the rear.

Once again he drove out towards the craggy coastal landscape that had been the scene of the past week's events. By the time they reached their destination, he had given Fjeld all the details.

They followed the path to the cluster of cottages. It had been a bitterly cold night, and in the shaded areas a thin layer of ice remained on the puddles, with patches of frost on the grass.

Jostein Hammersnes was standing in the doorway when they arrived, two packed travel bags sitting on the ground beside him.

'Going somewhere?' Wisting asked, nodding towards the luggage.

'It's too cold out here now the frost has arrived. The cottages here aren't built for cold weather.'

315

'I have something belonging to you,' Wisting said, producing the glass pendant from his jacket pocket.

There was no sign of the enthusiasm or pleasure Wisting had anticipated. 'My goodness,' Hammersnes said, accepting it. 'How did you get hold of this?'

'I've been to Lithuania,' Wisting explained. 'The thieves who stole it have confessed, but most of the other stuff they took is gone.'

Hammersnes weighed the glass ornament in his hand. 'Thanks,' he said.

'I've something else for you.'

Wisting took a photograph from his other pocket and held it out. It was from the petrol station where Jostein Hammersnes bought a hotdog before driving to his cottage. The CCTV camera was located approximately in the middle of the premises and showed Hammersnes full-length in front of the counter as he was handed his receipt and change.

Jostein Hammersnes took hold of the photo, peering at it. His pale features took on a bewildered expression. 'We've talked about this before. It was a dead end, you said. I dropped the receipt somewhere along the path, and you thought for a while that it was the murderer who had lost it.'

Wisting nodded. 'We put it aside. But it wasn't a dead end.'

'What do you mean?' Jostein Hammersnes attempted to return the photograph but Wisting did not take it. 'It really didn't have anything to do with the case,' he said. 'A dead end.'

'Your shoes,' Wisting said, tapping the photograph with his forefinger, his fingertip touching the curved logo. 'Nike Main Draw trainers. That's the same type of shoe that tramped around in the blood at the crime scene.'

The hand holding the picture began to shake.

Wisting's gaze fell onto the rubber boots Jostein Hammersnes had pulled on outside his trouser legs. 'Where are

316

those shoes now?' he asked, taking the photograph back.

Hammersnes shook his head without answering. His eyes were evasive.

'I think you burned them after hearing the news that the police had secured the killer's footprints.' In his mind's eye Wisting saw the dark smoke rising from the chimney and remembered the foul smell inside the cottage.

'I believe our technicians will be able to obtain fragments of rubber or other remnants, so we already have the evidence we need. All the cottages that were broken into were thoroughly examined. The crime scene examiners almost carpeted the floor with footprint foils. They found the same footprints here as in the blood, but thought the perpetrator was one of the burglars who had been in both places.'

Jostein Hammersnes cleared his throat, but said nothing. He leaned forward, knees bent, his body swaying rhythmically. His pupils had contracted, and his eyes fluttered to and fro like those of a trapped pine marten. The silence between them was palpable, on the point of fracturing, when it fleetingly appeared that Hammersnes' eyes saw something behind Wisting.

Turning around, Wisting looked in the same direction and then glanced back at Jostein Hammersnes. The man standing silent on the verandah swallowed. His gaze involuntarily slanted down towards the two travel bags. One had the logo of a savings bank on the side. The other was a black nylon sports bag.

Wisting unzipped the sports bag, pulled a blue towel from the top, and drew with it two thousand kroner notes that fell onto the wet grass. Inside the bag were bundles of banknotes, with the muzzle of a revolver protruding.

Behind him Wisting heard something smash. He wheeled around to see shards of coloured glass scattered across the verandah.

75

Thrusting his hands into his pockets, Wisting felt the cold wind against his face. Heavy grey clouds rolled in from sea. Line emerged from the cottage, setting down her luggage at the top of the staircase.

'Will you see to the shutters?' she asked. 'I just need to sweep the floors, and then I'm ready.'

Wisting lifted a shutter into place in front of the large living room window. His mobile phone rang. The display told him the identity of the caller. Thomas Rønningen introduced himself with his full name.

'Congratulations,' he said. 'I can't say I'm surprised at the case being solved, but I'm certainly impressed with the unbelievable investigative work that's been done. You've every reason to be proud.'

Gripping the phone between his shoulder and chin, Wisting thanked him as he hoisted the second shutter into place. Line waved at him from inside the living room.

'I understand you were the one who interviewed them and got the confessions,' Rønningen continued.

Wisting mumbled something about it being almost by chance it had turned out that way. Thomas Rønningen made some observations about police work and about what had emerged in the media, as Wisting raised the final shutter. The resolution had been what it almost always was once they knew it: simple.

Jostein Hammersnes had arrived at the cottage in the late evening to discover there had been a break-in. While he was

318

stomping around in the ransacked interior of his cottage, he heard something sounding like gunshots. He grabbed the poker from the companion set in the hearth and headed over to Thomas Rønningen's cottage. There too the burglars had struck. He went inside to take a closer look at the damage and, while he was there, a bloody, masked man had come lurching in, a revolver in one hand and a bag in the other. In his panic Hammersnes hit him over the head, first once, then twice. Then a third time as the injured man staggered to his feet.

The bag that fell from the masked man's grasp was open. Hammersnes saw the money inside and left with both the revolver and the bag.

'This whole case fascinates me,' Rønningen said. 'How a number of events interact and create a kind of chain reaction. What impresses me most though, is how you got the two murderers to confess.'

Wisting moved the phone from his shoulder to his hand and looked out to sea, following a cargo ship with his eyes. He knew he was good at conducting interviews: it came from years of experience, but there was something else he did not hesitate to call intuition.

He recognised it in colleagues too. Some had a talent, while others never became truly expert. Some simply knew which questions would set the conversation going, and could adapt to the person they were interviewing. Others might learn the techniques, attend training courses, study video footage, even become competent, but never more than that.

It never ceased to fascinate him how different police officers conducted themselves in an interview room. What the successful ones had in common was creativity, perseverance, a sense of logic, genuine curiosity. And intuition.

Wisting understood that a lie was the easiest way out of trouble for the majority of people, and so his aim was always to persuade the other person there was no possibility of lying his way out of his predicament. When the interviewee realised that telling the truth would bring relief, the battle was won.

'It's something like what you do in your programme,' he said. 'You usually persuade your guests to tell you more than they intended.'

'Interesting that you see it like that,' Rønningen said. 'I was thinking of having crime as my next theme, and hoped you would be a guest.'

Wisting opened his mouth to answer but Rønningen went on: 'It's going to be quite different from the usual, with me, the programme host, first feared to be the murder victim, but later regarded as a suspect, and you, the investigator, getting to the truth.'

Thomas Rønningen babbled on enthusiastically. 'I'd like to make a programme where the viewers are left with the thought that we could all commit crimes, just like Hammersnes. My God, I knew the man! We were neighbours. He was a quiet, unassuming IT guy. God knows what got into him, but on that evening he became a murderer and a thief.'

It was a good idea, Wisting thought, and might possibly make people reflect a little on what turned someone into a criminal.

'What do you think?' Thomas Rønningen asked.

Wisting skirted around the cottage, pushing the shutters firmly shut. 'I think it could be brilliant,' he said, 'but you'll need to find someone else.'

'But *you* are the whole concept,' Rønningen protested. 'It wouldn't be the same without you.'

'All the same, it'll have to be without me.'

Line emerged from the cottage, and Wisting drew the conversation to a close. He made it clear his decision was final, but thanked him anyway.

'What was that about?' Line asked.

Wisting shook his head. 'Nothing,' he said with a smile. 'Just some final pieces of the puzzle.'

Closing the door, Line locked it behind her. Wisting watched her as she turned the key and slid the bolts into place. The wind had turned, and was now blowing from the east.

When she was ready, he lifted her large bag and put his arm around her shoulder, leading her along the path away from the sea. He was already looking forward to their return, after winter.

The William Wisting Series

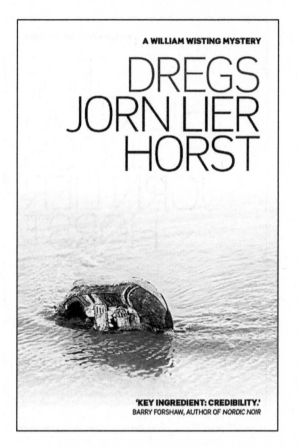

A WILLIAM WISTING MYSTERY

DREGS
JORN LIER
HORST

'KEY INGREDIENT: CREDIBILITY.'
BARRY FORSHAW, AUTHOR OF *NORDIC NOIR*

Police Inspector William Wisting has many years of experience, but he has never seen evidence like this. Four feet washed up on the beach... from four different victims?

'*Dregs* is immensely impressive. The writer's career as a police chief has supplied a key ingredient: credibility.'

Barry Forshaw

The William Wisting Series

A WILLIAM WISTING MYSTERY

THE HUNTING DOGS

JORN LIER HORST

'ONE OF THE MOST BRILLIANTLY
UNDERSTATED CRIME
NOVELISTS WRITING TODAY'
JOAN SMITH, *SUNDAY TIMES*

WINNER · THE GOLDEN REVOLVER TOP NORWEGIAN CRIME NOVEL 2013
WINNER · THE GLASS KEY TOP NORDIC CRIME NOVEL 2013

Years ago William Wisting closed one of Norway's most widely publicised criminal cases. Now it is discovered that evidence was planted and the wrong man convicted. It is Wisting's turn to be hunted.

WINNER: The Glass Key
(Nordic novel 2013)
WINNER: The Golden Revolver
(Norwegian crime novel 2013)
WINNER: The Martin Beck Award
(Best crime novel in translation 2014)